Jessica Manson

The Corruption Series Book Two
Beautiful Corruption

Copyright

Beautiful Corruption is a work of fiction. All names, characters, locations, and incidents are the products of the author's imagination or are used fictitiously. Any resemblance to actual events, locales, or persons, living or dead, is entirely coincidental.

BEAUTIFUL CORRUPTION: A NOVEL

Copyright © 2018 by Jessica Manson

All rights reserved.

Editing by KP Editing
Cover design by KP Designs
Published by Kingston Publishing Company

The uploading, scanning, and distribution of this book in any form or by any means — including but not limited to electronic, mechanical, photocopying, recording, or otherwise — without the permission of the copyright holder is illegal and punishable by law. Please purchase only authorized editions of this work, and do not participate in or encourage electronic piracy of copyrighted materials. Your support of the author's rights is appreciated.

Table of Contents

Copyright..3

Table of Contents..5

Chapter One 11

Chapter Two...17

Chapter Three 23

Chapter Four 29

Chapter Five 36

Chapter Six 42

Chapter Seven 50

Chapter Eight 59

Chapter Nine..67

Chapter Ten..74

Chapter Eleven...82

Chapter Twelve...88

Chapter Thirteen..95

Chapter Fourteen...104

Chapter Fifteen 110

Chapter Sixteen..117

Chapter Seventeen...122

Chapter Eighteen 125

Chapter Nineteen...134

Chapter Twenty 140

Chapter Twenty-One 146

Chapter Twenty-Two...152

Chapter Twenty-Three..160

Chapter Twenty-Four 167

Chapter Twenty-Five... 173

Chapter Twenty-Six.. 181

Chapter Twenty-Seven....................................... 186

Chapter Twenty-Eight.. 192

Chapter Twenty-Nine... 199

Chapter Thirty 205

Chapter Thirty-One 213

Chapter Thirty-Two.. 219

Chapter Thirty-Three.. 224

Chapter Thirty-Four 231

Chapter Thirty-Five 239

Chapter Thirty-Six.. 244

Extras 248

"What would an ocean be without a monster lurking in the dark? It would be like sleep without dreams." - Werner Herzog

"Don't let anyone tell you love isn't worth having because I see forever in your future."

- Words from the wisest woman who was too beautiful for earth, my mother, Cindy Greene

Chapter One

Corruption of the heart caused by someone you love, and trust unconditionally is the worst pain anyone could ever go through. I had learned to accept the death of my parents when they were taken from me by a car accident. But I would never accept them being murdered. Once the tears cleared, anger took over and I wanted to retaliate, but I knew I couldn't. I have a baby growing inside of me and I must think of its wellbeing first.

I collected myself and hid the pictures and the letter that someone left me in one of the books on the shelf of the library. No one would ever find them there. I checked myself in the mirror and then made my way back to Tristan who was sitting on the stairs waiting for me.

"Is everything ok?" he asked.

"No. Can I speak to you privately?" Daveh hurried off but I didn't trust that we wouldn't be heard. "Is there someplace we can go? Away from here?"

"Sure." He headed for the front door and I followed. We got in his car and drove for twenty-minutes. When we finally stopped, we were surrounded by trees. I knew no one would hear us out here, they wouldn't even be able to find us. He turned to me, "What's going on Lilith?"

I began to cry, and he placed a hand on my shoulder. "How close are we? I mean friendship wise?"

"We are very close, and you are my best friend. What's this about?"

"How close are you and Odin?"

"We used to be close but have grown apart since you came into the picture."

"Were the two of you so close that he would tell you his deepest darkest secret?" I asked, trying to find out if he knew the truth.

"No, we were close but not that close. Him and Cal are that close though. Why do you ask? Lilith what's going on?"

I looked at him meeting his eyes. "Odin murdered my parents." He didn't respond. He sat there looking down playing with the steering wheel. "Did you know?"

"Not completely."

"What do you mean not completely?"

"I assumed. One day Odin was sent on a mission by his father. He wasn't allowed to take any of us with him except Cal. They were gone for a few days and when they came back, they said we were moving to Maine for our next mission. When I asked what the mission was about, I noticed Odin and Cal exchange a weird look, but all they said was that we had to go and protect you. I was okay with protecting you. We watched you for a long time in the distance. We took shifts watching your house at night after school. It was my easiest mission since you didn't really have a life, no offense."

"Some taken but continue," I said.

"One day Odin decided to send Ambi over to you to see if you knew anything about your life. He wanted to know if you knew about being a vampire yet. When he learned that you didn't know anything, he decided to go after you. He knew he had to make you fall in love with him before Parker arrived. He knew he was coming, and he needed to stop the connection you and Parker would form. Once I met you and found out that your parents were killed in a car accident, I put two and two together. I wasn't positive, but I had a feeling Odin was the cause of their deaths. He had to get you away from them, so he would have a chance with you. He needed you vulnerable and weak."

"Tristian, I trusted him with everything I had. I confided in him. I told him things I have never told another person. I loved him and now I have the devils baby growing inside of me. I can't stay here. There is no way I will let Odin, or his sadistic father raise my baby."

"Are you sure this is what you want?"

"Yes. I'm sure."

"Okay then I will help you."

Beautiful Corruption

"You don't have to do that. When I leave, all hell will break loose and if they know you helped me, they will kill you. I love you and I can't let them kill you."

"Then I will come with you. I will help you run, hide and raise this baby. I would do anything for you Lilith and I won't let you go through this alone."

"You would do that for me? Why?" I asked surprised at his offer.

"Because I love you," he said meeting my eyes. "I have loved you for a long time Lilith."

"Tristan..." I was cut off when his lips met mine. He kissed me gently with pure love. It wasn't a passionate kiss, just simple, but I could feel it in my soul. He did love me, deeply. I pulled away from him and rested my head on his shoulder. "Thank you," I whispered.

"For what?"

"Helping me." I sat back on my side of the car. "We need to come up with a plan. We won't be able to just walk out the front door with all our stuff. If they know we are leaving they will try to stop us."

"We can grab just the things that are most important. We can store it in my trunk and each day add something else. When we are ready, we can sneak out at night while everyone is asleep. They won't know we are missing until morning and by then we will be long gone."

"How will we get out of Italy?"

"I have some connections. I will check with them and see about getting us a private jet."

"I really hope this works."

He turned to me. "Lilith you must act like everything is normal with Odin until we are able to leave. Can you do that? Can you act normal even though you want to rip his head off?"

I thought about Odin touching me and my stomach turned. I didn't want to be near him let alone having him touch me. "I will try my best," I said as if trying to convince myself.

"Okay and remember I am right next door if you need me for anything. No matter what time of day." I hugged him, and he pulled me closer. I knew I could trust Tristan. He never did anything to betray my trust like Odin had.

We left the woods and headed back toward the house when I had a question, "Once a Sacrament is complete, can it be undone?"

"In the coven, no. The Sacrament is complete, and you are about to break the biggest law of the coven."

"What will happen if they catch me once I leave?"

"If they catch you, you will be brought back to Odin and he will get to choose your fate. But you will be punished by his father and his father will want death. They don't take too kindly to the females leaving the coven. It's kind of like…"

"If I can't have you no one can," I said cutting him off.

"Exactly."

"What happens if I end up with someone else?"

"Then there will definitely be death for you and whoever you are with." I let his words sink in for the rest of the ride home.

When we pulled up to the house, I noticed Odin's car sitting in the driveway. Panic filled me, "Tristan wait. I can't do this."

"Yes, you can. Just do what you're good at lately. Go tell him you don't feel well and go take a nap," he said with a smile.

We got out of the car and headed toward the door. Before we could reach it, Odin came running out of the house. "Where have you been? I have been so worried."

"Tristan took me sightseeing. There was no need to worry," I said. Odin wrapped his arms around me and it took everything I had not to pull away from him. I let him hug me, but I could only hug him back loosely. My insides turned making my stomach upset.

"Why didn't you tell anyone where you were going?" he scolded.

"Odin I am not a child. I am free to come and go as I please," I snapped.

I heard Tristan in my mind, *Easy Lilith. Be mad but don't lose control.*

"I know you can do whatever you want but with Slaaneth's army after you, you should always let someone know where you will be. We need to be able to protect you. And we can't do that if we don't know where you are."

"Fine, I'll let someone know the next time I plan on leaving."

"Good," he said with a smile. He pulled me in for a kiss and what I felt shocked me. There was nothing, no heat, no electricity. The butterflies I felt every time our lips met were gone as well. All my feelings of love for him were replaced with hate and rage. When he finally pulled away from me, he looked at me questioningly. I knew he felt I was different. "Daveh said some guy brought you a package today, she said the guy said it was urgent. What was it?"

Damn you Daveh, I thought. "It was just the deed to my parents' house. Mr. Tassel had it delivered."

Odin nodded then turned to Tristan, "I would like to have a word with you privately." It wasn't a question and I could hear the authority in his voice. We all walked into the house and Odin ushered me upstairs while they entered the library. When the door closed, I ran over trying to listen in. The door was too thick; I couldn't hear a word.

I spoke to Tristan with my mind, *"Tristan I want to listen in."*

"Okay," he said back.

I wasn't just able to hear what was being said, I could see Odin. It was as if I were looking through Tristian's eyes. "What were you thinking taking Lilith off these grounds?"

"She wanted to see some of Italy. You weren't here. You are never here for her Odin."

"And what, you thought you would step up and play hero for her again?"

"Lilith is a big girl and very capable of making her own decisions."

"Lilith is *my* wife and you *will* learn to keep your distance. Understand?"

"Lilith and I are friends. You can't take that away from us. Don't be threatened by that Odin, it's not a good look for you."

Odin stepped closer to Tristan's face, "Stay away from her or I'll send you on a mission you will never return from."

15

Jessica Manson

I burst through the door rage fueling my body, "I swear on everything I love Odin if you so much as try and send him away I will never forgive you. Tristan is my best friend and I will not let you hurt him."

"Lilith I..."

"Save it Odin. You will not threaten him again. You will not try to intervene in our friendship again. Do you understand that if you mess with him you will lose me forever?"

"I know how he feels about you Lilith. He is in love with you."

"I know. And Tristan and I have an understanding about that. He will never try anything with me. He knows I am a married woman and he respects that."

"I can't trust that he won't try to have you."

Frustrated I turned toward Tristan, "Do you have any intentions of taking me away from Odin?" I asked. He shook his head. "Do you have any plans on trying to take me to your bed?" He shook his head again. "Do you want to interfere with my marriage?"

"I would never come between the two of you. Odin, I do love Lilith and she knows it, you know it. But I respect the bond between the two of you. I have no intentions other than being her friend," he said.

"Fine. The two of you can continue your friendship but no more secret trips together," Odin said.

"And you won't send him away?" I asked.

"No," he said reluctantly.

"Good. Then no more secret trips," I agreed.

I turned to leave the library, "Lilith can I talk you?" Odin asked.

"Not now. I'm still pissed. I'm going to go take a nap. Maybe when I wake up, I'll be ready to talk." He nodded and hung his head as I walked away. The rage inside of me made me exhausted and I needed sleep.

Chapter Two

When I woke up Odin was sitting on the couch in the sitting area of our room. He looked stressed and unfocused. I adjusted the covers causing him to look over at me. "Hey," he said softly.

"Hey."

"Can we talk now?"

"I guess."

He walked over and sat next to me on the bed, "Lilith I am sorry for how I reacted earlier. I just hate seeing him get to spend so much time with you. My father has me so busy with the coven I'm never home. And I understand now that me not being here for you has pushed you into this friendship with Tristan. I was jealous. I'm sorry."

"Odin, Tristan and I were friends before we even moved here. Why are you just now jealous?"

"Because I'm never here for you. When I'm not here who do you go to when you have nightmares?"

"Tristan."

"When you need something, who do you go to?"

"Tristan."

"And when you need comfort when I'm not around who gives you that?"

"Tristan. But Odin…"

He cut me off, "I appreciate that he can be here for you when I can't, but I know he is in love with you. He does these things because he is in love with you. And it kills me to know that I can't be here for you like he can."

"No Odin, he does them because he is my friend. My best friend."

"Do you love him Lilith?"

"Yes, but in the way, one would love a brother."

"Do you have feelings for him?"

"Not in the way you think I do."

"Can you honestly say that I have nothing to worry about between the two of you?"

I grabbed his face between my hands and made him look me in the eye. "You have absolutely no reason to think I would ever leave you for Tristan. I am madly in love with you Odin. You are the only person I want to be with." I thought I may just puke from my own words, but I had to make him believe me. So, I kissed him. I kissed him like I didn't know he killed my parents. I didn't think the kiss through because he climbed on top me and pulled my shirt off. I couldn't turn him down; he would know something was wrong. So, I gave into him.

He ran his hand along my stomach, inching closer to my breast. I tried to feel the same way I used too but I couldn't. I had nothing for him but hate. I pulled away from him, "Lilith what's wrong?"

"I don't feel well. I think I'm coming down with something."

"You have been sick for some time now. We need to get you to the doctor."

Panic filled me, if he took me to the doctor, they would find out I am pregnant. "No."

"Lilith, something is wrong with you. You have been extremely exhausted since we moved here. All you do is sleep. And you are constantly sick to your stomach. Wait, you don't think you could be pregnant, do you?"

He cannot find out I'm pregnant. "No. I actually took a test this morning because I thought that might be it but I'm not. I think the move just put a big strain on me."

"I still think you need to see a doctor," he pleaded.

"If I am still like this in a week, I will go see one. I promise."

"Okay I can give you a week but if you are not better by then I am going to take you myself." I nodded in agreement then he kissed me on the forehead. "I'm going to go see what Cinzia made for dinner. Care to join me?" he said holding out his hand. I took it and he led us to the kitchen.

When we were getting close to the kitchen my mouth started to water from the smell of the food. When we entered the room, the radio was blaring and Cinzia was dancing over the stove while stirring whatever she was cooking. "What are you cooking?" I spoke loudly so she would hear me over the radio.

"Mrs. Lilith, you about scared me to death," She said wiping her hands on her apron.

"What are you cooking?" I asked again with a giggle.

"Well Ms., Mr. Odin asked me to cook something you would like. He told me that you are from the south, so I made fried chicken, mashed potatoes, butter beans, turnip greens and cornbread. I also made some banana pudding for dessert."

"Wow, really?" I haven't had food like that since I moved to Maine.

"I must say, it was hard work. It takes a lot to make food like this," she said laughing. "Dinner will be ready in about ten minutes."

"Thank you. I will get everyone to the dining room."

As Odin and I left the kitchen I asked, "You had her make all of that?"

"You haven't been eating much lately and I figured if you had something to remind you of home, you would be able to eat."

"Thank you. I can't wait to try it. My mouth is already watering." Odin went to the third floor of the castle and I went to the second, so we could gather everyone for dinner.

Once everyone was seated Cinzia and Genevra started bringing out the food. Everything looked so delicious I couldn't help but lick my lips which caused Cal to start laughing at me. "What?" I asked.

"You must be starving," he said.

"Why do you say that?"

"Because your eyes got big and you licked your lips like you were ready to devour every bit of this food."

"A girl has got to eat Cal." We started piling our plates. I got some of everything while the others took everything but the turnip greens. They looked at them like they were disgusted. The chicken was juicy and cooked to perfection with a hint of spice behind it. The potatoes weren't lumpy which was good because I hated lumpy potatoes.

Jessica Manson

Everything was cooked just how I liked it. "I don't know how she did it, but this food is amazing," I said to no one in particular.

"It is tasty," Odin said.

"It's greasy," Ambi complained.

"That's what makes it so good. Nothing like a little fat to add some flavor," I said with a smile. When we were done with dinner, Cinzia brought out the banana pudding. It was topped with whipped cream and cookie crumbs, just the way I liked it. "Oh, my gosh that looks good." I was the first to dig in. "Mmm, y'all have got to try this," I said with a full mouth. The guys laughed at me while Ambi just looked disgusted.

With a full belly and no plans, I decided to read a book in the library. I got comfortable on a bean bag and was beginning to get lost in the book when a knock sounded at the door. "Come in," I called out.

Odin walked into the room, "My dad just called, and he needs me to come to his office. Would you like to come with me?"

I didn't want to go with him, but Odin knew I wanted to see where he worked. And if I was pretending everything was normal between us, he knew I would want to go. "Sure," I said.

A big smile played across his face, "Great." We headed for the car and toward his father's office.

"Your father works in a house?" I asked confused as we pulled up to a house instead of the office building, I was expecting.

"No, he works from home."

"So, this is where you come when you go to work?" He nodded in response. "Not what I imagined. I thought you actually worked in an office building," he laughed at me.

We got out of the car and headed inside. It was a fairly sized house. The outside is yellow with white shutters. There were flower beds along the house that was filled with brightly colored flowers. They reminded me of when Odin took me to Croatia. As we stepped inside Draven greeted us. He pulled me in for a hug squeezing me a little too tight.

"How is my favorite daughter-in-law?"

Beautiful Corruption

"I'm your only daughter-in-law," I joked.

With a laugh, he said, "Yes but you are still my favorite."

"What did you need me for?" Odin asked.

"Well I guess straight to business then. Lilith if you don't mind, you can wait in the living room. Get comfortable and make yourself at home."

They headed toward the back of the house, so I went into the living room. I was flipping through the channels on the TV when I heard a noise coming from behind a door off of the living room. I walked over to the door and stuck my ear to it. Another sound came from behind the door. I knocked lightly. There was shuffling so I slowly opened the door.

A woman sat in a chair in the middle of the room staring blankly at a TV. "Hello," I said. She had black hair like Odin's, but it was starting to gray, and she had the same glowing green eyes Odin wore. They were just as breathtaking on her as they were on him. She was elegantly beautiful.

She looked at me and smiled. "Hello," she said softly. "Who are you?"

"I'm Lilith, Odin's wife."

Her eyes lit up. "You married my boy?"

"Yes mam'," I said shyly.

"Come sit with me dear." I walked in and sat next to her. "It is so nice to finally meet you. Odin talks about you all the time."

I smiled, "Forgive me, but I don't know your name," I said embarrassed.

"I'm Adreana."

"It's nice to finally meet you."

"Same to you. So, tell me, how has my boy been treating you?" I told her what I thought about Odin before I found out what he had done. No matter how bad he betrayed me I wasn't going to down grate him to his mother. She told me stories about when he was a child. She told me that one time she had cleaned a sliding glass door so well that when he ran through the house to go outside and play, he ran right into

21

the door falling flat on his butt. We were laughing so loudly we didn't hear Odin and his father walk into the room.

Draven cleared his throat, "What's going on here?" he said with a look of admiration.

"I'm sorry I didn't stay in the living room?" I said feeling like I shouldn't have come in here.

"It's quite alright Lilith. Drena, how are you feeling?" Draven asked.

She ignored his question and looked at Odin, "I like her," she said smiling. "You better do everything in your power to keep her."

"I plan on it," Odin said as he walked over to me and wrapped his arm around my waist. "She's definitely a keeper."

"Well son, Lilith, I will see you out." Odin kissed his mom on the cheek before leaving the room.

"It was nice to meet you Adreana," I said.

"Same to you dear. And I hope I get to see more of you," she said as she pulled me in for a hug. She whispered in my ear before I pulled away from her, "Be careful Lilith. Don't let Draven get your baby."

I pulled away from her shocked. "What?" I asked quietly.

"Come now Lilith, you must be going," Draven said. Reluctantly I walked toward Odin and he took my hand as Draven walked us out to the car. "Lilith, you have to know that Drena is sick. She says things she shouldn't. She has gone mad."

"I didn't mean to impose on her. I heard a noise and was curious as to what it was. I'm sorry for not staying put where you said."

"It's alright my dear. I'll be seeing you soon." He stepped into me giving me a hug. I got in the car and shut the door. He and Odin shared a few words before Odin got in next to me and drove us home.

Chapter Three

The ride home was awkward because Odin kept smiling at me. Becoming tired of the smiling, I asked, "What Odin? Why do you keep smiling at me like that?"

"I am just really happy right now?"

"About what?"

"My mom. She hasn't said a word in over a year. When we talk to her, she just stares blankly at that damn TV. Not only did she speak to you, but she spoke to me. And she was smiling. You don't know what this means to me," he said excitedly.

"All in a day's work," I joked.

"Ah Lamia Mea I love you so much." He grabbed my hand in his and kissed the back of it. "I am so excited I can barely contain myself." I couldn't help but laugh at him. Seeing him this excited made it easy to forget about his betrayal.

When we arrived home Odin immediately started telling everyone about his mom. Everyone started getting just as excited as he was. It was contagious.

"Did you put a spell on her to make her talk?" Gunner asked.

"No, I would never do that," I said feeling offended.

"Are you kidding Gunner, all it takes is her smile to make anyone fall in love with her. Right Tristan?" Odin said jokingly.

Tristan and I shared a look before I spoke to him with my mind, *"He must be in a really good mood to joke about that."*

"I know. It really is amazing that you were able to get her to speak. She hasn't spoken to anyone in a very long time."

"All I did was talk to her."

"Yes, but she talked back," Odin said still wearing a huge grin. I flopped onto the couch and started flipping through the channels. Tristan sat beside me while everyone else was still making a big deal out of nothing.

"There is nothing on TV," I said throwing the remote down onto the coffee table.

Jessica Manson

"Want to play Skip-Bo?" he asked. "I think I might actually win tonight."

"Sure, but don't plan on winning."

He walked away to get the cards and I headed to the kitchen in search for some more banana pudding. While I was bent over digging in the fridge some arms grabbed me from behind causing me to scream out and flail. "Jesus Lilith, it's just me," Odin said.

"Don't do that. You about gave me a freaking heart attack."

"I didn't mean to scare you."

I pulled the pudding out of the fridge, "Want some?" I asked still flustered.

"No thanks."

"Good. That means there is more for me."

"It's good to see you eating and keeping it down."

"I guess the ba..." I cut myself off. I almost messed up and told him about the baby. "I mean Cinzia really knows how to make my favorite. This stuff is delicious."

Just as he was stepping in for a kiss Tristan walked into the kitchen, "You ready to lose?" he asked.

"No, I'm ready to win." I pulled away from Odin and grabbed my food, "We are playing cards, want to play?"

"No thanks. Have fun," he said.

When Tristan and I sat down at the table I started talking to him with my mind, *"I almost accidentally told Odin about the baby."*

"He didn't catch on, did he?"

"No. But earlier today before we went to his dad's he asked me if I was pregnant because of how I haven't been feeling good lately. He wants to take me to the doctor."

"What did you say?"

"I told him no obviously. But he said if I'm not better by next week he will take me himself."

"Then I guess that gives us one week to get things in order."

"There is something else."

"What?"

"Odin's mother told me to be careful and to not let Draven get my baby. Why do you think she would say something like that?"

"I don't know."

"Tristan, I'm scared. What if they catch us? I can't let them have my baby."

"I promise you with every fiber in my body they will never get your baby. At least not while I'm alive."

"Thank you."

"You two sure are quiet in here. You guys usually play a very intense and loud game," Latham said.

"Would you like to join us?" I asked.

"Sure." The three of us sat there playing cards for the next two hours until exhaustion took over me.

I excused myself from the game and went upstairs to take a hot bath. I ran the water as hot as I could stand it before stepping in. Sitting in the hot bath immediately relaxed me. I put my earbuds in and tuned everything out around me. Closing my eyes, I started to doze.

The music faded, and laughter took its place. I wasn't angry or scared of Slaaneth anymore. Meeting him in my dreams was such a common occurrence I was growing accustomed to it. "Slaaneth."

"Lilith, nice to see you again."

"Can't say the same. What do you want this time?"

"Still the same thing. I want your baby Lilith."

"Why?"

"It's my ticket to freedom. Your baby carries my blood. I can smell it."

"You aren't going to touch my baby."

"I will have that baby. I will take it when it is born just like I should have taken you."

Jessica Manson

"My baby will not be a sacrifice, so you can get out of hell. I will kill you first."

He laughed so close to my face I could smell his rotten breath. "Kill me? You could never kill me."

"I will do whatever I have to do to keep you away from my baby."

"This is getting boring. Till we meet again Lilith."

I woke up just as Odin walked into the bathroom. "May I join you?"

I pulled my earbuds out, "What?"

"May I join you?"

I closed my eyes and took a deep breath trying to control the frustration. "Sure."

He got undressed and slipped in behind me before asking, "Lilith, what's wrong?"

"Nothing. Why do you ask?"

"All day you have been avoiding me. Every time I touch you, you freak out. Did I do something to make you mad at me? Is this still about Tristan?" His voice had so much hurt in it I almost felt sorry for him.

"No, it's not that. I'm just in a bad mood today."

He started massaging my shoulders, "Maybe I could make you feel better." He kissed the side of my neck while moving his hands lower down my back. His touch didn't create the heat it used to, but it still felt nice. He began to run his fingers up and down my arms pulling me to lean on him. With my back laying on his chest, he lathered the loofah with soap and began to wash my chest.

When my chest was covered with soap, he dropped the loofah and took my breast into both hands squeezing them gently. I moaned from the touch. He slid his hands down my stomach until he reached my center. He gently caressed me sending a sensation through my body. He nibbled on my ear, squeezed one of my breasts and massaged my middle at the same time causing pleasure to flood through my body. When I reached my level of satisfaction I cried out with ecstasy.

Odin got up and stepped out of the tub. He pulled me up into his arms carrying me to the bed. He threw me down and flipped me over facing away from him. He pulled me onto my knees while he stood next to the bed. He thrust into me moving forcefully in and out. I couldn't help but cry out from the pleasure. The sex was quick, and it didn't take long for either of us to reach a level of release.

I crawled under the covers kicking myself for having sex with him. I knew I had to act like everything was normal but was having sex with him necessary? Odin crawled in beside me. "Are you sure everything is okay?" he asked.

I laid my head on his chest, "Yes. Everything is fine."

"I don't know. Something feels off about you."

"Baby, I promise you everything is fine," I said kissing him gently on the lips. We lay there in each other's arms until he fell asleep. When I was sure he wouldn't wake up, I slid out of his arms slowly. I grabbed a few things I knew I wanted to take with me. I grabbed the necklace my parents gave me, my iPod and a few of my favorite hoodies and I threw them into a duffle bag. I also threw in a couple pairs of blue jeans and t-shirts.

Before sneaking out of the room I spoke to Tristan with my mind, *"Are you awake?"*

"Yeah."

"Good. I'm coming to your room." When I walked into Tristan's room, he was standing by his bed in nothing but his boxers. He was gorgeous. His body was lean, but he was built. His abs sent heat flooding through my body. He fumbled with his clothes while I stood there and drank him in.

He looked a little embarrassed. "Sorry, I wasn't expecting you that fast."

"Sorry. I barged in."

"What did you need?"

I pointed to my head letting him know to listen, *"I have my things ready for when we leave. Can I leave it in here?"*

"Yes."

"If we could leave as soon as possible that would be great."

"Tomorrow I will make a few calls and let you know."

"That would be great. Goodnight."

"Sweet dreams, Lilith," he said with a smile.

When I crawled back in the bed Odin rolled over, "Where did you go?"

"To the kitchen for some water." I was really getting good at lying but somehow, I don't think this is a good thing. I was ready to leave right now. I didn't want to lay in this bed next to him. I didn't want to hear his voice or see his face. I wanted to hurt him. I wanted to see him suffer. I wanted to watch him beg for mercy as I caused him excruciating pain.

He snuggled up to me and I wanted to push him off. I could feel my powers stirring inside of me. I was beginning to learn that my powers are connected to my feelings. Whatever feelings I have, my subconscious calls on whatever power fuels that emotion. And right now, hate was radiating inside of me and the witch inside of me was itching to unleash some fury. I rolled over facing away from him staring at the wall until sleep took me under.

Chapter Four

I didn't wake up until well past eleven. I was anxious to see if Tristan had any news yet. The sooner I got out of this house the better. I rushed into my bathroom and took a quick shower. I dried off and threw my towel in the hamper. I walked back into my room naked and to my surprise, it wasn't empty.

"Tristan what are you doing in here?" I asked.

"Lilith. I am so sorry. I thought you heard me say I was coming in."

"No, I didn't. What do you need?"

"Do you want to put some clothes on first?" he asked embarrassed. I didn't mind being naked in front of him. He didn't make me feel like I needed to hide. He may have been uncomfortable with my nakedness, but he never once took his eyes off my body. I didn't mind him looking either. I confidently walked over to my dresser and slowly slid on a pair of red lacy panties. I then took out the matching bra, I slipped it on but didn't fasten it. I walked over to where he stood and asked for his help. With shaking hands, he clasped the bra for me letting his hand rest on my back for a few seconds. I walked over to the closet, grabbed some clothes and let him watch me slowly get dressed.

I don't know why I was teasing him, and I can't explain my line of thinking, but I knew he liked it. The bulge in his pants told me he did. "Now will you tell me what you needed?" I asked.

"What?" he asked with a cracked voice.

"You needed something, what was it?" I asked with a half grin and raised eyebrow.

"Oh, um." He gripped the back of his neck trying to remember.

"Do you need a minute?" I asked smiling.

"Shut up. It's your fault," he said laughing.

"What did I do?" I asked teasingly.

"You know exactly what you did."

"Okay fine, I teased you. But you liked it," I said pointing to his pants. He looked down and turned away from me. I didn't want him to feel ashamed. I walked over to where he stood, "Tristan don't be embarrassed."

"Lilith..."

I cut him off by pressing my lips to his. He tasted like candy, sweet and innocent. His lips were soft and puffy like little clouds. He touched my back gently and leaned in closer deepening the kiss. I wrapped my arms around his waist pressing his body against mine. I could feel the love he had for me in that kiss until he pulled away from me. "Lilith, what are you doing?" he asked in a whisper.

"I don't know," I said kissing him again. This time he kissed me harder sending tingles through my body and this time I pulled away, "Do you want me to stop?"

"Yes. No," he kissed me again. "Lilith, I want you," he said resting his head on my forehead.

"I know."

"What are we doing?"

I looked him in the eyes. "I think I might be getting feelings for you Tristan."

He didn't say anything. He didn't need to. The smile that displayed across his face said enough. "I have news."

"About what?"

"I called one of my friends and he can have us a jet out of here tonight?"

"Are you serious?" I asked excited.

"Yes. When you are ready to leave, all I have to do is give them the word."

"I'm ready. Let's go tonight."

"Meet at the bottom of the stairs at midnight." He kissed me on the cheek before leaving my room. I was so excited it instantly put me in a good mood. I was ready to leave Odin. I was ready to be away from all of the lies and deceit.

Beautiful Corruption

I was sitting on pins and needles waiting for midnight. I was beginning to get nervous when Odin was still awake at eleven thirty. He was lying in bed flipping through his phone. I knew I would have to do something to get him to relax so he would go to sleep. I crawled up beside him in the bed and took his phone from him, throwing it at the foot of the bed. "What did you do that for?" he asked sounding frustrated. I didn't answer him. I laid my head on his chest and lightly ran my fingernails in circles on his stomach. This always relaxed him and never failed to cause him to fall asleep. "Mmm, that's nice."

"Relax and enjoy it."

"Are you trying to put me to sleep Mrs. Edgerson?"

"No. I'm trying to cuddle with you, so I will fall asleep," I lied. He started tracing his hands up and down my arm and within a few minutes I felt his body start to relax. Soon after, he started to snore. I slowly slipped out of his arms. I didn't bother changing out of my night clothes for fear of waking him. I slipped into my shoes forgetting socks and quietly snuck out the door. I headed down the stairs watching over my shoulder.

Tristan was waiting for me at the bottom of the stairs even though we still had ten minutes. "Ready?" I asked.

"Are you sure about this? Is leaving him what you really want to do?"

"Are you backing out? You don't have to go with me. I can do this on my own."

"No, I'm not backing out. I just wanted to make sure you were completely sure."

"Of course, I'm sure. He killed my parents Tristan. I can't be with him after something like that."

"Okay, then let's go," he said with a smile.

We headed for Tristan's car and when we got outside a light upstairs caught my eye. Ambi was looking out her window watching us. "Tristan, we have to go now." I said scared she would wake Odin.

"What's wrong?"

Jessica Manson

"Ambi is watching us." I looked back at her window, but she was gone. We ran to the car and jumped in as quick as we could. As he pulled out of the driveway, I watched Ambi run outside. "Faster Tristan!" I yelled.

Ambi ran back into the house. I knew this time she would wake Odin.

Tristan was driving so fast everything passed by in a blur. We came to a gravel road and drove down it where a guy was waiting for us. "We are going to switch cars, but we should be quick since they know we are gone now. Odin put a tracker on all of our cars, so he would know where we are at all times."

Tristan didn't bother to make introductions. We threw our stuff into the trunk of the new car and drove off. Wasn't long after that my phone started ringing. I dug it out of my purse, "It's Odin," I said.

"Don't answer it." I didn't. I sent it to voicemail. He called three more times after that, each time leaving a voicemail. I could only imagine what he said. I wasn't ready to listen to them yet. Just as I was putting it back in my purse, I got a text message.

WTH Lilith?

I left you a package in the library. You should go look at it, Odin.

Where are the two of you going?

Odin please just go look at the package.

Earlier when Tristan told me we would be leaving today, I made copies of the pictures I had of Odin killing my parents. I left them for him on my desk in the library. I'm sure everything will make sense once he sees them. About ten minutes passed before he started calling again. While Odin was calling my phone Ambi was calling Tristan's. "You can answer it," I said.

"I'm not sure that would be a good idea."

"One of us needs to talk to them eventually."

"Yeah maybe, but right now I think we should get as far away as we can before we do that."

"He knows now," I said.

"Knows what?"

"That I know he killed them."

"How would he know that?"

"I left him copies of the pictures."

"Well I guess he was bound to find out sooner or later." I got another text message but this time it was from Ambi.

Seriously? WTF? You won't get away with this, you traitorous bitch. And you can tell Tristian that he is as good as dead.

As long as there is breath in my body, no one will touch him.

I should have killed you when I had the chance.

I could say the same.

Odin tried calling again. When I didn't answer, he text me again.

Lamia mea, please. You must let me explain. It isn't what you think it is. I am so sorry baby. Please answer your phone. I can't live in this life without you. You are my everything and losing you will crush me. Please come back and let me explain. I need you. I need us.

Tears started to flow down my face. I wish I would have never found out. I wish Odin hadn't done the things he did. I loved him very intensely and he used to be everything I needed, wanted and loved. But he ruined that. He ruined me, us. The love I had for him faded so quickly once I learned the truth.

Tristan reached over and grabbed my hand. "Are you okay?" A peaceful sensation flowed through me. I realized I had hardened my heart toward Odin only to maybe fall in love with Tristan.

"I'm fine. It's just that this is the second time in my life that I have been betrayed by a guy in the worse ways possible. Why does this keep happening to me? Do I have stupid and vulnerable written on my forehead?"

"I can assure you that you don't. I don't know what happened to you in the past, but I will say that both guys are the ones that are stupid. To risk losing a girl like you is crazy. If I had you, I would never do anything to hurt you."

"I honestly believe that. I know you would never hurt me. But then again I am a fool."

"You're not a fool Lilith."

"I am so messed up right now. My husband killed my parents, I'm carrying his baby, we are on the run from him, people want me dead, Slaaneth wants to kidnap my baby and I am in love with you. How did my life get turned so upside down?" I was scolding myself as soon as the words left my mouth. I couldn't believe I just told him I was in love with him. Tristan didn't say anything, he sat silent in the driver seat still holding my hand. The silence between us was becoming awkward. "Say something," I whispered.

"We're here," he said. My stomach dropped, and my body filled with embarrassment. I knew he loved me. He didn't keep it a secret, not even from Odin. So why didn't he say anything when I told him I was in love with him too? "Ready?"

"Yeah."

We were parked near a small landing pad where a jet waited for us. Before getting on Tristan turned to face me, "We need to leave our phones here. Odin will be able to track us if we don't." I dug my phone out of my purse and handed it to him, he then handed it to another friend that I didn't get introduced to. "Let's go."

The jet was a lot smaller than Odin's making us sit next to each other. I took the window seat, so I would have a distraction from my

Beautiful Corruption

embarrassment. We didn't speak until we were in the air. I had to be the one to break the silence. "Where do we go from here?"

"Montana."

"Why Montana? There is nothing in Montana."

"Exactly. Do you think Odin would think to look for you there? Besides one of my connections has a cabin there that they will let us stay in for however long we need to." Tristan sounded kind of snippy toward me and with my feelings hurt I didn't respond to him, I just turned to stare out the window again.

Jessica Manson

Chapter Five

We sat awkwardly in silence. Rejection hurt. Especially from someone you thought loved you back. A single tear slid down my cheek and I quickly wiped it away. Another one fell, then another. Soon I was crying from both eyes. I turned my body toward the window pulling my knees up to me resting my head on them. I didn't want Tristan to see me crying but it didn't matter that I turned away from him, he knew. He placed his hand on my back and said, "I can't stand to see you like this. Can we talk?"

"What is there to talk about? I think your silence said enough," I said with a weak voice.

"Lilith, you don't understand. I didn't say anything because I know you are not ready to go there with me. You are not ready to be with me and I understand that. And I don't expect anything from you. I love you. I have loved you for a very long time. I have waited, and I can wait again. Your happiness is all that matters to me."

"Tristan, I didn't tell you I love you because I thought that is what you wanted to hear. I didn't tell you I love you because it wasn't true. I told you I love you because you love me. And I told you I love you because I can sit next to you and not say anything and be at peace. I love you because you are special to me and I feel amazing when I spend time with you. You give me goosebumps in a way no one ever could." *Except Odin,* I thought to myself. "I feel safe sharing my secrets with you. I appreciate that you think about my feelings before you say or do anything. But most of all I love you because I trust you."

He sat there looking at the floor taking in my words. He finally looked up at me. "Do you know why I love you?" he asked."

"No, I don't."

"I love you because the world is less scary when I am with you. Knowing you gives me courage. You are the first and last thing on my mind every day. I love you because if something serious happens to me, you are the first person I want to call. And I love you because I hear your voice even when we are not in the same place. I can be me when

Beautiful Corruption

I am with you. And because your smile makes me smile. I can feel it when your heart sings because it makes mine sing too. You are my best friend and you mean the world to me. And I love you because I want to love you."

"You and I became close friends really fast after I married Odin and I fell in love with you a long time ago but as I said I was with Odin. I kicked myself every day for being in love with two men when maybe I should have only been in love with you." I am so confused. I love Odin and Tristan at the same time. And if I love two people at the same time how can I be sure of what I feel for either of them is real?

He leaned over and kissed me softly on the lips. It wasn't a kiss filled with passion or heat, instead it was filled with something else. It was a small kiss, but it had a big impact. His kiss was filled completely with love. Unconditional, unjudging, perfect love. You could tell he didn't want me for my body, he wanted my heart.

When we finally landed, there was a beautiful brunette waiting next to a car for us. When she spotted Tristan, her eyes lit up like she was seeing the love of her life. She ran up to him and threw herself into his arms. Jealousy ran through my veins when she spoke with a seductive voice. "I have missed you Tristan. Why do you always stay away so long?"

"Nice to see you too, Harper," Tristan said. "This is…" She cut him off by kissing him. It was a deep passionate kiss. Tristan tried to pull away, but she just held on tighter. Anger raged through me causing me to snap my fingers. She started screaming without opening her mouth.

I walked over to her and got in her face, "Keep your filthy lips off of him. Do you hear me?" She nodded that she understood so I snapped my fingers again giving her lips back.

"You crazy bitch. Tristan, you're just going to stand there and let her do this to me?" she said angry. I turned to walk away from her and she grabbed my hair pulling me back.

Tristan ran up between us so fast he was a blur. "Let go of her now Harper."

Jessica Manson

"The bitch used magic on me Tristan and you expect me not to retaliate?"

I could feel the vampire and the witch in me start to wake up. They were getting ready to attack. "Tristan, you have about five seconds to get her off me." I warned him knowing it was coming fast.

"Harper if you know what's good for you, you will let her go now."

"No," she said bitterly.

"Four...five." I spun around to face her. I was ready to fight when Tristan stepped in front of me.

"Lilith don't do this. If you fight you will lose the baby," he said sincerely.

Harper loosened her grip on my hair, "She's pregnant?"

"Yes, Harper. She is, and we have to go. Now," Tristan said.

We finally got into the car and drove away. Tristan drove for two hours before we reached a hidden gravel road. It was so small our car barely fit on it. It took us another thirty minutes down this road before a small cabin came into view. It was made out of large logs and had a red tin roof. I couldn't wait for it to rain. Rain hitting the tin is my favorite sound. It is relaxing and calming. There were large pillars along the porch that were made of rocks. The cabin was completely surrounded by trees but off to my right I could hear water.

Tristan grabbed our things from the car, "Come on, I could use a shower," he said as he led me toward the house. I could smell the dust as soon as he opened the door. The air was so thick with it, it took my breath. The inside wasn't as cute as the outside. The living room and kitchen were one room and the walls were brown paneling. The floor had darker brown tiles and the furniture was all tan. The house was in desperate need of color and light. It looked like no one had been here for years. "I'll show you to your room."

Tristan led me down the hallway that looked exactly like the living room. There were three doors, one on each side of the hall and one at the end. "Which one is mine?" I asked.

He pointed to the door on the right, "That's you, that's me and that's the bathroom."

Beautiful Corruption

I walked into my room and wanted to walk right back out. The walls were red, and the furniture was black. It reminded me of my room with Odin. I turned and walked across the hall into Tristan's room. He was just setting his things on the bed. His room was a light shade of green and the furniture was a horrible shade of brown. It was perfect. "Will you switch rooms with me?"

"What's wrong with yours?" he asked.

"You'll see."

He grabbed his things and walked across the hall, "Oh."

"Yup. Thanks for switching with me," I yelled after him.

"No problem," he said standing in my doorway. "I'm going to shower, need anything before I go?"

"No thanks." When I heard the water running, I walked into the living room/kitchen and looked through the cabinets. Tristan must have had someone stock food for us because there wasn't an empty cabinet in the house. There was even a pantry that was full, and the freezer and fridge were also stocked with all of my favorites.

My stomach growled at the sight of all the food. I looked under the sink to find some cleaner. I grabbed the bottle of dusting spray and started dusting. I needed a clean area, so I could make myself something to eat. When I was done dusting everything, I started to clean the countertops,

I turned the water on to wet a rag when I heard Tristan scream. I ran to the bathroom and threw the door open, "What's wrong? What happ…" I cut myself off when I noticed his naked body. I bit my bottom lip as my eyes landed on his member. Tristan was gorgeous. His body full of muscles was calling for me to touch it and I wanted to so badly.

He cleared his throat and wrapped himself in a towel. "Did you turn on the water?"

"Mm hmm," I said still looking at his member.

"The water turned ice cold. You almost froze my nuts off Lilith."

"That would have been a tragedy." I was still looking at his body lost in a daze.

39

Jessica Manson

"Are you okay?" he said with a laugh. When I didn't answer, he walked over to me, "Lilith? What's wrong?"

"What? Nothing's wrong. Are you okay?" I felt like an idiot. I was staring at him like a kid staring at a candy store. "I'm hungry." I turned and walked back into the kitchen without saying another word. I could feel my cheeks burning red. I finished wiping down the countertops and pulled out stuff to make a sandwich.

Tristan walked into the kitchen wearing a white t-shirt and some night pants. Thankfully he had clothes on, but it didn't help the way I felt on the inside. I tried to keep my eyes focused on my sandwich, but it was hard to do. When I was done making my food I walked over and sat on a bar stool. He walked over and started to fix himself the same thing. I watched how his muscles flexed in his arm as he lay the turkey on the bread. They twitched as he spread the mayonnaise. I could see his chest muscles move through his shirt as he cut his sandwich in half and I have never been so turned on in my life.

When he was done making his food he came and sat next to me. His elbow brushed against my arm when he sat down sending a tingling sensation straight to my center. My body was reacting to him in a way that I knew wasn't safe. It was hard to breath sitting next to him and that's when he noticed I was being weird. "Are you okay?" he asked.

I couldn't look at him, "I'm fine." He turned and looked at me placing a hand on my shoulder. His touch was enough to make my body lose control. I jumped up from the stool and walked over to the fridge. "Want something to drink?"

"Sure," he said with a raised eyebrow. I got up and grabbed us two sodas. When I handed him his, our fingers touched causing me to look him in the eyes. That was all my body could take. I was on him so fast he didn't see me coming. I kissed him hard and he slipped his tongue into my mouth causing me to moan in reaction. The sweet familiar taste of his kiss was still there. He pulled me closer into him and slowed the kiss down. He began to kiss me softly. His kiss was filled with so much love it calmed my body down. It was amazing how he knew what I needed when I needed it. He knew I wasn't ready to have sex with him yet but if we continued to kiss like we were, it wouldn't take much more for me to be ready.

He slowed the kiss down so much that our lips were barely touching. He gave me one last peck before pulling away from me. "I'm sorry I attacked you like that," I said looking away from him.

"Don't be sorry. I enjoyed it," he said with a smile. "Who knew you could be so aggressive?"

"I don't know what came over me. I was just...I mean I saw your..." frustrated I couldn't find the right words I closed my eyes. The pictures of him standing in the bathroom wet and naked came flooding back. Gosh he was so sexy. "I'm just sorry okay."

"Okay," he said with a laugh.

"What's so funny?"

"You."

"What did I do?"

"You are sexually frustrated at me."

"And you think that is funny?"

"You're cute when your flustered."

"Goodnight Tristan," I said as I walked back to my room.

Jessica Manson

Chapter Six

The next few days were quiet. There have been no signs of Odin finding out where we were so Tristan and I spent the days relaxing. I knew we were getting a little bit too comfortable and we were letting our guard down, but it was nice spending time together.

We decided to sit by the lake to watch the sun set behind the trees. Just as I was relaxing, I smelled something in the breeze. It was an awful stench. It smelled like rotten garbage, but also musty. "Do you smell that?" I asked; the smell was making me sick to my stomach.

"Smell what?"

"It smells like…" I turned to my right and came face to face with a bear. I grabbed for Tristan without making any sudden movements. The bear walked closer to me, smelled me, then stepped back. He suddenly changed. A naked man stood in the bear's place. He was buff and covered in tattoos. His black shaggy hair falling into his brown chocolate eyes. "What the hell?" I screamed.

Tristan got up and stood in front of me. "Who are you and what are you doing here?" he asked the man.

"I'm here for the girl," the man said.

"What do you want with her?"

"I was sent to bring her back."

"So, Odin is working with shifters now?"

"I don't work for Odin; I work for Draven."

"Well, you can tell Draven she's not coming back."

"You will hand over the girl or I will kill you where you stand boy."

I stepped in front of Tristan, "You will not touch him, and I am going nowhere with you. You will leave now, or you will not survive coming here," I said through clenched teeth.

The man laughed. "What will a puny little girl like you do to me?" he said stepping closer to me.

I closed my eyes and took a deep breath. When I opened them again the vampire in me had taken over. With one swift thrust of my hand I stood holding the man's heart. He looked at me with shock before

Beautiful Corruption

falling limply to the ground. "Kill you," I answered even though he was already dead.

"We have to go Lilith. They know we are here. You go get your stuff while I take care of his body." As I walked away, I heard a splash; Tristan had thrown him in the lake.

I grabbed my things as quickly as I could. When I came out of my room Tristan was waiting for me by the front door talking to someone on a phone, I didn't know he had. He hung up when he saw me. "You ready?" I asked a little out of breath.

"Go grab whatever food you want to bring. We are going to be on the road for a long time." I walked over to the kitchen and started grabbing whatever food I could while he loaded our things into the car. When he came back inside, he helped me carry the food I had had chosen to take with us. We hopped in and headed down the long skinny dirt road back toward civilization.

"Where are we going?" I asked curious as to what our next destination would be.

"I have a friend waiting with another car. Once we switch, we will drive to New Mexico. A friend has a house we can use."

"So, there are shifters in this world too?" I asked.

"Yes, among other things."

"What types of other things?"

"Well, fairies for one."

"Seriously? Like Tinkerbell?"

He laughed at me before saying, "They aren't little flying glowing things if that's what you mean. They are regular people like us. In fact, you already know two."

"Who?"

"Daveh and Razi."

"No way. They are fairies?"

"Yes."

"What else exist in this world?"

"Trolls, mermaids, werewolves to name a few."

43

Jessica Manson

"What? How did I live my whole life in this world and never know about any of this?"

"You were human. Humans can't know about us."

"So, there's more?"

"More what?"

"You said that was just to name a few. So, there are more creatures than that?"

"So much more. And I hope we never run into any of them."

We drove in silence for a while and I could tell Tristan wanted to talk about something but wasn't sure how to approach me. It was starting to become awkward between us. I had to say something if he wouldn't. "What is it Tristan? I know you want to say something."

"I was just thinking."

"About what?" I asked.

"About how you ripped that guys heart out with such little force. Usually it takes at least some effort to rip someone's heart out." I didn't respond to him. I was still shaken about what I had done. I actually killed someone with my bare hands. "How are you handling that?" he asked concerned.

"I'm a monster Tristan."

"No, you're not. You did what you needed to do to save the three of us Lilith. I would have done the same thing if you would have given me the chance."

"I'm sorry I stepped in but every time someone threatens you something comes over me. I feel protective over you for some reason. Same thing happened when Odin threatened to send you away. I was ready to kill him then too. I don't understand why I am that way about you."

"I think it is sweet," He said as he took my hand in his and kissed the back of it.

I know what I am and sweet isn't it. I am an abnormality of my kind. I am a savage beast. I hate what I have turned into. I need answers on how to control what I can do. The demons inside of me are always begging to come out. They control me when it should be the other way around.

Although, I do love the fact that Tristan can love me despite what I have become. He can look past the beast that dwells inside me. And he has offered to help raise my baby that doesn't even belong to him. He is even willing to wait till I'm ready before trying to start a relationship with me. He knows I am in love with him and he understands what I have been through, which makes me love him more. Lost in my thoughts I started to doze.

Out of nowhere I was standing on a cliff and laughter surrounded me. I was getting sick of Slaaneth's games. He always invaded my dreams and it was getting tiring. "What do you want Slaaneth?" I asked a little more than frustrated.

"You already know the answer to that question."

"Yes, I know. You want my baby and me dead. What's new?"

"So, snippy today my Lilith."

"Why are you here?"

"Just checking in on my saving grace."

"You will not get your filthy hands on my baby. What do you not understand about that?" I yelled.

"Why are you so convinced that I won't?"

"Because I plan on killing you," I said confidently.

His laughter was so loud it made my ears ring. "You are so sure you can kill me. How?"

"I don't know yet. But I will find a way."

"My sweet naive Lilith, so new, so confident, so willing to take me on. Even though we both know you don't stand a chance against me."

"Naive? You're the one who is naive. You think because I am new to being what I am that I can't take you on? Don't underestimate me Slaaneth, I may be a newbie but this newbie plans on killing you."

He came closer to me. Our faces merely inches apart. His breath, hot against my cheeks, smelled like rotten flesh. "You child will die before ever seeing your child's face. You will die before hearing its first

Jessica Manson

cry. You will be dead before getting to hold your precious child. I will make sure of it."

I lunged for him, but he disappeared, and I jolted awake. I placed my hands on my stomach making sure my baby was okay. "Are you okay?" Tristan asked startled.

"Yes. I just need to check something. I need silence please." I closed my eyes and concentrated. I was listening for a heartbeat. In the silence of the car I could hear a faint thump, thump. I let out a slow sigh of relief as I realized my baby was okay. I would do whatever I needed to do to make sure Slaaneth never got his hands on my baby.

"Is everything okay?" Tristan asked again.

"Yes. I was just checking on the baby."

"How is it?"

"Hungry. Can we stop to get some real food? These chips just aren't doing it for me."

"Sure. I'll try to find an exit. But is it okay if we hit a drive thru? I'd really like to get as much driving in as I can."

"That's fine with me."

It took us forty-five minutes to find an exit with decent food. By the time we got to the drive thru, I had to use the restroom. I told Tristan to order me a burger and some fries while I ran inside. When I walked into the restaurant the lobby was empty except for one woman sitting in a booth facing me. She kept her eyes on me as I entered the bathroom.

In the middle of midstream the door to the bathroom opened. Someone walked over to my stall and was standing in front of the door. Panic filled me as I watched their feet. I pulled my pants up and tried to control my breathing. The person leaned up against the door. "What do you want?" I asked.

"He sent me to warn you."

"Who did?" I asked completely confused.

"Slaaneth," she said with a giggle. "He wanted you to know how easy it would be for him to kill you and take your baby," I whimpered as fear took over my body. "There is no need to be scared today. I'm

Beautiful Corruption

just here to warn you. Remember, he is always watching, and he always knows where you are."

The woman walked out of the bathroom leaving me alone. When a knock sounded at the door, I jumped, and a small scream escaped from me. "Lilith? Are you okay?" I ran out of the stall and straight into Tristan's arms. "Hey, what's wrong?" He asked in a tender but concerned voice.

"Can we go please?" I asked through tears. I finally realized that Slaaneth could do whatever he wanted to me unless I killed him. He would always be there in the shadows stalking me. He had reign over my dreams while his followers had my consciousness.

I was torn between telling Tristan about Slaaneth's threat. I wanted to tell him, but I didn't want him to have to worry about something else. He was already stressed enough with Odin and his father looking for us. I didn't need to add to it.

"Are you going to tell me what happened back there?" Tristan asked once we were back on the highway.

"It was nothing," I lied.

"Lilith, something clearly upset you. Tell me what happened."

"I just don't want to add another problem to your plate. It's full enough."

"We are in this together. Whatever happens to you, happens to me. Tell me."

"Fine." He listened intently as I told him about the dream and about the woman in the bathroom. "I'm scared he will be able to get my baby before I can stop him."

"I will never let that happen."

"But how was he even able to find us in the first place? How would he know we would pick that place? How would that lady know to be waiting for me and who I was?"

"I don't know. But I do know that we will do whatever we can to protect your baby. We are in this together."

"There is just so much to take in. Maybe we should have waited until I killed Slaaneth before leaving. I mean there is so much to deal with now. We are constantly running from Odin and his father and Slaaneth. This much stress can't possibly be good on the baby."

"If you want, we can always turn back. You know Odin will forgive you."

"I don't want to go back to Odin, Tristan. He betrayed me in the worst possible way. And besides how could I spend a second with him when I am in love with you? All I was saying is that I wasn't prepared for all of this. Even though I knew Slaaneth was after me I didn't think he would actually try anything until after the baby was born. I thought we had time."

"We have been driving for hours. Want to stop for the night?"

"Sure." I was exhausted, and we had been driving for seven hours and it was already late when we left the cabin.

Tristan found us a hotel and got us a room with two beds. I was fine with that since I didn't trust being left alone. I was afraid Slaaneth would send someone to attack me.

"Mind if I shower first?" I asked as soon as we entered the room.

"Go ahead."

I grabbed my clothes and headed for the bathroom. I let the water steam before stepping in. I let the hot water run over my body trying to relax, but nothing would calm the worry inside of me. Someone wanted to take my baby, while someone else wanted me and Tristan dead. Would Odin find us? What would happen to us if he did? A thousand questions ran through my mind causing me to zone out until the water ran cold. I quickly washed up and jumped out. After I dressed and brushed my hair I walked back into the room. "I may have used all of the hot water accidently," I said to Tristan as I got into my bed.

"Accidently?" he asked with a grin.

"Yes accidently. I was lost in my thoughts until the water turned cold."

"Are you sure you're okay?"

"Yes, I'm just worried."

"I'm here if you need me. I'm a good listener."

"I know. Thank you. Goodnight Tristan."
"Sweet dreams empress."

Jessica Manson

Chapter Seven

When I woke up the water in the bathroom was running. I assumed Tristan was in the shower. I got up and looked at myself in the mirror above the dresser and I was shocked by my appearance. My hair looked like a rat's nest and I had dark circles under my eyes. I looked exhausted. I also looked like I had lost ten pounds overnight.

The water turned off and a sudden sharp pain went through my stomach. The pain was so intense I doubled over and let out a scream. Tristan came running out of the bathroom wrapped only in a towel. "Something is wrong with the baby Tristan," I cried out. He got dressed so fast he was almost a blur.

He picked me up and carried me in his arms to the car. Once we were inside, he sped out of the hotel's parking lot. "I saw a sign for a hospital on the way in last night. We will be there soon Lilith. Just hold on okay."

The pain was so intense I was rocking back and forth trying to ease it. I was losing my baby and there was nothing I could do about it. Within minutes we pulled up to the hospital. Tristan parked right in front of the emergency door. He pulled me out of the car and ran inside. "Help her, please," he pleaded with the first nurse we saw.

"Calm down sir and tell me what's wrong." The lady said sitting behind the desk.

"She is pregnant. She may be losing the baby. Help her!" Tristan cried out.

She called someone on a radio before saying to Tristan, "Lay her on that bed. Someone is on their way to get her." Tristan did as he was told and as soon as I was laid down a man came through a set of double doors.

"I'm Liam, I will be her nurse today. Can you tell me what happened?" he asked as he wheeled me through the same double doors he just came from.

"She is pregnant and is having pains. I'm afraid she might be losing the baby."

Beautiful Corruption

"How far along is she?"

"We don't know. We just found out she was pregnant. She hasn't seen a doctor yet."

"I see. Has she been under any stress lately?"

"Yes."

"Can you tell me about that?"

"No."

"Okay then, what was she doing before the pain started?"

"She had just woken up. The pains started immediately."

Liam wheeled me into a room and another nurse stepped in to assist him. "I'm going to start an IV on you. We need to get some blood work. We will also need you to get fully undressed and into this gown," he said as he laid the gown on the bed at my feet. "I can help you if you need my assistance."

"No thank you. Tristan can help me," I said taken aback by his offer. I know he was probably just being a good helpful nurse but the way he said it sounded dirty, provocative even.

"Okay, I'll step out and let you get changed. I'll be back in five minutes." When he was gone, I breathed a sigh of relief. I looked at Tristan, "Do you mind helping me get into that?" I looked at the gown disgusted.

"Of course, I'll help you. You shouldn't feel like you have to ask."

"Tristan, do you think my baby is okay?" I asked scared.

"I don't know. I hope so," he said sounding perplexed. Tristan pulled my shirt over my head and then helped me stand to pull off my pants. When I stood, a pain surged through my stomach causing me to cry out. My knees went weak and I leaned into him. Our bodies were so close as he held my almost naked body in his arms protectively. "Let's hurry so you can lay back down." He slipped the gown around me, so I could discretely slip out of my bra and panties.

"Thank you," I said grabbing onto his hand as he tried to walk away. "Will you stay with me?"

Jessica Manson

"I'm not going anywhere." He pulled a chair next to my bed just as Liam came walking back into the room. He was holding a bag with clear fluid in it, a bunch of little packages and some little tubes.

"Okay let's start that IV," he said with a little too much enthusiasm. "We will need to get your blood work as well. Once the results of that come back a doctor will be in to examine you."

"How long does the blood work take to come back?" I asked already anxious to get out of there.

"Anywhere from thirty minutes to an hour. But because you are pregnant with abdominal pain you will be moved to the top of the list. Your blood work will take priority over everyone else's."

Liam stuck my arm but missed my vein. The pain caused me to flinch. "Ouch," I cried out.

"I'm sorry. The vein seemed to have rolled. I'll try the other arm." Liam scooted to the other side of my bed making Tristan move away from me. This time he got the IV in. Once he was finished drawing my blood, he stepped out of the room again. While we waited for the results a lady came in to collect my information. Once she was gone, with Tristan still holding my hand, I drifted off to sleep.

I was standing in pitch blackness. I couldn't see anything in front of me. I could feel someone there with me. A shiver crept up my spine. "Hello," I called out. The person stepped closer to me; now I knew who it was by their presence. "Right now, is not a good time for you to make claims on my baby Slaaneth. I in fact, just might be losing it."

"You can't let that happen Lilith. You must take care of the baby."

"You know I'm not surprised I'm losing my baby. You have me under so much stress and stress isn't good for the baby."

"I know. That is why I brought you back here. I will keep my distance until it is time for you to have the baby. I will not get in your way. My army will back off as well."

"Why? Why have you decided to leave me alone now?"

"Because Lilith, I need the baby healthy and strong, but most importantly, I need it alive."

"So, you will not bother me again throughout my pregnancy?"

Beautiful Corruption

"No. I will not return until it is near your due date. Take care Lilith. And take care of the baby."

I jolted awake in shock just as Liam was walking back into the room. "Test results are back; the doctor is on his way in." Just as the words left his mouth the doctor came into the room. He was fairly young and very attractive with his brown wavy hair and light green eyes. I couldn't help but think about Odin's eyes when I saw him.

"Hello, Lilith. I am Doctor Reed. How are you feeling?" he asked.

"Thirsty," I said with a dry mouth that felt like I had been licking sand.

After pinching the tops of my hands and ankles he pressed his thumb into the tops of my feet. He then pressed gently on my stomach, "Does this hurt?" I shook my head. "Well, there is a reason you are feeling thirsty. Your test results have come back. You are dehydrated. Your baby needs fluids to stay healthy. Are you drinking enough water?"

"Not as much as I should," I said suddenly embarrassed.

"I would like to keep you here over night, so we can get some fluids into your system."

"Am I going to lose my baby?" I asked nervous of what his answer will be.

"As long as you get some fluids in you, your baby should be fine. But I would like to set up an ultrasound for in the morning."

"Okay," I said joyfully. The doctor and Liam both left the room. I was relieved that my baby would be okay. The joy filled my body threatening my heart to explode with it. Tristan squeezed my hand tight. I hadn't realized how scared he was for me. I turned to look at him, "Everything is going to be alright."

"I should have taken better care of you and the baby," he said with dread in his eyes.

"This isn't your fault. It's mine. I should have been drinking more water. You take great care of us just by being by our side." He rested his forehead on our still clasped hands. "Tristan please don't put this on yourself. It is my fault. And you heard the doctor, everything is

53

Jessica Manson

going to be fine." He gently kissed the back of my hand sending a tingle up my arm that reached all the way to my heart. He actually felt guilty about a baby that isn't even his. I realized he loved this baby just as much as I do, and he has no connection to it other than me. I knew then that he would love this baby unconditionally as if it were his own.

"Lilith, I need you to make me a promise."

"Anything," I said willing to give him whatever he wanted.

"I need you to promise me that you will take better care of yourself and the baby. And I too will promise to take better care of the two of you."

"I promise," I said looking straight into his eyes.

Liam came back into the room with a wheelchair. We have a room ready for you. Tristan helped me get into the chair while Liam hooked my IV bag to the attached pole of the chair.

Tristan left me at the hospital to go get our stuff and to check us out of the hotel. I spent the rest of the afternoon lying in bed with my feet propped up. I lay there watching TV until he returned. I was too afraid to go to sleep without him by my side. It wouldn't have mattered anyway because the nurses disturbed me every hour on the hour to check my vitals.

Tristan came back and almost immediately had fallen asleep propped up on a chair. He was lightly snoring, and the sound was making me sleepy like a lullaby to a baby. Once I finally drifted off, I had the best uninterrupted sleep. It had been so long since I slept that good. There were no visits from Slaaneth as promised.

I didn't wake up until a lady came in to take me for my ultrasound. I called Tristan's name to wake him and he jumped to his feet on alert. "Do you want to go with me for the ultrasound?"

A huge smile spread across his face. "I would love to." I got into another wheelchair and the lady drove me to the elevator. She took us down three floors and when the doors opened the hallway had an eerie feeling to it.

I grabbed Tristan's hand and spoke to him with my mind, *"Something doesn't feel right."*

"What do you mean?"

"I don't know. Something just feels…off."

"Everything is okay. I'm right here beside you. Nothing is going to happen while I'm here."

His words didn't console me. I gripped his hand tighter afraid if I let go something bad would happen. I could feel eyes on me and a shiver crept up my spine. I was eager to get off this floor. We entered a room with a big machine and a hard bed in it. The lady instructed me to lay down and lift my gown to my chest. I was thankful when Tristan looked away as the bottom half of my naked body was exposed. The only thing not showing were my breast. The lady finally came over with a sheet and covered me from my middle down leaving only my stomach exposed.

She then squirted a cold gel onto me and placed some kind wand looking tool on my stomach. She started moving it around pressing down firmly. She stopped when she found what she was looking for. "You look like you are about eight weeks along," she said. "Want to hear the heartbeat?"

"Yes," Tristan and I said in unison making me laugh. It warmed my heart to see him so involved. The lady turned the volume up so we could hear. It was amazing. I have never felt so much love for one person in all my life, especially one that I have never met before. I watched Tristan's face light up and had to fight the urge to hold back tears. I listened to the heartbeat holding my breath making sure I created a memory of this moment. But then the heartbeat started to sound funny. It was almost like there was an echo to the heartbeat.

"Why does it sound like that? What's wrong?" I asked panicked.

"Hold on just one moment. Don't worry that sound is perfectly normal," the lady said with a smile on her face.

"Then what is? Why does it sound like that?"

She turned the screen toward us, so we could see the baby. "It sounds like that because there are two heartbeats. You are having twins."

I almost passed out from shock. "Twins? Are you sure?"

Jessica Manson

"Yes dear, twins. The proof is on the screen." I looked at the screen again and sure enough there was two little bean sprouts growing in my belly. Tears filled my eyes. The lies and betrayal from Odin that I thought corrupted my heart, in this moment, turned into a beautiful corruption. He had stolen my life from me, but he gave me the most precious gift anyone ever could. Not one but two babies grew inside of me.

I looked over at Tristan hoping he still wanted to stick around. When I looked at him, I watched a single tear escape from his eye. He was just as happy as I was. "Tristan."

"Yeah?" he asked never taking his eyes off the screen.

"That's our babies," I said letting my own tears fall.

"Ours?" he asked finally looking at me.

"Ours. If you will still have us."

"Of course, I will." He leaned down and kissed me gently. "You have made me the happiest man in the world. I wouldn't give it up for anything." I kissed him again but this time letting him feel what I was feeling. The kiss grew and was becoming very passionate. We forgot about the lady being right next to us until she cleared her throat.

"Would you like a picture of the babies?" she asked breaking the awkwardness.

"Yes please," I said. "How far along do I have to be to find out what they are?"

"Usually around sixteen to twenty weeks. It will all depend on how the babies cooperate."

Once the pictures were printed, I got back in the wheelchair and we headed back upstairs. When we stepped out into the hallway, I had the same eerie feeling as before. I looked around the hallway and noticed a shadow standing a few feet down.

I was eager to get out of the hallway. "Can we walk a little faster? I want to get out of here." They sped up their pace while I kept my eyes on the figure down the hall. It was a guy hidden in the darkness of a doorway. I couldn't see any of his features, but I knew he was watching me. We reached the elevator, but it seemed like it was taking forever to open. I watched as the figure took a step closer. It was as if he was taunting me.

The doors finally came open and I rushed them inside. Just as the doors were about to close the man stepped in front of it. He stared at me with a wicked smile. I could smell him; he was a shifter. Odin had found us, again. Panic filled me. Tristan and I had to get out of the hospital. I was anxious to get back to the room, so I could tell Tristan, but then I remembered I could already speak to him. *Tristan, they found us again. We have to get out of here.*

"Okay. Stay calm. We will leave as soon as we get back to the room."

I grabbed his hand. I was terrified. There was no telling how far away Odin was from us. We finally got back to my room and I immediately got dressed. We were just about to leave when a knock sounded at the door. The person didn't wait for an answer before walking in. "Well, hello. Leaving so soon?" My heart fell when Brant and Latham stepped inside.

"Just let us go. No one has to know you found us," I pleaded.

"You know we can't do that," Latham said.

"I can't go back there. He killed my parents," I said furious. Latham's body stiffened like this was news to him while Brant seemed unaffected. I looked at Latham closely, "You didn't know, did you? He didn't tell you?"

"No. He failed to mention that detail," he said.

"So, you see why I can't go back to him. I won't."

"Why are you in the hospital anyway?" Brant asked.

"I got sick and had to stay overnight."

"What happened?" he insisted.

"Nothing I am just a little dehydrated. Everything is fine."

"We should get going," Latham said.

"I'm not going with you!" I yelled.

"Yes, you are. Odin is waiting," Brant said.

"I don't care. I. Am. Not. Going," I said making sure to enunciate every word.

Jessica Manson

"We can do this the hard way or the easy way. But either way, you *are* coming with us." When had Brant become so vial? I have never seen this side of him.

I stood there eyeing the both of them while I spoke to Tristan in my mind, *"What do we do? We can't go back there. They will kill you and take my babies."*

"Can you put a sleeping spell on them?" he asked.

"Oh, my Gosh, why didn't I think of that? Cover your ears. Last thing we need is you falling asleep with them."

I recited the same sleep spell on Latham and Brant that I had used on the mover.

Awake by day, At rest by night,
I thank the Gods, Turn out the light,
I pray to thee, O holy one,
Let him sleep, and his day be done.

"What are you doing?" Brant asked right before he fell to the ground sleeping. Latham looked at me and smiled then nodded right before he fell over next to Brant.

Chapter Eight

We ran as fast as we could without raising suspicion from the hospital staff. We jumped in the car and headed south once more toward New Mexico. Tristan drove as fast as he could to get as far away from Latham and Brant as we could before they woke up. "How do they keep finding us? We got rid of our phones and keep switching cars. How is he doing it?" I asked panicked.

"I don't know. Maybe they have Kira tracking you."

"She can do that?" He nodded. "Then what is the point of us even running? We will never be free of them. Our babies will never be safe." A big grin played across his lips. "What has you smiling like that at a time like this?"

"You called them ours," he said still smiling.

"Because they are ours. Yours and mine."

"Lilith, I know this is bad timing but, I love you. I love our babies. I will raise them and treat them as if they are my own. According to me, they already are mine. I am the only father they will know. And I want to spend the rest of my life with you. Running forever or one day finally being free, I will always be by your side." My heart warmed by his words. He had taken on so much in such a short amount of time.

"I love you too Tristan and I couldn't pick a better father for my children." I grabbed his hand and pulled it to my lips, kissing the back of it. I didn't let go and he didn't pull away. Tristan is everything I thought Odin was. He has shown me unconditional love. He has proved himself to be worthy of my love. And I do love him. I think I have been in love with him for a while now, but I was also in love with Odin. I couldn't understand at the time how my heart could love two men at once. I had no choice but to ignore my feelings for Tristan.

Odin's love came with passion, but Tristan's love came with something that I needed more. Trust. Sometimes, trust trumps passion.

We had driven for hours and there was no sign of anyone following us. I started to relax and was beginning to drift off every now and then.

Jessica Manson

I tried to stay awake, but my body was so exhausted. Sleep finally took over drawing me into a deep abyss.

I could hear murmurs in the distance. It was so dark I couldn't see anything. The murmurs grew louder until it turned into something else. Chanting. Finally, three witches stepped in front of me. "Welcome Lilith. It is time you joined us." The woman that spoke sounded so sure of herself as if she just knew I would do whatever she demanded of me. She must be the leader of the three.

"Who are you?" I asked feeling like I have seen them before.

"We are a part of you. You need to join us, so our coven will be complete."

"Join you? I will not join you or anyone else. Why can't you people just leave me alone to live in peace?"

"You can have peace once you have joined us. We can give you everything your heart desires Lilith." The girl on the left of the leader said.

"I have everything I need already."

"Join us now or we will hunt you until you do." The leader said through gritted teeth.

"I am not joining you. Hunt me if you must but I will not be a part of your coven."

"One day soon, you will join us Lilith. You will see."

"Fuck!" I yelled as I was jolted awake. As if I didn't have enough people chasing me already now, we have to add witches to the mix.

Catching Tristan off guard when I yelled, he swerved almost hitting a passing car. "Lilith what's wrong? You scared the shit out of me."

"Sorry."

"What happened? Are the babies okay?"

"Yes. They are fine. I have good news and some bad news. Which do you want first?"

"Good news."

"Good news is, Slaaneth isn't going to bother me again until it is time for me to have the babies."

"And the bad news?"

"Now some witches are after me."

"How do you know that?"

"They came to me in a dream just like Slaaneth does. They tried to get me to join them."

"Why do they want you to do that?"

"I don't know. But I think it's time I talked to Parker. He seemed to know a lot about witches. Maybe he can help me."

"I don't think it is safe to contact him," Tristan said sounding worried.

"We have to. He may be the only person with answers." An idea occurred to me, "Do you think it is possible that I can reach out to him the same way Slaaneth and the witches visit me?"

"I don't know. Do you know how to do it?"

"No. But I have learned that if it is quiet enough and I concentrate hard enough I can sometimes do the things I want. Did I ever tell you that I summoned my mom once?"

"No!" he said excited.

"The day I was at the house alone waiting for the movers. She is the one that told me how to kill Slaaneth."

"If she told you how, then why haven't you done it yet?"

"Because she said the answer lies within me. The answer will reveal itself when I am ready to listen. I just haven't figured it out yet."

"So, you need a quiet place with no distractions?"

"Yes. Any places come to mind?"

Since leaving Montana, we had already passed through Wyoming and were well into Colorado. "As a matter of fact, one place does come to mind." He immediately pulled out his phone and called someone. It sounded like he was making reservations. "Everything is set. It is a little off course, but we can be there in less than an hour."

"Where are we going?"

"Tristan smiled, "It's a surprise."

"Fine, don't tell me," I teased. "I hope this works. It's the only way to reach him undetected."

Jessica Manson

It felt like we drove more than an hour before we got to our destination. When we stopped, I quickly got out of the car to get a better look at the view. It was breathtaking. Tristan had brought us to a resort that sat next to a red mountain, the Palisade Monolith. It was in close proximity to nothing. "Is this okay for some quiet?" Tristan asked.

"Are you kidding? This is perfect."

"Well come on, let's get checked in." After checking in Tristan turned to me and said, "They only had one room with one bed. Is that okay? The rooms here have couches that I can sleep on."

"That's fine. I'm just ready to relax a little."

Inside our room was almost as beautiful as the outside. Everything in the room was done in earth tones. The walls were a soft sage green with soft yellow curtains. The furniture a dark wood. Everything here seems so earthy. I sat on the bed to feel it's softness and it made me miss Odin's bed. His bed was so soft and fluffy it was like sleeping on clouds. If I am ever able to stay in one place long enough, I would have to get me one like his.

Laying on the bed my stomach was yelling at me. I had forgotten to eat today. "Hungry?" Tristan asked with a raised eyebrow. I nodded, and he walked toward me holding out his hand. "There is a restaurant downstairs."

The restaurant was just as beautiful as everything else in the resort. The lighting was dim giving off an intimate feel. The walls were a golden yellow and chandeliers hung over every table. Everything was elegant, and it looked pricy. I felt underdressed in my jeans and t-shirt, which brought back memories of the first-time Odin took me out to eat; the first time we had a real conversation. He took me to a fancy restaurant where there to I was way underdressed.

Even the menu was elegant. Nothing jumped out to my taste buds, so I decided to get the Dry Aged Bison Rib Eye while Tristan settled on the Broken Arrow Ranch Venison Oscar. Hopefully the food didn't taste as bad as the names sounded.

When the food came out, I was surprised at how wonderful it looked. The plates were elegantly designed. And the taste was insane.

The name did no justice for how the food tasted. I was expecting something I wouldn't like but it was exquisite. When I was done with my meal, I decided on getting the Chocolate and Hazelnut Mousse Cake. By the time I was done eating, I was stuffed; my hunger fully satisfied.

"That was amazing," I said more to myself. "How did you know about this place?"

"It is my secret hideaway. I come here when I need time to myself."

"Well are you ready to go see if I can reach out to Parker?" We headed back to the room and got comfortable on the bed. "Wait Tristan, this is a stupid idea. What if Parker isn't asleep? I won't be able to reach him if he is awake."

"This isn't stupid, and you will never know if you don't try."

With his words, I closed my eyes and tried to concentrate. I focused on what I needed to do. I searched for Parkers subconscious. I got nothing. I opened my eyes frustrated and sighed. "This isn't working."

"Try Bristol."

"Okay, but I don't think it will work."

"Of course, it won't if you don't believe."

"What are you a Disney movie now?" I asked joking.

"Ha. Ha. Very funny."

"Okay, silence." I closed my eyes again and focused on Bristol this time. I called out her name with my mind. I was about to give up when I zoned in on her subconscious. It felt as if I was inside my own mind walking around. Like an out of body experience. I could see myself walking toward her. She stood in a field of wildflowers smiling up toward the sky. I felt bad for interrupting her dream. "Bristol," I called out to her.

She turned to face me, "Lilith? What are you doing in my dream? How did you get here?"

"Oh, my God Bristol." I ran up to her and threw my arms around her neck. I was overjoyed that I had actually done it. "I am so glad I found you."

"What are you doing here?" she asked again confused.

Jessica Manson

"I need to get in touch with Parker, but this is the only way. It is too dangerous to contact him by phone. Odin may have bugged him."

"We heard you left Odin. What happened? He came to us looking for you."

"He did? What happened?"

"Odin, Ambi, Latham, Brant, Cal and Gunner showed up at our house and demanded for us to let them search for you. We told them we haven't heard from you, but they didn't believe us. They tore our house apart looking for you Lilith. What happened?"

"Odin killed my parents. I couldn't stay with him after finding out the truth and I knew Odin wouldn't just let me walk away. So, Tristan and I ran. Bristol, I have to get in touch with Parker. If I tell you where we are can you and Parker meet us there?"

"Of course."

"It is very important that you be discreet. No one can know about this. If they find us, they will kill Tristan and me."

"I understand," she said with reassurance.

I told her where they could find us, and she said they would leave immediately. With having their own private jet, they would be there in the next few hours. "Bristol," I called out before returning to myself. "Thank you." She nodded as I was zapped back into the room with Tristan.

"Did it work?" he asked impatient.

"They will be here in a few hours."

"You actually did it? That's amazing. It is so impressive how strong your powers are becoming. All you have to do is want a power to work and it does."

"It doesn't terrify you?" I asked remembering how Odin told me once that the powers I had inside of me scared him.

"Not at all. Just the opposite. I think what you can do is amazing." He seemed to have a new joy within him and it warmed my soul. He was so cute when he was excited. He jumped up and walked over to me, pulled me into his arms and spun me around. "You are simply amazing."

64

Beautiful Corruption

I couldn't help but laugh at his playfulness. He placed my feet on the floor slowly causing me to slide down his body. His closeness made my breath catch. Our eyes met and lingered on each other. He leaned in and kissed me gently on the cheek. When he tried to pull away, I pressed my lips to his lightly. His tongue grazed my lip causing me to deepen the kiss until our tongues met.

He pulled my body closer to his wrapping his hands around my waist. His hands slid up the back of my shirt and I started to lose myself in his touch. I ran my hands up his arms and slid them into the sleeves of his shirt. I reached around him to feel his back. I removed my hands and pulled his shirt over his head. His lean body spoke to mine and called for me touch him. I ran my fingers from his chest to his belly button feeling every muscle.

He pulled my shirt off and picked me up in his arms. He sat me gently on the bed and climbed on top of me. "Lilith." He called my name so softly it sent butterflies through my body making me kiss him. I reached down and unbuttoned his pants letting him know what I wanted. What I needed. My body has longed for his for far too long. I was tired of waiting. "Are you sure about this?" he asked.

"Never been surer of anything in my life." He kissed me again before taking my pants off and standing to remove his own. He climbed back on top of me. He kissed me from my stomach up to my neck until he found my lips again. He sat me up and unclasped my bra then slowly removed my panties.

He rested on top of me kissing me and I opened myself up to him. He entered me slowly. He moved at a slow pace while never leaving my lips. Our bodies never unwrapping from each other. His touch was so gentle it made me crave more of him. Sex with Odin was filled with passion and our hunger for one another. It was aggressive. But sex with Tristan wasn't any of that. It was gentle. Every caress, touch, glance was filled with pure love. It was more than just two people having sex with each other. It was our trust and commitment to one another. It was our hopes, our dreams and a promise to make it through whatever the future may throw at us.

Jessica Manson

Tristan was able to satisfy something inside of me in a way Odin hadn't been able to in a long time. Odin satisfied my physical lust, but Tristan was able to satisfy the trust I needed to feel. He was able to fill a void I hadn't realized was there. We made love to each other with every part of our bodies. Love radiated from us. It was in our breath, our touch, our heart beat. We stayed tangled in each other for hours before our bodies gave out from exhaustion. I rested my head on Tristan's chest letting sleep take me away.

Chapter Nine

When I woke up Tristan was still asleep. I quietly slipped out of the bed and went into the bathroom. I turned the water on as hot as I could stand it and once the water was hot enough, I stepped in. A smile formed on my lips as I thought about making love to Tristan. What we did was beyond what I thought was possible for two people. It lasted hours and was the best sex I had ever had even though I have only had one other lover before him. We reached a connection so deep it was like we could feel each other's souls.

I can't figure out if I am lonely, heartbroken or just desperate to be loved by someone I can trust.

I loved Odin so deeply and he meant everything to me. I never in my wildest dreams thought about betraying him. I loved Tristan while I loved Odin, but my heart only beat for Odin. Tristan never had a chance with me no matter how I felt about him deep down. But, all of that changed when I found out that Odin killed my parents. The moment I found out, every drop of love I felt for him turned to hate. My heart didn't beat for him anymore. The weird thing is, is my heart isn't even broken over him, it is just filled with so much anger and hate toward him.

Maybe when the hate leaves, my heart will finally bleed. Maybe then I will be able to feel the pain I need to feel.

I know it is quick and I was trying to wait, but I think I am ready to give myself to Tristan fully. I want to be with him mind, body and soul. Last night proved that to me. He has been beside me through so much. And is willing to stand beside me through so much more. Tristan is the calm to my storm.

When I was about to turn the water off Tristan stepped into the shower with me. "Hi beautiful," he whispered in my ear as he wrapped his arms around me from behind.

"Hi." I leaned into him resting the back of my head on his shoulder.

Jessica Manson

He kissed my neck softly as he whispered in my ear, "Last night was amazing."

"Yes, it was."

Without saying another word, he turned us, so he was under the water. He let the water run over his head and I found it sexy. I washed his hair for him while our eyes stayed locked on each other. Once I rinsed the soap out of his hair, I kissed him gently on the lips before stepping out of the shower.

As I walked back into the room, I heard a knock at the door. "Just a minute," I yelled out trying to get dressed as fast as I could. When I opened the door Parker and Bristol stood on the other side. I hugged both of them at the same time catching them off guard. "I'm so glad you're here."

"Nice to see you too," Bristol said pulling away from me. "You going to let us in or do we have to stay out in the hall?"

"Sorry. I was just so excited to see you," I said as I stepped to the side letting them in.

Parker stopped in front of me looking at me intensely, "How are you holding up? Bristol told me about Odin," he asked.

"I'm holding up for now."

"I'm here for you Lilith. If you need anything, anything at all, don't hesitate to ask."

"Well, I have tons of questions I was hoping you could answer for me."

"I can try."

Tristan walked out of the bathroom wearing only a towel. The sight of him made my heart speed up. He looked extra sexy with his hair disheveled and dripping a few water drops that landed on his chest and ran slowly down to his stomach. I couldn't peel my eyes away from him and Parker couldn't take his off me. Parker watched me watch Tristan dig in his bag for his clothes. The muscles in his chest and arms twitched as he pushed the clothes from side to side.

Parker cleared his throat making me remember Tristan and I weren't alone. Embarrassed, I looked up at Parker who wore an expression I couldn't read. Tristan laughed as he walked back into the bathroom to get dressed.

"What questions do you have for me Lilith?" Parker asked.

"First, I'm hungry. Would the two of you like to join me for breakfast?" Before heading for the restaurant, I knocked on the bathroom door. Tristan opened the door wearing only his jeans that were still undone. My mouth watered at the sight of him and my body longed to fill his against mine again. "We are going for breakfast, care to join us?" I asked.

He pulled me into the bathroom and closed the door behind us. "I can't stop thinking about last night," he said as he pulled me in for a kiss.

"Me either," I said as I pulled away from him.

"How are my babies this morning?" he asked as he rubbed my stomach.

"Hungry. Are you coming with us?"

"Yes. I'll meet you down there once I'm dressed." I turned to walk away when he pulled me in for one lighter kiss. "I love you Lilith."

"I love you Tristan." He smiled and finally let me go. When I stepped back into the bedroom Parker and Bristol both, gave me a questioning look. "Let's go. Tristan will meet us down there," I said before they could ask any questions.

When we got to the restaurant it was empty except for the workers. The emptiness made it comfortable for me to ask some of my questions. "So, Parker, is it okay to ask a few questions now or should I wait?"

"Sure, as long as no one hears us."

I didn't hesitate, "What will happen to me if Odin catches me?"

"It will be up to him what he wants to do about what you have done. But typically, if a mate leaves it is usually punishable by death."

"But what if the Sacrament was performed under false pretenses? I mean it's not like I didn't have a good reason for leaving him," I said trying to defend myself.

Jessica Manson

"That is true, but in the coven's eyes you are the one that betrayed an oath. What Odin did before the Sacrament was performed doesn't matter in their eyes. You will be the one punished, not Odin."

"But that isn't fair. I shouldn't have to be with someone just because they say I do."

"I agree," he said in my defense.

"Could I become the mate of someone that wasn't chosen for me?"

"How do you mean?"

"Say for instance, if I wanted to perform the Sacrament with Tristan, could I since he was not chosen to be my mate?"

"No. The Luminaries chose the mate for you. Odin was chosen for you, so you have to be with him. And let's say something happens to Odin, like he dies, the Luminaries would choose another mate for you. You don't get to choose. You have no say whatsoever."

"But I got to choose between you and Odin."

"That was different. Two mates were chosen for you, so you had no choice but to choose."

"But if the Luminaries choose for me, how was there a mistake? How was two chosen for me?"

"I don't know. It never made sense to me but who am I to question anything?"

I couldn't help but wonder if Odin was ever really chosen for me. Did the Luminaries really make a mistake? "So, what happens to Tristan for helping me?"

"The same thing that will happen to us if we get caught, we die."

"They can't do this. They can't force me to stay with Odin. They can't kill my friends for simply helping me." I was hoping Tristan had been wrong about them wanting to kill us.

"They can Lilith and they will."

The waitress finally came over to take our drink order. When she left to get our drinks, Bristol said, "So you and Tristan huh?"

"What about me?" Tristan said taking the seat beside me.

"Was just asking if you two are together now," she said with a smile.

Tristan looked at me searching for confirmation. "Yes, we are together," I said matter of fact. I spoke to Tristan in his mind, I needed an okay to ask about the babies. When he nodded, I asked Parker, "What will happen to my babies if I am caught by Odin?" Parker and Bristol both looked at me shocked with their jaws dropped. When they didn't speak, I asked again. "If Odin catches me and I get sentenced to death what will happen to my babies?"

"I'm sorry did you say babies? Like as in more than one?" Bristol asked.

"Yes, more than one. I am having twins." Parker still hadn't spoken yet.

"Oh, my gosh. That is so amazing. It is very rare for a vampire to have twins," she said.

I looked over at Parker, "Parker, what will happen to them?"

"Who's the father?" he said finally speaking.

"Odin. But I have no intention of telling him they are his. As far as he will know if he ever finds out, Tristan is the father."

"If he thinks they are Tristan's they will be sent away."

"Sent away where?"

"We don't actually know where they go. There have been rumors of babies created out of the bond were killed. They are considered to be abominations. But no one knows for sure what happens to them. The Luminaries make the call as to what happens to them."

"What if they think they are Odin's?"

"Then Odin and his new mate will raise them. His mate will raise them as her own."

"You mean they will think she is their real mother? They will be calling her mom?" I asked feeling heartbroken.

"You will be dead Lilith; they will never even know you existed." Tears started to burn the rims of my eyes. The pain of knowing my children may never know me killed me inside. The tears began to spill over right when the waitress came to take our order.

"I'm not hungry anymore," I said having lost my appetite.

"Baby, you have to eat. The babies need nourishment. Do you want to end up back in the hospital?" Tristan said.

"Fine. Just two scrambled eggs and some fruit please," I said still not wanting to eat.

When the waitress had all of our orders and walked away Parker's focus turned back toward me, "Lilith, I know what I have said to you is painful to hear, but it is the truth."

"They can't be that cruel. Odin would never do that. I think he honestly loved me. He just can't do it, he won't."

"Lilith, he will. Even if he chooses not to, Draven will. Draven makes all of Odin's decisions for him."

"What will happen if Draven or Odin are killed?" I asked feeling my anger start to take over me.

"I don't know. Someone will take Draven's place, but no one will know if he feels the same as Draven did. He may carry out Draven's orders, but he may not."

"Not if I kill him and take his place."

"You may kill him, but you could never be one of the Luminaries."

"Why not?"

"Because they are all men. There has never been a woman to serve as a Luminary."

"There is always a first time for everything."

"You can't be serious about this Lilith," Parker said sounding worried.

"I have two little angels growing inside of me that needs my protection. And I will protect them. I will do whatever I have to do to ensure their safety. And if that means killing Draven then so be it. I will not let them kill any of you or my babies. And I sure as hell will not let another woman raise my kids and make them call her mommy. They are mine and no one on this God forsaken earth will so much as touch a single hair on their heads."

"I will stand beside you with whatever choice you make. Those are my babies and I also will not let anyone hurt them," Tristan said.

Beautiful Corruption

"Me too. I mean I am going to be an aunt, I can't let anyone hurt them. And Lilith I consider you to be my sister, I won't let them hurt you either," Bristol said.

Parker didn't say anything. He just looked at us like we had lost our minds. "Parker, I need you. My babies need you. It will take all of us to take them out, we can't do it alone. Will you help me?" I asked pleadingly.

"Fine, I will help, but we need to be very careful. We must cover our tracks and be very discreet," he said.

"We need a plan," I said a little too excited.

Jessica Manson

Chapter Ten

When we finished breakfast, we headed back to the room to start working on a plan, but Bristol kept getting distracted. "How far along are you?" she asked.

"Eight weeks."

"Why were you in the hospital?"

"I thought I was having a miscarriage, so we went to the hospital. Turns out I was just dehydrated. They kept me over night, but then Latham and Brant showed up to take me back to Odin."

"If they showed up how are you not back with Odin?"

"I put them to sleep then we escaped."

"I see. So how long have you known you were pregnant?"

"Two weeks."

"How did you find out?"

"Slaaneth told me in a dream and I took a test to confirm it." She was asking her questions so fast it was hard to keep up with her.

"So how long have you and Tristan been official?"

"Since yesterday. But he was by my side way before that," I said as I caught a glance of him. He made my heart flutter with just a simple glance.

"Do you love him?"

"Yes, I do." Growing tired of her interrogation I tried to get back to the reason we were here. "So, does anyone have a plan yet?"

"I was thinking that maybe the two of you could come back to Italy with us and stay at our house. Odin has already searched it. He won't come looking for you there again. We could hide you until you have the baby. Plus, that will give us plenty of time to formulate a plan to take Draven out," Parker said.

"You mean stay locked in a house for seven months?" I asked not liking the sound of his idea.

"Unfortunately, yes. It is the only way to keep you safe. We will be able to have a doctor come to the house for visits for you. You need a doctor during your pregnancy Lilith."

74

"Baby this is a really good idea. No more running or hiding. We will be safe there. And you will be able to rest and relax with no worries," Tristan said.

"You do understand that you will have to be locked up with me, right?" I asked.

"Yes, I know, but as long as I'm with you and you are safe, I don't care."

"Fine, I'll do it."

"Yay!" Bristol said as she jumped up to hug me. "We will have so much fun."

"Yup being locked away for seven months sounds like a real hoot," I said bitterly.

Before heading back to Italy Bristol and I decided to spend the day at the spa here at the hotel while Parker and Tristan went horseback riding.

The plane ride back wasn't something I looked forward too. I was nervous to go back. What if Odin finds out that I am with them? They will pay with their lives if we get caught.

"Is everything okay baby?" Tristan asked sensing my uneasiness.

"What if this doesn't work?"

"It's the best option we have right now."

"Doesn't mean I am comfortable with it. As soon as we get there, we need to make an escape plan just in case Odin comes to search their house again."

"I agree with that."

Parker and Bristol came to sit in front of us just as the pilot announced that we were departing. I rested my head on Tristan's shoulder trying to rest, but it was no use. "Parker what can you tell me about witches?" I asked curious to see if he could help with the witches that are after me.

Jessica Manson

"Not really much more than what I have told you before. Witches only have one or two powers but no more than that. But of course, you are different. Why?"

"Because I have a coven that's after me. They want me to join them. They made it sound like they could make me, and they said they would hunt me until I joined them."

"They can't force you. You have to accept their offer of your own free will. Witches are tricky. They will find what you love most and hold it against you, so you have no choice but to join them," Parker said.

"It sounds like to me we need to add some witches to our hitlist," Bristol said. I liked her line of thinking.

"That may be true. Killing them too, may be the only way to stop them. But why do they want me so bad?"

"How many of them were there?" Parker asked.

"Three. They said they needed me."

"I see. They need their fourth."

"Their what?"

"Fourth. They need someone to complete their circle. Earth, wind, fire, water. If the four elements connect the witches will become very powerful. They will be unstoppable. As long as they cast together their powers would be unimaginable."

"Well, I'm already all of those things. So why do they need me? Why can't they just find some other witch to join them?"

"Exactly. They want you because you already have those powers. If you joined them, they would have power like never before. They want to see what it feels like to be you. You are stronger than any other witch in history. Why wouldn't they want you?"

"Don't they know I'm not one to mess with? I hurt people before I even know I am doing it." The words brought me back to when I hurt Ambi before I even knew what I was doing. I had planned on killing her and almost succeeded had it not been for Odin. Then I thought about the man whose heart I ripped out without thinking about it. It was so effortless, so easily done before I knew what had happened.

"Trust us, we know; we were their when you and Ambi fought," Bristol said.

"Not just her," I said as I hung my head in shame. "I ripped a shifters heart out," I said in almost a whisper.

"No way," Bristol said astonished.

"You should have seen the power she used. She ripped his heart out with no effort at all. I mean the strength she carries within her is magical. It is unlike anything I have ever seen before," Tristan said bragging me up. His bragging didn't make me feel any better about what I had done to that man.

"Parker, can you teach me how to control my powers? I can't control any of them except one. It usually just happens on its own. Usually when I get angry my body automatically calls for the vampire or the witch inside of me. They take over automatically."

"I don't know how to help you with that but give me time and I will find you answers."

With some of my questions answered I could relax a little bit. I still feared Odin would find us, but my thoughts of him got replaced with my desire to know more about the witches. I couldn't help but wonder what they would threaten me with to try and get me to join them. Then something occurred to me, I wondered which powers I already had went with the vampire or the witch part of me. "Parker, can I ask you a few more questions?"

"Sure."

"I was thinking about my powers and I don't know which ones are vampire and which ones are witch powers."

"What powers do you have already?"

"I can talk to people with my mind as well as read theirs."

"Telepathy. Could be both, witch or vampire."

"I can talk to people in their dreams. That is how I got Bristol to get you to me."

"Dream manipulation. Vampire."

"I brought you and Odin to me once with a snap of my fingers; what did you call that?"

Jessica Manson

"Conjuration. Witch."

"I can put people to sleep. I use a spell, but I feel deep down that if I thought it, it would just happen."

"Try it."

"On who?"

Parker looked over at Bristol who had in ear buds listening to music. "Her. She will never know it is coming and won't be able to block you."

I closed my eyes and tried to concentrate. I thought about what I wanted to do and focused on Bristol's face in my mind. I opened my eyes and peered at her. I mouthed one word, sleep. Bristol's eyes shut, and her head fell to the side instantly. "It worked! I did it!" I said overexcited. Tristan laughed.

"Mind stunning. Witch," Parker said with a smile. "Try causing Tristan pain."

"No. I can't do that to him," I said disgusted by his suggestion.

"Go ahead. I don't mind. I think it is a good idea to figure out what powers you have," Tristan said.

"Fine. How do I do it?"

"The same way you do everything else."

I closed my eyes again and this time focused on Tristan. When my mind was clear, I opened my eyes and looked at him, "Pain." He doubled over crying out in extreme pain. He was gripping the armrest so tight his knuckles turned white. I broke my focus from him feeling guilty about hurting him on purpose. "Tristan I am so sorry." He held up his hand to me needing a moment.

"Pain infliction. Witch," Parker said.

"I can move objects or people with my mind."

"Telekinesis. This one could be both as well. Now try to make Tristan do something by touching his arm."

"Make him do what?"

"Anything."

"Are you okay with that Tristan?" I asked still feeling bad for him.

78

Beautiful Corruption

"Yeah. Go ahead." I reached out and grabbed Tristan's arm. I thought about what I wanted him to do. He reached out and punched Parker in the arm.

"What was that for?" he said rubbing the spot Tristan had just hit.

"That was for making me cause him pain," I said.

"Okay. I get it. Now Lilith, try doing the same thing but this time use eye contact." I looked into Tristan's eyes and concentrated on what I wanted from him. This time I made him dance in his seat causing Parker and I to burst out into laughter. "What you just did was mind compulsion. By touch is witch, eye contact is vampire."

"This is starting to get fun," I said still smiling.

"Not for me," Tristan said still dancing in his seat. We laughed again, and I broke the eye contact between Tristan and me.

"Want to try more?" Parker asked.

"Yes. I need to know what all I can do."

"Try to make Tristan feel a certain way. It could me sad, happy, mad. Any emotion."

I focused again on Tristan and thought about how I wanted him to feel. I looked at him and he immediately broke down and started crying. Tears were flowing heavily down his face. I then changed the emotion and he burst out into laughter. He was laughing at absolutely nothing. I giggled at him as I broke my concentration from him.

"Emotional control. Vampire." Parker looked at me with a mischievous smile playing across his lips, "Want to try a fun one?"

"Sure."

"Concentrate on Tristan and try and see beneath his shirt."

"You mean like x-ray vision?"

"Yup. Just like x-ray vision." I looked at Tristan and focused on seeing what was beneath his shirt. When his chest came into view for me, I was shocked. I also couldn't help myself and looked further down. I could see him as if he were sitting in the seat naked. I smiled at his body and the dirty thoughts I had about it. "Lilith."

Parker called my name making me turn to face him. "Oh, my God," I yelled horrified. My eyes landed on Parkers naked body. When I tried

79

Jessica Manson

to look away my eyes landed on Bristol. I had just seen both Parker and Bristol naked. I closed my eyes, "How do I turn it off? I've seen way more than I needed to."

"Just stop thinking about it," Parker said with a laugh.

I slowly opened my eyes back up and thankfully everyone was wearing clothes again. "I never want to do that again. That was horrifying."

"It could come in handy at some point," Parker said with a laugh.

"Why would I need to see anyone naked?"

"You won't just see naked people. With x-ray vision, you can look through objects like doors or walls."

"Well in that case I'll use it."

"That's a witch's power by the way."

"Noted. Got anything else?"

"Try turning yourself invisible."

"Seriously. I can do that?"

"I don't know. Try it and we shall see. But I'm willing to bet that you can."

I didn't need concentration this time. I simply thought about being invisible and instantly was. "This is so cool." I wanted to see if this power went further. I thought about Tristan turning invisible too. The moment I thought it he also turned invisible. Then so did Parker. "This is the best power yet."

At that moment, Bristol finally started to wake up. I kept us invisible and decided to mess with her a little bit. "Guys? Where did you go?" She got up from her seat and looked around the jet for us. She walked into the back room searching. I got up from my seat and followed her. When I reached her, I tapped her on the shoulder. She spun around with a frightful look on her face. "Guys this isn't funny."

I made myself visible again and said, "Boo," Bristol screamed making the three of us laugh.

"That wasn't funny," she said.

"I'm sorry Bristol. I had to do it," I said still laughing. "Let me guess, witch power."

"Yes. Now try changing your appearance."

I thought about looking like Bristol. "Did it work?"

"Yes Bristol. There are two of you now," Parker said with a giggle.

"This one could work in my favor when Odin comes to take me back." I thought about pushing the power out onto Tristan.

"Holy shit," Bristol said. I looked at Tristan who now looked like Parker sitting beside me.

"That is amazing. I don't think any witch has ever been able to change the appearance of another without touch or some kind of spell before," Parker said. "This power is called glamouring. It too is a witch power."

"This has been fun, but I am starting to get tired."

"It seems as if you have more witch powers than vampire. There are a couple more powers I want you to work on, but that needs to be done when we are not fifty thousand feet in the sky. With a little bit of meditation, you should learn to control your powers. You will be able to call on them instead of having them take over you." With his words, I leaned my head onto Tristan's shoulder and was finally able to nap.

Jessica Manson

Chapter Eleven

When we arrived in Italy the nerves, I felt over Odin finding out I was back, was almost unbearable. My heart was beating so fast it felt like it would beat out of my chest. My hands began to shake, and my forehead beaded with sweat. I made Tristan hold my hand the whole way into the house for fear of an attack. Once inside the house I made Bristol and Parker close all the curtains before I started to settle down.

"Lilith, I want you and Tristan to be very comfortable here. This is your home just as much as it is ours," Parker said.

"Thank you. We appreciate everything you have done for us," I said giving him a hug. I held onto him a little while longer before asking, "What happened to you after the Sacrament? I've missed you."

"I know. I've missed you too. I'm sorry we stayed away. We just wanted to give the newlyweds time to yourselves."

"Yeah because that matrimony turned out perfect," I said sarcastically.

His arms grew tighter around me, "I'm sorry about your parents and about what Odin did to you. How are you really holding up?"

"My heart is hard Parker. I cried once when I first found out, but I have grown numb to it."

He pulled away from me. "You need to let yourself feel this Lilith. It isn't good for you."

"I will eventually, I'm sure."

"Come on, I'll show you to your rooms," Bristol said excitedly.

She led Tristan and I down a long hallway that had six doors in it. There were two doors on one side, three on the other and one in the middle at the end of the hallway. Bristol pushed open the first door to the left, "This will be your room Tristan," she said as he stepped in. We continued down the hall until we reached the second door on the right, "This is your room. I'm sorry there isn't a bathroom of your own in here. But the bathroom is the door at the end of the hall."

"This is fine. Thank you."

"My room is next door and Parker is right across the hall from you if you need anything. No matter the time of day or night. Okay?"

"Okay," I said as I smiled at her.

"Get settled in while I go have Drezzie make us some dinner."

"Bristol," I called out for her before she left the room. "Would you happen to have some comfortable clothes I could wear? All I have are my jeans."

"Of course. I'll be right back." She walked out of the room and was only gone for a second before returning. "Here these should do." She handed me a stack of clothes. "Anytime you need something to wear feel free to go into my closet and get what you need."

"I will need to find a way to do some shopping. I will need clothes, so will Tristan."

"I can go for you tomorrow. Just write down yours and Tristan's sizes."

"Thank you, that is very kind of you."

"Don't mention it. What are sisters for anyway?" she said as she walked out of the room again. I walked over to the bed and looked through the stack of clothes. She had brought me a black t-shirt, a pair of hot pink sweat pants and some very bright multi colored fuzzy socks.

I had just put on the last sock when a knock sounded at the door. "Come in," I called out.

Tristan walked into my room and closed the door behind him. He didn't say anything. He walked up to me and pulled me into his arms. He held me against him for a long moment before pulling away from me. He lifted me into his arms and laid me on the bed on my back. He lifted my shirt to expose my stomach. "You are already starting to show." He kissed my belly, "How are my babies?" he said speaking to my stomach. "Daddy can't wait for you to get here. I love you both so much and I haven't even met you yet."

Tears filled my eyes at his words. My heart warmed for him. He is truly an amazing guy. He loves us so much when he doesn't have to. He laid his head on my stomach while caressing it. I ran my fingers through his hair. "We love you too Tristan," I said wiping the tears away from my eyes.

He leaned over me, our faces only inches away from each other. "I love you Lilith. And these are *my* babies. No matter what happens, they are mine."

"Forever," I said. He leaned down and kissed me passionately. He climbed on top of me laying his body gently on top of mine. Our bodies started to heat up the longer we kissed. I pulled his shirt over his head exposing his chest to me. I bit my lip at the sight of his muscles. I ran my hand over them feeling each one slowly. He pulled my shirt off and kissed my chest.

I tugged on his jeans letting him know I wanted him to remove them. He stood up and took them off and then he removed mine. He climbed back on top of me pressing our skin to each other. He unclasped my bra and pulled off my panties. He then slipped out of his boxers. He kissed my body tenderly causing tingles to flow straight to my center.

My body yearned for his. I needed to feel him inside of me. When I opened myself up to him, he pressed himself inside me gently. He took his time pleasuring my body. He paid so much attention to my body. He kissed one of my breasts while caressing the other. From time to time he would gently bite my nipples causing a fire to surge through my body.

After forty-five minutes of showing my body all the attention, I used my super strength and flipped us over, so I was on top of him without breaking the connection. I slid back and forth on top of him slowly. I dug my nails gently into his chest causing a growl to escape him. I sped up when the feeling of euphoria started to take over my body. Moans were escaping me uncontrollably. I could feel Tristan swell inside of me. He was just as close as I was to our release. He placed his hands on each side of my hips and helped me slid back and forth faster. The muscles of my middle began to contract sending me into ecstasy. Tristan and I came at the same time making us both moan with pleasure.

I laid down on the bed beside him trying to catch my breath. He pulled me into his arms and I laid my head on his chest. We lay in each other's arms silently. We didn't need words to explain what we were feeling. We told each other how we felt with our bodies. No one would ever be able to make love to me like Tristan could. He poured every bit of his love for me into our sex. And it was perfect.

I was lost in my thoughts when someone knocked on the door. "Just a minute," I yelled out jumping off the bed trying to find my clothes.

"I just wanted to tell you dinner is ready. Take your time and meet us in the dining room when you are ready. We will wait for you," Bristol yelled through the door."

"Do you think she knows we just had sex?" I whispered to Tristan.

"Yes, she does," Bristol yelled through the door laughing.

My face burned with embarrassment. I was horrified. Tristan laughed at the shocked look on my face. "Oh, my God Tristan. That's so embarrassing. How am I supposed to face her at dinner?"

"Baby, she doesn't care that we made love. It's not like she's never done it before."

"I know. But still…"

"Still nothing. Come on let's go eat. I know my babies are starving," he said cutting me off.

"Fine," I said reluctantly as I headed toward the door.

When we got to the dining room Parker and Bristol were waiting for us. Bristol was wearing a huge grin on her face and the embarrassment washed over me again. "How are the two lovebirds?" she asked.

"Dandy," Tristan said smiling back at her. As we sat at the table waiting for the food, two guys walked into the room carrying trays of delicious goodness. The smell hit me making my mouth water and my stomach growl. My babies were hungry and couldn't wait to be fed.

Jessica Manson

The trays were filled with Italian foods. Spaghetti, Ravioli, Gnocchi, Risotto and Lasagna. They even made a pizza. "Wow, this is a lot of food for just four people," I said salivating.

"We weren't sure what you two liked, so we had them make everything," Bristol said.

I took a little bit of everything. It was a lot of pasta for one person to ingest, but it was so delicious. Everything was very tasty. "Oh, my goodness, this is so good," I said taking another scoop of Lasagna and Risotto. Just as I was about to dig into my second plate, the two men walked back in with trays of dessert. My eyes followed them as they sat the trays down. "Is that cheesecake?" I asked ready to dig in.

"Yes. Also, there is Tiramisu, Cannoli, Semifreddo and Zeppole."

I finished my second plate of dinner before taking some of every dessert. The desserts were so decadent and delicious. It was like heaven in my mouth with every bite. My eyes rolled back in the back of my head and a moan left me as I savored the taste. When my plate was empty, I couldn't help but take more. I silently hoped they weren't judging my pigging out. If they said anything, I could always blame the babies.

When my second plate of dessert was finished, I sat back and saw everyone was watching me with wide eyes. Embarrassment washed over me. I knew what they were thinking without even having to read their minds. "What?" I asked annoyed.

Tristan reached over and rubbed my stomach while a smile grew on his face. "My babies were hungry."

"I am eating for three, you know?" I said.

"I know. It's cute," he said.

"Cute? Me pigging out is cute?"

"Yes."

"What do the two of you want to do now that dinner is over?" Parker asked.

"I don't care what we do, but I am too stuffed for an active activity," I said rubbing my belly.

"How about a movie?" Parker suggested.

Beautiful Corruption

"Sounds good to me," I said. Parker led us to the basement where they had the TV room. When we stepped inside my jaw hit the floor. This was no ordinary TV room. This was an in-home theatre. They had a white screen with a projector. The white screen covered one whole wall of the room. They had large black leather theatre seats that reclined. There was a concession area that was filled with candies, sodas, and popcorn. Had I not eaten so much at dinner, I would definitely grab me some Goobers. "This is amazing," I said as I planted my butt into one of the seats on the front row.

"What movie would you like to watch?" Bristol asked.

"What do you have?" Bristol walked over to some floor to ceiling cabinets on the left side of the room and opened the accordion style doors exposing thousands upon thousands of movies. There would be no way for me to choose out of all those movies. "Y'all will have to choose, that is way too many movies for me to look through."

Bristol and I decided to let the guys pick the movie. I almost fell asleep while waiting the thirty minutes it took for them to choose. I groaned when they finally chose a dude movie about a man that is half man-half cyborg needing to save the world. Needless to say, I ended up falling asleep halfway through the movie.

Jessica Manson

Chapter Twelve

Chanting filled my ears as darkness filled my vision. Annoying as they were, visits in my dreams no longer scared me. Slaaneth visited me enough to keep the fear of them at bay. I knew the witches were coming and I wished I could wake myself up, so I could avoid them. I would have to ask Parker about how to do that.

It wasn't long until I was standing in the middle of a forest in front of the witches. "What do I owe the pleasure of this visit?" I asked in a bitchy tone.

"It seems you, Lilith, are in a foul mood so I will cut to the chase. Have you decided to join us?"

"Yes, I have decided, and my answer is the same as last time. I am not going to join you."

"You must," the leader snapped at me.

"I don't have to do anything I don't want to and I also know you can't force me. So, as I said before, I will not join you."

"You don't understand, you need to join us. That is the only way you will ever be safe." The girl to the left of the leader said.

"What could the three of you possible keep me safe from? For all I know you just want me, so you can use my powers."

"We will tell you everything when you join us."

"I. Am. Not. Joining. You," I said enunciating each word.

"You will and sooner than you think," the leader said.

Anger was starting to flood through my body and I could feel the witch inside of me screaming to be released. I let her. After all, this is just a dream.

I began to say a chant of my own:

Powers of the witches rise,
Course unseen across the skies,
Come to thee, I call you here,
Leave your witch, leave her bare.

"What are you doing? Stop it," the leader of the group shouted. Looking her in the eyes, I repeated the chant:

Powers of the witches rise,
Course unseen across the skies,
Come to thee, I call you here,
Leave your witch, leave her bare.

"Don't do this. Please," she begged. I held out my hand and absorbed the powers from the leader of the three witches. Tears began to fall from her eyes. "How could you steal my powers?" she asked in a weak voice.

"Maybe you should consider who you mess with next time. I told you I would not join you. Consider this a warning. I could do far worse things to you. Don't visit me again," I said as I snapped my fingers waking myself up. I guess I wouldn't need to ask Parker how to do that after all.

When I woke up, I was in my bed confused. One, how did I get to my room when I fell asleep in the theatre and second, had I really taken the witch's powers? I know it was a dream, but I could feel her power surging through my body connecting with mine. I jumped out of bed needing to talk to Parker.

When I opened the door, Tristan was standing on the other side. "Lilith, good morning. I was just coming to get you for breakfast," he said.

"Where is Parker? I need to see him right now," I said rushing past him.

"He is in the dining room. What's wrong? What happened?"

When I walked into the dining room and Parker saw me, he could tell something was wrong with me. He immediately asked, "What's wrong?"

"Can I hurt someone in my dreams?" I didn't hesitate to ask.

"What?" he asked confused.

"Can I hurt someone in my dreams?" I asked again.

Jessica Manson

"Hurt them how?"

"Can I steal another witch's powers in my dreams?"

He looked at me in shock for a second, "Yes. You can steal their powers, you can hurt them, and you can even kill them."

"Oh God, what have I done?" I asked myself as I sat down so I wouldn't pass out.

"What did you do Lilith?"

"You remember me telling you about the three witches that came to me in my dreams?" he nodded while Bristol and Tristan leaned in closer to listen. "They came to me again just now. I told them I wasn't joining them, but their leader is just so damn persistent. She said I would join them sooner than I think. The witch inside of me was raging to get out. I thought it was just a dream, so I didn't see the harm in letting her have a little fun. I started chanting. The leader begged me to stop but I didn't listen. I said the chant one more time and held out my hand. I absorbed her powers. I can feel them inside of me. She cried Parker. She was fucking crying while I stood there smiling in her face. But the worst part is, I liked it."

"Lilith, it is okay," Parker said.

"No, it's not. I took her powers. I am truly a monster."

"No, you're not."

"Don't you get it? I hate what I am. I have since the first time I hurt that innocent woman in Croatia. That's all I do is hurt people."

"Everyone has monsters inside of them trying to get out, but it is up to you to control it."

"The monsters you run from, you can see. But the monster I run from is me."

"If you call what you are a monster, then you will always be a monster. There is no turning back from it. But what type of monster you become is up to you."

"Baby, you would have had to fight her eventually. Isn't it better that you did it this way? I mean she is now one less witch we have to worry about attacking you." Tristan said putting his arm around my shoulders.

Beautiful Corruption

"I guess so. But I still don't feel good about it."

"No one said it would be easy doing these types of things, but you have faced harder and you will continue to face harder times. You ripped the heart out of a bear shifters chest. That was harder than taking the powers of a witch."

"He was going to kill you."

"I know. And you did what you had to do to protect me just like you did what you had to do to protect yourself. They would have done something horrible to get you to join them. They would have hurt your friends or killed someone you love. They probably would have threatened you with our babies. Witches are evil tricky bitches. Best you took the leader out now rather than later."

"Nice Tristan," I said as I got up and walked away from him pissed. I know he said witches, but I am part witch. He may have been directing his words toward them, but it didn't make me feel any better about the witch I carry inside of me. But what upset me the most is, I *am* an evil tricky bitch. I have ripped a heart out of someone, stolen someone's powers and attacked two people almost draining the blood from them.

I was digging through my duffle bag when a knock sounded at my door. "Come in," I yelled reluctantly.

"Are you okay?" Bristol asked.

"No, I'm not."

"Do you want to talk about it?"

"Not really," I said as I threw the duffle bag onto the floor and plopped onto the bed. "I shouldn't be here."

"What do you mean?"

"I shouldn't be willingly putting y'all in danger. Months ago, I was a loner perfectly capable of taking care of myself. I can do it again."

"We knew the risk when we agreed to help you. Whether you like it or not, we are your family Lilith and family sticks together."

"I know, but I can't let y'all risk your lives for mine. And I love Tristan so much it would kill me to lose him. We can't be together no matter how much we love each other."

91

Jessica Manson

"Why not? I'm sorry Lilith, but I don't see the problem."

"Because. Bristol, Odin will kill Tristan for helping me. And if he ever finds out that I love him he would bring him back from the dead and kill him again. I can't even begin to think about what Odin would do if he found out Tristan and I had sex."

"Do you love him? And I mean really love him."

"Yes, I do."

"Then don't let anyone make you feel like love isn't worth having because I see forever in your future."

"Thanks Bristol," I said still not feeling any better.

"Can I tell you a story?"

"Sure."

"It was the 18th century. Life back then had just began to transform from the industrial revolution. Most people lived in the countryside, making their living from farming. The more land you owned, the richer you were. But most people lived as subsistence or bare survival.

England suffered from gin drinking. It was cheap and easy to find. Back then no one needed a license to sell alcohol. It was many peoples only form of comfort. The estimated population in England was about 5 ½ million then so the towns grew larger bringing in new people every day. The population in my town of Liverpool was about 77,000.

Bodies of men called Paving or Improvement Commissioners moved into town to clean up our streets and improve our town. They even added oil lamps to our street lighting then up at night. That's when I met and fell in love with Solomon. I was only seventeen. When I first laid eyes on him I thought about how dashing he looked in his breeches and stockings. He was a gorgeous man.

We spent all our free time courting. We would spend afternoons in a field reading or going to horse races. We would visit the assembly rooms to play cards or go to balls. He had asked for my hand in marriage after only four weeks of courting me. I was so happy. I rushed home to tell my parents about my good news. They forbid me to see Solomon ever again. They said I wasn't allowed to marry him because someone would be coming for me on my eighteenth birthday.

Beautiful Corruption

I didn't understand why they wouldn't want me to marry him. He wasn't the richest man, but he had money. All of my friends were already married or were planning their weddings. I was so angry at them. I was planning on running away with Solomon, but my parents found out and moved me away. My heart was so broken. I had lost the only man I had ever loved.

My parents were right though. The day before my eighteenth birthday a man came for me. My parents handed me over with no questions asked. He took me to his home and explained that I would become his wife the next day. I was terrified and furious. I didn't know this man and my parents just gave me to him.

When my transformation started, that's when he explained everything to me. He told me what I was and why I had to marry him. Once the transformation was over, I wasn't mad or scared anymore. I was grateful."

"Grateful?"

"Yes. I was grateful that my parents had saved Solomon's life. And I forgave them for that.

I completed my Sacrament even though I didn't love Lafayette. He became my husband and over time I grew to love him. He became my best friend at first. He didn't pressure me into doing anything with him until I was ready. Gradually day by day I loved him more and more. And now today, Fate is my soulmate, my one and only. He is the light in my darkness. I love him with every part of my being.

I am telling you this because I see the same kind of love that I feel for Fate in you and Tristan. The two of you have something very special. I know you and Odin were connected, but the love you and Tristan have is unbreakable. It's a bond that can withstand the test of time. Don't give that up because you are scared. Tristan loves you and has decided to raise not one, but two babies that are not his. If that isn't love, then I don't know what love is."

"Bristol where is your husband now?" I asked realizing I have never met him before.

"He is still on a mission. He has been gone almost a year."

"Don't you miss him?"

"Of course, I do. I get to talk to him from time to time and his mission is almost over. He should be home by next month."

"I bet you are so excited."

"Impatient is more like it. I can't wait to see his beautiful face."

"I can't wait to meet him."

"Okay, enough story time. I came here on official business. I have shopping to do. Did you write your sizes down for me?"

"I did," I said as I grabbed the piece of paper and my debit card that Mr. Tassel gave me from the dresser.

"I don't need your money. Consider it a welcome home gift." She took only the paper before heading out the door.

Chapter Thirteen

I started digging through the duffle bag again but this time in a much better mood when another knock sounded at the door. "Come in," I yelled once again. It was Tristan who walked in this time. He shut the door and leaned his back against it looking at me. I started to speak, but he held his hand up stopping me.

"Lilith, when I said witches were evil tricky bitches, I was in no way referring to you. I am truly sorry for insinuating that."

"Tristan I…" He cut me off again and walked closer to me.

"I would never think you are evil, tricky, or a bitch. I love you. I love my babies. And…"

This time I cut him off by placing my lips to his. I kissed him until I was sure I would be able to speak. "Can I say something now?" he nodded. "I am sorry for getting mad at you. I knew you weren't talking about me. I was just mad at myself and blamed you for it. I love you Tristan. I want us to be in a real relationship with each other. I know we can't get married, but I already feel like I'm your wife."

"We can get married Lilith. Marry me. Today."

"I can't marry you. I'm married to Odin."

"Not by the eyes of the human laws. You are only married to Odin by the secret laws of the coven. We can get married as humans."

"Are you serious? You really want to marry me?"

"Lilith, you know I have loved you since I first met you. Odin may have claimed you as his from the time we got to Newport, but that day in the front yard I took one look at you and knew you were meant for me. You are my north star guiding my way, the mother to my children and the one and only true love of my entire existence."

"Then yes, I will marry you." He pulled me into his arms and spun us around in circles.

We laughed with joy until I had to make him put me down. I immediately ran to the bathroom to throw up. I hadn't eaten breakfast yet so there was nothing but stomach acid to get out. Tristan ran in behind me and held my hair back for me. When I was done, he got me

Jessica Manson

a cold wet rag. "Guess no more spinning for a while," he said smiling at me.

"Guess not. You know what would be nice?"

"What?"

"A hot shower. I have been trying to get my clothes together for the last hour, so I can take one."

"You get in and relax. I'll go get you some clothes."

"Thank you." Tristan set the water for me before leaving the bathroom.

I stepped in the shower letting the water hit me in the face first. I stood there letting the water wash away the nausea when Tristan came back into the bathroom with some clothes for me. He got undressed and stepped into the shower with me. He washed my hair for me then lathered the loofah with soap and washed my body. He wasn't being sexual with the shower time, instead he was caring. He was washing me because he knew I didn't feel good.

Once I was washed, he wrapped me in his arms from behind placing his hands on my small protruding stomach. "You don't know how long I have waited to be a father Lilith. You have blessed me not once, but twice with the greatest gift in the world. I will always love you for that." He said as he kissed my neck.

"If I didn't have so many people after me right now, my life would be perfect."

"When all of this is over, we will have the perfect life together. Just the four of us."

When we got out of the shower Bristol was back and emptying bags of clothes onto my bed. "That was fast."

"After years of being alive, you kind of master the art of shopping," she said.

"Alright, show me what you got."

"I got you ten packs of t-shirts in different sizes, so you can grow into them as you get bigger. I got tons of sweat pants. A woman must be comfortable while lounging. And I also got you some flowy dresses in case you feel like dressing up one day."

Beautiful Corruption

"Wow this is a lot of clothes."

"A woman can never have too many clothes Lilith." She had bought at least twenty pairs of sweatpants in all different colors of the rainbow. The dresses were the same way. Some had flowers, some had hearts, I even thought I saw one with balloons on it. I shuddered at the thought of wearing that one. "I also got you socks, underwear and some bras." She leaned in a little closer to me ear and whispered, "Some sexy, some not so sexy. You'll thank me for the not so sexy when your huge," she pulled back smiling at me.

"May I come in?" Parker asked.

"Sure. What's up?" I said.

"I just got off the phone with a doctor. She will be here this afternoon for your checkup."

"Great," I said excited. "Tristan let's go see what you got." We all headed over to Tristan's room. He had gotten a lot of clothes also but not as much as me. He had about ten pairs of jeans varying in colors from light denim to dark blue. He had multiple packs of shirts as well.

While I was thumbing through his clothes he turned to Parker, "Lilith and I would like to get married today under the laws of humans. Could you get us a priest?" I stopped messing with the clothes and looked at Parker waiting for his answer.

He stood there with a smile on his face, "Actually, I am an ordained minister. I can marry both of you right now. We just need two witnesses."

"I'll be one," Bristol said happily.

"We just need to find one more," Parker said.

"What about Drezzie?" I asked. "Why do you call him that anyway? It's an odd name."

"His real name is Driscoll. I got tired of saying that after a while, so I started calling him Drezzie," Bristol said.

"Yup, the nickname is definitely better," I said laughing.

"I'll go find Drezzie and give the two of you time to prepare your vows," Parker said.

Jessica Manson

"Actually, I would like to go traditional this time if that's alright," I said looking at Tristan.

"Traditional is perfect," Tristan said.

He then handed me a small black velvet box. "What is this?"

"My wedding ring." I opened the box that held a solid black titanium grooms ring. It was beautiful. "I have one for you as well."

"How did you get these if you can't leave the house?"

"I got Bristol to pick them up this morning while she was out shopping."

"How did you know I would agree to marry you?"

"I didn't. I had planned on asking you at a later time so while she was going out for us, I took my chance of getting the rings, so I would have them when the time came. But luckily for me, you suggested it this morning."

"Can I see mine?"

"Yes, when Parker tells me to place it on your finger."

"Hey that's not fair. You got to see yours," I whined.

"You will see it soon enough. Now go get something other than sweat pants on," he said pushing me out of his room.

I went into my room and looked slowly through the dresses again. I found a white one that was knee length. It was a baby doll style dress that had spaghetti straps and a lace embroidery along the breast of the dress and at the bottom. It was a very cute dress that was perfect for our simple union.

Bristol knocked on my door sticking her head in before waiting for me to answer. "Drezzie will be your second witness."

"Perfect. Would you do me a favor?"

"Sure. What is it?"

"My hair."

She laughed, "Of course." She curled my hair then pulled the very top of it back into a clip giving me a little bump on the top of my head. Simple, just like everything else. I put on light makeup to match.

"Everything is ready when you are," she said.

"I'm ready," I was excited to be marrying Tristan. This would be a marriage that actually would be recognized by human law. I know marrying him so soon is crazy, but the way my life is, it's now or never. Tomorrow we may be on the run again. We just don't know how much time we will have to be together and I want to spend as much of it as we can as husband and wife.

The union would be held in the dining room. When we walked into the room the dining table had been removed. Parker stood at the far end of the room with Tristan and Drezzie at his side. Tristan wore a white button-down dress shirt with a pair of his new jeans. He was so sexy standing there. I couldn't help but think about what happens later after we are married making a smile form across my lips.

I walked up and stood beside Tristan. "Ready?" he asked.

"Ready," I replied. Parker started the union.

When it was time for the rings Tristan pulled out a matching black velvet box. He took the rings out and placed them on my finger. The ring was breathtaking. It was a black oval diamond surrounded by small white diamonds. The band of the ring was white gold that had four white diamonds on either side of the black diamond. There was also another band the was white gold with fifteen white diamonds that completed the set. It was the most beautiful ring I had ever seen.

When we said 'I do' Tristan pulled me into him and kissed me like he was kissing me for the last time. When he let me go, he said, "Mrs. Rose, you have made me the happiest man in the world."

"Mrs. Rose, I like it," I said testing out the name.

"Well I would hope so."

"I love you Tristan."

"I love you."

Drezzie and the same guy from last night brought the table back into the room and started serving lunch. I was thankful because I was starving having missed breakfast. They served us baked Italian chicken, roasted seasoned potatoes, garlic pan fried green beans with homemade seasoned rolls. It was delicious, and I ended up eating two

Jessica Manson

plates again. The way my babies made me eat I would be as big as a house if I wasn't careful.

When we were done with lunch Drezzie brought in a small wedding cake. It was two-tiered white frosting with a little fancy design on it. It had three blue daisies on top made from gum paste as well as two that were sitting at the bottom. It was simple like the rest of the wedding.

"We weren't sure what flavor cake you like. The bottom tier is half strawberry and half chocolate. The top tier is half vanilla and half red velvet."

"It is perfect," I said taking a slice of every kind except chocolate. The cake was so moist and delicious. It was the perfect dessert to our perfect lunch.

When lunch was over Tristan and I decided to move his things into my room. Well it was more like he moved them, and I laid on my bed watching, trying not to fall asleep. By the time he was done moving his things in, our room was a wreck. Clothes were everywhere, including on top of me.

Tristan pulled the clothes off me and leaned in for a kiss. When he pulled away, he said, "You know the babies are officially mine now right?"

"What do you mean?"

"Because we got married under human law your last name will change. They will be able to carry my last name," he said beaming.

"Last name doesn't matter to me. They were yours before that."

"I know, but now I have two little beings that will carry on my family name."

"Have you thought of any baby names yet?" I asked.

"Not yet. I was waiting until we found out what we were having first."

"Me either. But I think we should go ahead and pick out names. We can each pick two boy names and two girl names. And out of the four pick which boy and girl name you like the best."

"Okay. But you don't expect this right away, do you?"

"Of course not. I will give you time to think about it. But sooner would be better." I don't know why, but I have a bad feeling that I won't have much time with Tristan. I don't know if it is just because of the stress we are under or if it is my witch's intuition.

"I think I have some names," Tristan said.

"That was fast."

"Well I really hadn't thought about it till just now when you said something. My names are Ava, Elizabeth, Elijah and Jackson."

"Why those names?"

"Ava Elizabeth was my mother's name and Elijah Jackson was my father's name."

"They are beautiful names."

"Thank you. Do you have any picked out yet?"

"I was thinking Zoey, Avery, Carter, and Hayden. And no, they don't have any meaning behind them like yours do. I just like them."

"Well there, we finally have baby names to choose from," He said smiling at me.

Parker stood in the doorway knocking on the doorframe, "The doctor is here Lilith."

"Okay, we will be right out." I kissed Tristan once Parker walked away. "Ready to check on our babies?"

"Of course, I am," he said with a smile on his face

We walked into the living room to meet the doctor. She was a short woman about late thirties to early forties. She had shoulder length brown hair that was starting to gray a little. She held out her hand toward me. When I took it, she said, "Hi, I'm Dr. Johnson."

"I'm Lilith. This is my husband Tristan."

"It's nice to meet you both. So, tell me Lilith, how have you been feeling?"

"Tired mostly. I get sick every now and then. But it is nothing like it was in the beginning."

"What happened in the beginning?"

Jessica Manson

"I couldn't eat anything except crackers. I slept constantly. I probably slept eighteen hours a day. I was extremely sick to my stomach."

"I see. Now, that is normal for pregnancy. Do you know how far along you are?"

"Approximately seven to eight weeks."

"Have you seen a doctor before this?"

"I had to stay the night at a hospital last week."

"What for?"

"Dehydration."

"Okay, is there a place you can lay down, so I can measure your stomach? I need you to lay flat for me."

"Sure," Tristan and I led her to Tristan's old room and I laid on the bed.

She pulled my dress up and pulled out a measuring rope. "You are growing very fast to only be this far along. I am going to listen to the heart beat now." She pulled a little device from her bag that looked like it had a microphone attached to it. She pressed the microphone looking thing to my stomach and moved it around a little bit until she found the heartbeat. "Strong heartbeat. 176 beats per minute. Very nice," she said.

"So, everything is okay?" I asked.

"Yes. Everything seems normal. I will send over an ultrasound machine to keep here for my visits. I will be back in two weeks to do an ultrasound. I am also going to write you a prescription for some nausea medicine in case you need them. But you are not required to take them. Also, I am going to get you started on some prenatal vitamins. These will help the babies grow strong and help with their development. Plus, it will give you a little extra of what they are taking from you."

"Thank you," I said getting up from the bed.

We walked her to the door, "Expect the ultrasound machine in about a week and I'll see you in two. Take care of yourself Lilith. Have a good day."

"You too, thank you again for coming," I said as she walked out of the house. The visit was quick and straight to the point, leaving me feeling like the wind had been knocked out of me.

Jessica Manson

Chapter Fourteen

The rest of the day was uneventful, and I spent most of the afternoon in the theatre room relaxing. I had finished two movies when Tristan came in to join me. He cuddled up into the seat with me. He wrapped his arms around my waist pulling me into him. He began to kiss my neck slowly sending tingles throughout my body. He lifted me in his arms and carried me to our room.

Once the door was shut behind us, he didn't waste any time undressing me. I unbuttoned his shirt and watched it fall to the floor at his feet. He pulled me against him pressing my bare breast to his exposed chest. The heat from the contact set my body ablaze. Our hearts beat against each other frantically. He tangled his fingers into my hair pushing my lips against his in a long devouring kiss.

Our hands tangled as we fought to unbutton his pants. Once he was naked, he laid me on the bed and climbed on top of me. I could feel the hardness of his shaft against my thigh. He ran his hands over my body feeling every inch of me until they found my center. He rubbed in a circular motion until I cried out and my body spilled desire.

With my legs shaking he entered me slowly. He moved in and out of me and I moved my hips to match his rhythm. My head hummed, and my eyes rolled in the back of my head. He quickened his pace causing me to cry out. His naked hips pressed against me as he leaned in and kissed me; his teeth nipping at my bottom lip.

My muscles were beginning to contract and I knew I was getting close. "Tristan," I called out his name causing a growl to escape him. "Come with me," I begged. He sped up moving in and out of me so quickly I couldn't control the moans leaving me. He pumped and pushed harder until I felt like my insides exploded with euphoria. He released inside of me at the same time I spilled out onto him.

Tristan lay beside me on the bed, we smiled at each other as we tried to control our breathing. Letting my body relax completely I started to hear murmurs. I sat up on the bed and tried to focus in on what I was hearing. It was then that I recognized the voices. "Oh no," I said.

Tristan shot up beside me, "What's wrong."

I looked at him my body filling up with fear, "They're here."

"Who's here Lilith?"

"Odin." I closed my eyes focusing on Parker and Bristol. I spoke to them with my mind letting them know Odin had found us.

The house was completely surrounded. Odin and Draven were at the front door getting ready to knock. Ambi and Latham took the back of the house while Gunner and Dex took the left and Brant and Cal took the right. There was nowhere for us to run.

Parker and Bristol burst through the door just as Tristan and I were getting our clothes on. "What do we do?" I asked frantically. "If they catch y'all they will kill every one of you."

"We can take the back way out," Parker said.

"No, we can't they have the house completely surrounded. Just let me go out and turn myself over to them. While they are taking me y'all can run."

"No way Lilith. I'm not letting you face them alone. If you go then I go too," Tristan said.

"You can't Tristan. I can't lose you. He will kill you."

"I don't care. I will not let you go out there alone."

"He's right. If you go, we all go," Bristol said.

"Bristol, you can't go out there. Fate will be back soon. If you go you will never see him again. Y'all have to let me do this."

"No way," Tristan said sounding frustrated.

"Baby please. I can't let them hurt you."

"Lilith, I do not care. I am going with you."

"Fine," I said reluctantly.

"I'm going too," Parker said.

"So am I," Bristol said.

I shook my head in disbelief. It didn't matter what I said they wouldn't listen to me. How can you save someone if they won't let you?

Jessica Manson

"Then let's get this over with." We walked to the front door and just as Odin was about to knock, I opened the door.

"Thank God Lilith. I have been looking for you everywhere," Odin said lifting me into his arms for a hug.

"Put me down and don't touch me," I said pulling myself out of his arms. As I stepped back Tristan wrapped his arm around my waist protectively. Odin's eyes switched back and forth between Tristan and me. "Let me guess you are here to force me back."

"Lilith, you and Odin preformed the Sacrament. That bond is unbreakable. You cannot just run out on him like you have done," Draven said with an official tone.

"Odin betrayed me. He killed my parents."

"Yes, it seems so, but that doesn't change the coven's rules," he said. The rest of the group had come around to the front of the house. Draven nodded at Brant. Brant then walked over to me and grabbed me by my arm and started pulling me toward a car.

"Get your hands off her," Tristan yelled as he tried to fight Cal and Gunner off of him. They threw him in the back of a van as Latham and Dex dragged Parker and Bristol over to join him. "Let her go," Tristan was yelling as he banged on the windows of the van.

Tears began to spill from my eyes as I watched them drive away. Ambi got in behind the wheel of the car while Draven got into the front. Brant slid in on my right as Odin got in on my left. "What's going to happen to them?" I asked.

"They will pay for kidnapping you," Draven said.

"They didn't kidnap me. I left willingly. You can't hurt them," I cried out. "Odin please don't hurt them," I pleaded.

"It is out of my hands. There is nothing I can do."

Draven turned in his seat and clamped a metal bracelet around my wrist. "This will keep you from using your witch powers."

"You can't do that?" I shouted.

Brant leaned over and whispered in my ear, "He just did." He was still pissed at me for escaping him at the hospital. He was enjoying this.

106

Anger boiled over in me. I punched Brant in the nose then turned toward Draven. I punched him in the back of the head several times before Odin pulled me off of him. "Let me go," I yelled.

"Feisty, isn't she?" Draven said with a smirk across his face as he fixed his hair.

"Fuck you," I said calmly in his face.

Odin pulled me back to him. "Calm down baby."

"Don't you ever call me that. You lost that privilege when you killed my parents." Odin kept his arm around me but turned his head to stare out the window.

We finally reached the castle and my heart lifted a little when I saw the van sitting in the driveway. Odin stepped out of the car and walked over to Brant's side before Brant stepped out. He pulled me out and each of them took one of my arms. Draven led the way while Ambi took the rear.

They led me into the castle and down the long hallway that led to the kitchen. We stopped in front of one of the large waterfall pictures that hung on the wall. Draven pushed on one of the bricks in the wall and a doorway opened.

We took some stairs that led us down to a part of the house I didn't know existed. When we reached the bottom of the stairs we stood in an open room. Along the walls were multiple cells. I spotted Tristan in one. I broke free from Odin and Brant and ran to him. I grabbed onto the bars and he wrapped his hands around mine. "Let him go," I begged.

"We can't do that. Step away from him and follow us," Draven said.

"No. I'm not leaving him."

"Step away Lilith," Draven said more authoritative.

"No," I shouted reaching my arm through the bars to hold onto him tighter.

"Baby listen to them. You have to step away before they hurt you," Tristan whispered to me.

"No. I'm not leaving you," I said as tears streamed harder down my face.

Draven walked over to me and said once more, "Step. Away."

Never letting go of Tristan I turned and looked Draven in the eyes. "I'm. Not. Leaving. Him," I said enunciating each word. Without saying a word, he backhanded me causing me to fall to the floor.

"Don't hurt her," Tristan yelled. Draven walked over to me and was ready to kick me when Tristan yelled again, "Draven don't. She's pregnant."

Draven stepped away from me. Odin walked over, helped me up then pulled my shirt up to expose my protruding belly. "Lilith?" he said in a whisper.

I pulled my shirt down and ran back to Tristan. "You shouldn't have told them."

"They were going to hurt them," he said trying to caress my cheek.

"Them?" Odin asked. I didn't answer. I kept my focus on Tristan. "Lilith, how far along are you?" I still didn't answer him. "If those are my babies, I have the right to know," he said sounding angry at my silence.

Finally, I turned my focus on him. "These are not your babies. And they never will be. Tristan is their father. They will carry his last name not yours."

"They are my babies. You will not keep them from me."

"You will have to kill me to get your filthy hands on my babies."

"You didn't think his hands were filthy when you were making those babies," Ambi said. I ignored her.

"Damn it, Lilith. Those are my babies. Don't be this way."

"Don't put this on me. You lost all your rights when you betrayed me."

"I'm tired of these games. Brant, lock her up," Draven said.

Brant walked over and grabbed my arm. "This way empress," he said pulling me toward a large wooden door. He opened the door and pushed me inside. The room had a large bed, a dresser, and a small bathroom. He shut the door behind me leaving me alone. I could hear Odin and his father talking outside the door.

"You can't leave her down here. She is pregnant with my children," Odin said.

"She may be your mate and she may be pregnant with your children, but she broke the laws of the Sacrament. She must be punished," Draven said.

"Let me punish her in my own way. Don't leave her down here."

"Tell me son, how do you plan on punishing her? She left you and ran off with another man. She is pregnant with your seed, yet she refuses to give them your last name." Odin didn't say anything. "You wouldn't punish her. You are too soft. I will handle it from here. I will oversee her punishment. And I will see to it that you get your babies Odin." The voices faded leaving me in silence.

My heart ached to be with Tristan. I longed to feel his arms wrapped around me. I wish we would have had more time together. I walked over to the bed and lay down. Exhaustion took over me and sleep wasn't far behind.

Jessica Manson

Chapter Fifteen

When I woke up, I was confused where I was at first. When reality hit me, my heart sank. There were no windows, so I couldn't tell how long I had slept. I heard screams coming from the other side of the door. It sounded like Bristol. What were they doing to her? I needed to get out of this room. I needed to help them.

When I got to the door the screaming stopped. I tried to open it, but it was no use. If I could get this bracelet off, I could teleport out of here. I tried using my strength to break it, it didn't budge. I tried pulling it off, but it cut into my skin. After getting pissed I didn't care about it cutting me. I pushed down as hard as I could. It sliced through my skin on my thumb and above my pinky.

The pinky side of my hand was the worst. The bracelet cut a huge chunk out of my skin, but the blood made it easier to slip off. The bracelet fell to the floor along with my skin. Blood poured from my hand leaving a trail as I ran into the bathroom to get a towel to stop the bleeding. I had bled through the towel before I even got it wrapped around my hand, so I grabbed another towel before running to the door.

I wish to go
I wish to fly
Take me to the other side
Take me there before I die

I wish to go
I wish to fly
Take me to the other side
Take me there before I die

When I was done chanting, I was thrown across the room landing against the wall. A scream escaped me during mid throw. As I was picking myself up Odin rushed into the room. "What happened? Are you okay?"

A pain surged through my belly. "I think the babies might be hurt."

Odin rushed to my side and lifted me in his arms. He ran with me up the stairs and into the library. They had turned the library into a doctor's office. He laid me on the bed then yelled for someone to get the doctor. "Everything is going to be okay baby. We have a doctor who will be here twenty-four seven while you are pregnant."

I tuned him out and tried to speak to Tristan with my mind. *"Tristan. Baby, are you there?"* I called out trying to reach him. I was relieved when I heard his voice.

"Baby I'm here. Are you okay? What happened? I heard you scream then all of a sudden Odin was running with you upstairs."

"I tried to teleport through the door, so I could get you out, but my spell didn't work. Instead I was thrown against the wall. I think the babies may be hurt."

"Oh, God please no," he begged. He wasn't pleading with me. He was speaking to a higher power. *"Baby please tell me they are going to be okay."*

"I don't know. A doctor is coming to check on them."

"Okay baby. Let me know as soon as you know something."

"I will. Hey Tristan. What are they doing to y'all down there? I heard screaming."

"Don't worry about us baby. Just make sure our babies are okay."

The doctor walked in and I was shocked to see Dr. Johnson standing in front of me. Now I understood how Odin found us. "Lilith, nice to see you again."

"Can't say the same doc."

"Can you give us a few minutes for me to check her?" she asked Odin. When he stepped out of the room, she turned to me. "You don't understand. When I left your house, I was stopped at the end of the driveway. They already had the house surrounded. They threatened to kill my family if I didn't tell them what I was doing there. I tried to lie, but they had a witch with them."

111

Jessica Manson

"Kira."

"Yes. She told them I was lying. I didn't have a choice. I'm so sorry."

"It's okay. They brought us here against our will too."

"I thought you told me Tristan is your husband?"

"He is by human law. And Odin is my husband by coven law."

"Tell me what happened. Why is Odin so frantic?"

"I tried to do a spell but was thrown against a wall instead. There is pain in my belly."

"In that case, I am going to bring Odin back in here to help undress you. I don't want you moving to much before I can examine you."

"I don't want him touching me."

"I understand, but I have to get you undressed and you can't move. It may hurt the babies worse."

"Fine."

She called Odin back into the room, "Help me undress her but be careful. She needs to move as little as possible."

Odin walked over to me and looked at me for my permission before he started to undress me. "Just do it. But don't touch me and I mean it." He sat me up gently and pulled my shirt over my head. He laid me back down and slid my pants off. I was naked in front of the man who killed my parents. He didn't take his eyes off my body. He stared at me and desire filled his eyes. "Odin," I called his name. "What is that?"

"What is what?" he asked.

"Is that blood on my pants?" Panic started to fill me. This was it; I was losing my babies.

"Now some blood is normal. Let's check you out before you panic," Dr. Johnson said. She rolled over a big machine, "I am going to do an ultrasound on you. This will be cold since I don't have a warming machine here," she said as she squirted some cold goo onto my belly. She pressed something to my belly and started moving it around. "I'm not getting a good picture. I will need to use the vaginal wand."

"What is that?" I asked scared of her answer.

"I will do the ultrasound from the inside. I will insert this vaginally, so we can see the babies better." She laid the bed down flat and had me

Beautiful Corruption

bend my knees and lay them to the side. "This shouldn't hurt, but you will feel some pressure." She didn't give me time to breathe before inserting that thing inside me. I felt violated, but I knew we needed to make sure the babies were okay.

Odin placed his hand on my shoulder trying to comfort me. I pushed his hand away from me. "I said don't touch me."

"I'm just trying to comfort you," he said.

"That's what I have Tristan for," I snapped.

"Do you think he is going to take my place? He is not your husband, I am."

"He is my husband."

"What do you mean he is your husband?"

"We got married under human law. He is my husband. Remember when I told you yesterday, they would carry his last name? That is because that is my last name now."

"You are already married to me. You can't marry him."

"I am only married to you under the coven's laws Odin. It's not recognized by human laws so there is no name change. No divorce needed. Technically we aren't even married. But Tristan and I are. We are legally married."

"If you will look here you can see the babies," Dr. Johnson said interrupting our argument.

"Are they okay?" I asked.

"They are fine. But there is a very small tear in the ambilocal sac. You are losing a little bit of fluid. You will need to be on bedrest and monitored at least twice a day for a couple of weeks. You are nine weeks along Mrs. Rose." The look on Odin's face when she called me that was priceless. He was pissed, and I thought it was hilarious.

"Thank you."

"Odin, you can help her get dressed then carry her back to bed. The babies can't handle any stress so no fighting with her."

As Odin was dressing me, I asked, "Odin, can I please see Tristan when we get back down there?"

"No," he said quickly and flatly.

Jessica Manson

"Odin please. I need to see him."

"No Lilith. My father would kill me."

"Grow some fucking balls Odin. You are a grown ass man. You don't have to do everything daddy says."

"Don't be like that. You know I can't let you see him."

"Why not? I just need to make sure he is okay."

"Come on let's go. You need to get back to bed." He lifted me into his arms and carried me back down stairs. I tried to see Tristan in the cells, but I couldn't. Odin was moving too fast. He took me back to my room and laid me on the bed. "What happened to your hand?"

"I took the bracelet off."

"Here let me heal you."

"You can do that?"

"Yes, but I would have to bite you."

"I am not letting you bite me."

"Lilith it's the only way for me to heal you and you are still losing blood from it."

"Fine," I said holding out my hand to him.

He gently unwrapped the towel from my hand. "Jesus Lilith."

"Yeah, yeah I know. Now can we get this over with." My hand looked disgusting with a large chunk of skin missing from it. He pulled my hand to his lips and sunk his teeth into my palm. I cried out in pain. He drank from me, tasting me. He looked up at me as he drank my blood and our eyes locked. He longed to feel me again. I could see it in his eyes. I looked away from him reassuring him my answer was no.

He pulled away from me, "There. See healing already. Now do you want to tell me how this happened?"

"I got the bracelet off."

"Why did you take it off?"

"So, I could get out of here."

"Did you try using magic in here?"

"Yes. But it didn't work. I got thrown against the wall."

"My father used the same metal behind the walls throughout the room that was used for the bracelet. That's why you were thrown."

114

Beautiful Corruption

"Odin, you can't keep us here. Why would you force me to be your wife?"

"Because you are my wife. Lilith, I love you and I know you still love me. We were good together."

"Your wrong. I don't love you anymore. My love for you died the day I found out you killed my parents."

"I can make you happy, make you rich. I can give you and the babies a life that Tristan can't."

"We have our own money. We don't need yours. And Tristan already gave me a better life than you. He gave me what you didn't, a choice."

"Well, well. What have we here? Is the happy couple reuniting?" Draven said with a smug smile on his face.

"What do you want Draven?" I asked with ice in my voice.

"Bring her Odin. It's time she sees what their punishments are."

"She can't. The doctor said the babies can't handle any stress."

"Do not disobey me. Bring her now," Draven said.

"I'm sorry Lilith. We have to go," Odin said. Odin lifted me into his arms again and carried me back out into the opened area where the cells were. They were still empty.

"Where are they?" I asked Odin.

"You will see them soon enough." We walked over to a door under the stairs. I hadn't even noticed it was there. Draven pushed the door open and stepped aside for us to enter. My heart fell at the sight of Tristan, Bristol and Parker.

Tristan was on his knees chained to the wall. Bristol was strapped to a metal table naked. And Parker was tied to a chair. They were all covered in dirt and blood. They looked like they had been down here for weeks instead of just a day.

"I think it is time we get started," Draven said walking around the room. "Who shall go first?"

"Leave them alone." Tristan finally raised his head at the sound of my voice. Tears filled my eyes as I watched blood pour from his nose and mouth.

115

Jessica Manson

"I think I will start with her. She is a pretty little doll isn't she." I watched as Draven climbed on top of Bristol and unbuttoned his pants. He forced himself inside of her and she let out a scream.

Anger boiled inside of me and I forced myself out of Odin's arms. Draven was so focused he didn't realize I had snapped my fingers freeing Tristan from his chains. I snapped my fingers a second time and freed Parker from his chair. I walked closer to Draven and flicked my wrist throwing him against the wall. With one snap of my fingers the chains wrapped around his wrist holding him captive just as they did Tristan.

"Odin do something. Get me out of here," Draven yelled.

Before Odin could grab me, I threw him into the chair that held Parker. I lifted my hands into the air and without touching them, I moved Parker, Bristol and Tristan outside the door and shut it, locking me in with our kidnappers.

It was my turn to have a little *fun*.

Chapter Sixteen

I walked over and looked Draven in the eyes before back handing him the same way he did me. "That was for yesterday."

"Do you think you scare me?" he said with a smile across his face.

"I am going to kill you and take your place as the next head Luminary."

His smile turned into a loud laugh. "You think you will be a Luminary? You are a girl. Women don't serve as a Luminary."

"They will after today. I plan on making you pay for all the hurt you caused me and Tristan. When I am done, there will be nothing left of you."

"Let me ask you something Lilith. Do you know why there were two mates chosen for you?"

"I think I do, but why don't you enlighten me?"

"Odin was never chosen for you. Parker was your only chosen mate."

"What are you talking about?" Odin asked looking at his father for answers.

"He is saying he lied and forced the Luminaries to lie too. He wanted my power."

"See, I needed you on our side. We needed the power. I made a sacrifice. My son for you."

"You are a shitty father."

"I did what I had to do. Eighteen years ago, when I found out your mother was pregnant with you, I knew you would be different. I made the choice then to have two mates chosen for you. Parker was your original mate. But the only way I could have you in my family was to give you Odin as well. I had a witch cast a spell on Odin so the first time you lay eyes on him you wouldn't be able to resist him. You should have been drawn to Parker, but the spell worked. Odin of course had to do all of the work. The spell was only to make him irresistible. Odin had to put in the effort to win your heart."

"You mean she isn't mine?" Odin said with sadness in his voice.

Jessica Manson

"No, she never was," Draven said with no regret.

"Why did you need my powers? There are no wars upon you. No one to fight off."

"The Luminaries had decided once you were on our side, we would start a war of our own. We wanted power. We craved it. The coven's all around the world would bow to us."

"You were going to use me to win a war for you?"

"Yes. You are very powerful child. We weren't expecting you to find out about your parents. We also weren't expecting you to run off."

"Why did you make him do it?"

"Make who do what dear?"

"Why did you make Odin kill my parents?"

"We needed to get you away from their protection. We knew as long as you were living with them, we would never get to you."

I looked over at Odin. He was heartbroken at the realization at what he had been tricked into doing. Even though my heart was hard toward him, I couldn't stand to see him like that. I opened the door and with a flick of my wrist he flew out of the room still strapped to the chair. I shut the door behind him not letting anyone in.

Draven rose from his knees and walked toward me as far as the chains would let him. "I will kill you and your babies once I am free."

Without hesitation, I kicked him in the knee popping it backwards. He fell to the floor screaming in pain. "You won't get the chance." I kicked him in the face as hard as I could. Banging started at the door. Everyone was yelling for me to let them in. I guess the group had arrived. "Seems we have visitors. Too bad they won't be able to save you."

Just as the words left me, the door flew open. Brant charged toward me, but I stopped him in his tracks with a snap of my fingers. Ambi was next to enter the room followed by Dex, Gunner and Cal. I tried to stop them but was unsuccessful. They dragged me back to my room. Before shutting the door on me Ambi said, "You will die for this bitch."

"Fuck you," I spit at her. I was locked up once again. I should have killed Draven when I had the chance. Now he was going to kill

118

everyone I love. Tristan, Parker and Bristol would pay for my fighting back.

It has been ten days since they locked me back up in this room. I haven't heard from Draven or Odin since I attacked them. They haven't even let the doctor see me. The only contact I have had is when Brant and Ambi bring me my food, but they don't speak to me. They just slid the tray of food in and quickly leave.

I haven't been able to reach Tristan with my mind either. I know Parker said my telepathy is both, vampire and witch, but I can't seem to tap into it just as a vampire. I seem to be more in tune with the witch side of me, but I can't use it from fear of hurting my babies again. Maybe I can't access the vampire side because it needs to be fed. I crave the taste of blood every day now. I can smell the human doctor and the fairies all the way down here as they move about upstairs. The desire to feed from them makes my throat burn. I need to taste them.

I could hear someone moving around outside my door. I walked over to see if I could figure out who it was, but they never spoke, only fumbled around. "Hello. Who's there?" I asked through the door. "Can you get Odin for me? Please." Whoever was there never answered me but the moving around stopped.

I lay on the bed and tears filled my eyes. I missed Tristan so much. I longed to be held in his strong comforting arms. One of his hugs would be nice right now. I miss our conversations. I miss how we used to talk every minute of every day. I miss having our own private conversations with our minds. I wish I was there with him or him here with me. Truth is I just want to be with him anywhere. Missing him is the worst feeling in the world.

With my body needing to feed it has made me weak. The slightest movement wears me out. And it doesn't help that my belly seems to grow bigger by the day. None of the clothes they stored for me in here

Jessica Manson

fits. My belly was growing, but my body was becoming weaker by the minute. And with my body so weak it is hard for me to stay awake for more than an hour.

I was just about to fall asleep when Brant showed up with a tray of food for me. He slid it in and was about to close the door when I called out for him. "Brant, wait."

He peeked inside the door. "What?"

"Don't worry I don't have enough strength to hurt you or to run."

He stepped inside the door and took one look at me, "What is wrong with you? You look like shit."

"I need help Brant. Can you get Odin for me? Please" I begged.

"I'll see what I can do, but he refuses to see you."

"Please. Just try."

"Okay. I'll try," he said walking back to the door.

"Hey Brant," I called after him one more time.

"Yeah."

"I'm sorry for putting you to sleep back at the hospital and for punching you in the nose." He nodded before walking out of the room. I walked over to get the tray of food, but my legs gave out causing me to fall to the floor. I tried to lift myself, but it was no use, I didn't have enough strength. My head started spinning and black dots appeared in my vision. I laid on my back to try to get the room to stop spinning, but that just made it worse. The black dots grew until my vision faded completely and I blacked out.

In and out of consciousness I could hear voices outside the door. I tried calling for help but it took so much strength it would cause me to black out again. When I finally came to, I peered at the clock and noticed I had been passed out for five hours. I started to feel relieved because I knew it was almost time for Brant to deliver my food. I lay on the floor for fifteen more minutes before Brant showed up. He opened the door and slid the tray in. This time he did something he has never done before, he actually looked inside my room.

He looked around for me and when his eyes finally landed on me, they grew wide with horror. "Son of a bitch," he yelled. "Get Odin.

Now!" he shouted to someone on the other side of the door. Brant rushed to my side. "Lilith, are you okay?" I couldn't speak so I shook my head the best I could. "What happened?" he asked not realizing I couldn't speak. I started to black out again. My eyes rolled into the back of my head causing Brant to pull my head into his lap. "Stay with me Lilith. Odin is on the way."

Tears rolled down my cheeks because I could feel myself slipping away. I knew my time had come. I could feel my body shutting down. Tristan's face flashed before my eyes and I longed to see his beautiful face one last time. I needed to feel his hands on my cold body, to feel our hearts beat against one another one more time.

Tears fell harder as I realized that would never happen. I would never see him again. I would never feel his body against mine. I would never hold his hand again. And I would never be able to tell him goodbye. My heart broke for him. He would never see our babies born. He would never hold them in his arms. He would never hear them call him daddy.

All of the moments we shared together, each and every beautiful memory flooded back to my mind. Hopefully the love we had for each other would be enough to outweigh my death for Tristan. I'm not leaving him because I want to, I'm leaving him because this life has no other plans for me. He was the best part of my existence.

My breathing and my heart beat slowed. My death was getting closer. My hell was almost over. I looked at Brant and our eyes met. I told him goodbye with my eyes and tears formed in his. He knew as well as I did, it was over. I motioned for him to lean closer to me. I used the last bit of my strength to whisper in his ear, "Tell Tristan I love him and tell Odin I am sorry." The most painful goodbyes are the ones that are never said and never explained.

"No, you don't Lilith, don't you fucking die on me." He pulled me into his arms and started running with me as death took me under.

Jessica Manson

Chapter Seventeen

-Odin-

I was upstairs when I heard Brant yelling for me. I ran out of my room to see what all of the commotion was about. When I found Brant, I saw Lilith laying in his arms motionless. I ran to his side and tried to take her from him, but he wouldn't let her go. She wasn't breathing, and her heart had stopped. She was gone.

I felt my own heart stop as I yelled for the doctor. Brant ran with Lilith into the library and laid her on the table. Brant pushed me out of the way to examine her. I was frozen with the fear of losing her. I just got her back; I couldn't lose her again. I fell into a chair as all of my strength dissipated.

This is the second-time death has come to claim my lamia mea. And this time he seems to have been successful. Dr. Johnson rushed into the room and took over where Brant had started performing CPR. My vision became groggy and everyone in the room disappeared. I became lost in the memories I shared with my beautiful Lilith.

I thought about the first time I ever laid eyes on her. Her beauty was beyond any I had ever seen. Her big gray eyes sparkled with the sadness behind them. I remembered saying to myself that I could make this girl happy. Make her sadness be a thing of the past.

But I never did that. If anything, I made her sadness worse. She hated me and had every right too. I was a monster. I was the one that killed her parents. And I would never get to say I'm sorry or make it right. I would never get the chance to prove to her how wrong I was.

My love, my life, was now gone. Forever taken away.

Fear gripped me as I realized that one day I wouldn't be able to remember her smile, her laugh. I would forget the way she always smelled like strawberries. A room would never light up the same way she could make it when she entered it. She is my light; the thing that keeps me going. With Lilith gone my world would be in total darkness.

I felt the tears as they slid down my face. There was no stopping them, and I didn't care who saw them. A hand landed on my shoulder to comfort me, but I pushed it off. I got up without thinking about where I was going; my feet having a mind of their own led me to the cells.

-Tristan-

As I slept, I heard someone calling my name. I put the pillow over my head trying to drown out their voice, but they just got louder. "Tristan. Something has happened."

I jumped up at the sound of his voice. "Odin? What are you doing here?"

"Something has happened?" he said in a slight whisper.

"What? Is Lilith okay? The babies?" I could tell he had been crying and panic sunk in. If he was here and had been crying something bad must have happened. Odin hung his head not saying anything more causing anger to fill me. "What happened Odin? Tell me now," I yelled.

"Lilith, she..." He shook his head as if he was trying to will himself to say the words. "She's gone."

"What do you mean gone? Where did she go? Did Draven ta..."

"No. She is dead," he said cutting me off.

"No. No. She can't be. It's not possible," I said not believing him.

"She is."

"No. No. No. No. No," I yelled as I fell to my knees. "She can't be"

"I'm sorry Tristan. I wish it wasn't so," Odin turned and left without saying another word.

The pain I felt was indescribable. She was only mine for a short time, but I loved her more than anything in this world. The pain that I felt for losing Lilith only got worse as I realized what else I had lost. My babies.

Jessica Manson

I would never hold them in my arms. I would never be called daddy. There would be no one to carry on my last name. No cries in the middle of the night. No diapers to change. No little hands to hold. No one looking at me for advice. No talks about the good and bad in life. There would be nothing. My life as I knew it was over.

Chapter Eighteen

-Lilith-

When I came to, I was laying in the library. I had an IV in my arm and some type of machine strapped to my stomach. My stomach was huge. It looked like it had grown three times its size overnight. I tried to sit up, but a pain shot through my head causing me to lay back down. "You shouldn't try to sit up. Your body is still recovering," Brant said walking out from behind the bed I was laying on.

"What happened?"

"You died."

"What? How? Was it because I needed to feed?"

"No. You were poisoned. You needing to feed was your body telling you that blood would heal you," Dr. Johnson said walking into the room. "How are you feeling?"

"My head hurts."

"That is normal after coming out of a coma."

"What do you mean coma?"

"Once we brought you back, I put you in a coma to give your body time to recover. You were dead when Brant got you to me. Had he waited any longer I wouldn't have been able to save you. Once we realized you had been poisoned, I suggested putting you in a coma so you could heal without the stress of everything else going on with you."

"How long have I been in a coma?"

"Seven months. Your body needed more time to recover than we thought."

"Seven months? I have been out for seven months?"

"Yes dear."

"Who poisoned me?"

"We aren't sure yet."

I looked at Brant. "Where is Tristan? Please tell me Draven hasn't killed him."

"Tristan is fine. He is still locked up in the cells," he said.

125

Jessica Manson

"Can I see him?"

"You know I can't do that."

"Brant please."

"No Lilith. If I do that, I will be in a cell right next to him."

"Where is Odin?" I asked hoping that maybe he would let me see him.

"I'll get him for you," Brant said walking out of the room.

"You know those two never left your side the whole time you were in a coma. The only time they left you was to shower, which is where Odin is now. They ate their meals in here beside you. They both slept in here on the floor. They even took turns reading to you," Dr. Johnson said. "They love you, you know?"

"I know. But that doesn't make up for what they have done."

"I know sweetie, but maybe it will make it a little easier. It takes a strong person to say sorry, and an even stronger person to forgive. I know forgiveness is not always easy. Sometimes it feels more painful than the wound we suffered. But you will never know how strong your heart is until you know how to forgive who broke it. There is no peace without forgiveness Lilith."

"How do I forgive Odin when he killed my parents?"

"Martin Luther King Jr. once said, 'Let no man pull you low enough to hate him.' Lilith forgiveness is a virtue of the brave. Forgiveness is not something we do for other people. It is something we do for ourselves. Forgiveness does not change the past, but it does change the future. You will begin to heal when you let go of your past pain and forgive those who have wronged you. You deserve peace Lilith. It is time to let it go and move on."

As I was pondering over her words Odin rushed into the room. "You're awake," he said stating the obvious. "How are you feeling?"

"A little headache. Odin, I would like to see Tristan." I didn't waste time letting him know I needed to see him. "But can I have a word with you privately first?"

"Sure."

Beautiful Corruption

"I'll be right down the hall if you need me," Dr. Johnson said as she left the room.

"What is it Lilith?"

"I'm sorry I walked out on you. I'm sorry I didn't give you the chance to explain yourself."

"No Lilith, I'm sorry. You were right that day you told me I needed to grow some balls. I let my father run my life and by letting him do that I lost the only person I ever loved. I'm sorry about your parents. If I could take it back I would."

"Odin, I need you to understand something. I did love you. I loved you with every fiber in my body. But the day I found out the truth my heart hardened toward you. But some things Dr. Johnson said to me made me realize that in order for me to be truly happy, I need to forgive you. And I do, I forgive you Odin. I can't love you the way I did and I'm not saying we will be bff's instantly, but I want us to try and grow as friends. I want to try and get past this."

"Friends huh?" he asked with a smile on his face.

"Odin, y'all are the only family that I have, and I lost all of that when I left you. I miss all of y'all. And yes, I want to be your friend. That is the best I can give you."

"Then friendship is what I will take," he said standing to give me a hug.

"Can I please see Tristan?" I begged.

"Can you walk?"

"I'm willing to try."

"Let me get the doctor to unhook all of those wires from you and I will take you to see him."

I grabbed his arm before he walked off. I pulled him in for another hug, "Thank you so much Odin."

He pulled away smiling at me, "I'll be right back." I couldn't help but smile as he left the room. I was finally going to see Tristan. I missed him so much it hurt.

Odin and the doctor returned, and she quickly unhooked me from everything. "Lilith, you need to be extremely careful. You could go into

127

Jessica Manson

labor at any moment." When I tried to stand, I almost fell. Odin reached out and caught me. Being in a bed for seven months had my legs like noodles.

"I will carry you," Odin said. He lifted me in his arms and headed for the door.

Dr. Johnson stopped us just before we exited, "Lilith, would you like to know the sex of the babies?" she asked.

"Yes, I would," she told me and my eyes watered. I knew instantly what their names would be. "Take me to Tristan," I said excited.

"Can I ask you something?" Odin asked.

"Of course."

"I know these are my babies."

"Odin, we have already talked about this," I said cutting him off.

"I know. Let me finish. Like I was saying, I know these are my babies and you want Tristan to be the father. I am willing to let that happen if I can be a part of their life too. Why can't they have two fathers?"

"How about being their uncle?" I suggested.

"I am their father Lilith. I deserve to be a part of their life too."

"I'll think about it."

"I guess I will take what I can get for now."

We reached the bottom of the stairs and my heart fell to the pit of my stomach. I was nervous to see Tristan after so long away from him. What if he didn't feel the same about me? What if seeing me this huge makes him turn away from me?

Odin walked me up to his cell. He had his back to us. "Tristan." He turned around quickly when he heard my voice.

"Lilith? Baby."

"Can you stand and hold on to the bars?" Odin asked. I nodded, and he set me down. He walked to the other side of the room to give us privacy.

"Baby I have missed you so much," Tristan said walking over to me.

Beautiful Corruption

"I've missed you too." He rubbed his hand against my belly and the babies started kicking. "It seems they are happy to see you too."

"They are growing good," he said with a smile.

"I know, I am huge. The doctor said I could deliver at any moment."

"I can't wait to meet them."

"Me either. We have to get you out of here. They can't keep you locked up like this."

"As long as they are doing right by you, I don't care what happens to me."

"I care what happens to you. I love you Tristan."

"I love you too baby. More than you will ever know."

"The doctor told me what we are having. Do you want to know?"

"Hell, yes I do."

I met his eyes and smiled. "We are having an Ava Faye and an Elijah Eugene. Your parent's first names and my parent's middle names. Do you like them?"

"They are perfect," he said with tears in his eyes. "I wish I could kiss you right now." I kissed my finger and pressed it to his lips. "That's not the same."

"I know, but it will have to do until I can get you out of here."

Odin walked back over to us, "We better get you back upstairs."

"Thank you for letting me see her," Tristan said to Odin.

Odin nodded then looked at me, "Ready?"

"No, but I guess I have no choice," I turned to Tristan one last time, "I love you baby."

"I love you too."

Odin lifted me into his arms and carried me away as tears streamed down my face. I missed Tristan already and who knew when I would get to see him again. "It's okay Lilith. You will see him again," Odin said as if he was the one that could read minds now.

"I don't just want to see him Odin. I want him to be free."

"I know. In time, maybe."

"How is Bristol and Parker?"

Jessica Manson

"Hanging in there just like Tristan. My father has stopped the punishments for now. He actually hasn't been here for a couple of months. He calls daily to check in though."

"I hate your father Odin."

"I know."

We didn't speak again until we got back to the library. Odin laid me on the bed. "Thank you for taking me to see him. I know how hard us being married must be on you."

"I've had seven months to think about it and it was hard to accept at first, but I have accepted it. I have moved on. Speaking of moving on I have to tell you something."

"What?"

"Don't be mad okay?"

"Odin just tell me what it is."

"You said we were friends and friends can tell each other things, right?"

"Odin damn it. Just say it."

"I've gotten back together with Ambi. After all she is my intended mate."

"Seriously?" I asked surprised.

"Are you mad?"

"Are you happy?"

"Yes."

"Then no, I'm not mad. I'm happy for you. You deserve to have your happy ending just like Tristan is mine," I lied. I was mad. It could have been anyone but her and it wouldn't have phased me. But her? The woman that has threatened to kill me more than once? How could he be with *her* of all people?

"Thank you. That means a lot coming from you. I'll go get the doctor, so she can hook you back up."

While he left the room, I tried to get comfortable on the bed, but it was no use. Sharp pains were shooting up my back making it impossible for me to sit still. The pain intensified causing me to cry out. Brant ran into the room. "What's wrong Lilith?"

Beautiful Corruption

"It hurts." Just as the words left my mouth fluid spilled from between my legs. "I think the babies are coming." Brant stood there in shock not moving. "Brant, get the doctor," I yelled causing him to run from the room. Within seconds he was back with Odin and the doctor following him.

"I told you it would be any moment," the doctor said with a smile on her face.

"It hurts," I said squirming. Odin walked over and held one of my hands while Brant held the other. The pain felt like my insides were being twisted, pulled, and squeezed all at the same time. It felt like menstrual cramps times a million. It felt as if my hips were being pulled apart. "Oh, my god it hurts so bad," I cried out as tears fell from my eyes.

I squeezed Odin's hand as tight as I could. The pain was unbearable. "Breathe Lilith." I released my breath not realizing I was holding it.

"I need Tristan. Odin please get Tristan." Odin nodded at Brant and he left the room.

"I need to check your cervix Lilith. I need to see if you have dilated any," Dr. Johnson said. "Odin, we need to get her undressed." Odin did as the doctor said and undressed me. I was naked except for a sports bra that covered my breast. "Lilith when I tell you to, take a deep breath for me okay." I nodded in understanding. She lifted my knees into a bending position and laid them to the side. "On three take a deep breath. One. Two. Three." I breathed in as she inserted her hand inside of me. "It looks like these babies are eager to come out. You are dilated eight centimeters already."

Just then Brant and Tristan came into the room. Tristan took Brant's place holding my hand. "Hi baby. How are you feeling?"

"Peachy fucking keen." The guys laughed even though I wasn't trying to be funny.

Tristan pressed his lips to my forehead. "I love you baby." I looked up at him and pressed my lips to his. I missed his sweet taste. My body filled with heat the longer I kissed him.

A shooting pain caused me to break away from him. I screamed out as the pain intensified. "I can't do this. It hurts so bad."

"You can do this baby. We are right here to help you."

"It's hot in here. I'm hot," I said getting frustrated. Brant got me a cold rag and held it to my forehead for me. "Thank you," I said trying to look up at him. "I feel an extreme pressure down there," I said turning away from Brant to look at the doctor.

"Let me check you again. On three remember," Dr. Johnson said. She lifted my knees again. "One. Two. Three." She inserted her hand once more. "Wow that was fast. I feel a head. Are you ready to start pushing?"

"No, but let's get this over with."

"Brant run and get Ambi. I will need her assistance like we practiced." He left the room and was back within a couple of minutes, Ambi right on his heels. "Ambi suit up. It's time to deliver some babies," the doctor said excited. "On three you give me a big push Lilith. Odin, Tristan, you two hold her knees back as far as they will go. Brant keep that rag to her forehead and one hand behind her back." They all nodded at her instructions. "Ready Lilith? One. Two. Three. Push."

I pushed as hard as I could. I pushed until I was out of breath. I sucked in another breath and pushed again. "Aghhhhhhhhhh," I screamed as the first baby popped out of me.

"Relax. Breath Lilith. It's a boy." She handed the baby to Ambi so she could clean him up. "Ready to push out baby number two?" I nodded. "On three again okay? Guys ready to do this again?" They nodded.

"Baby you are doing great," Tristan said in my ear. "Let's do this one more time okay."

"Okay," I said.

"Here we go. One. Two. Three. Push." I pushed again with all the strength I had left in my body. My Ava came a little easier than her brother. When she came out, I relaxed my body laying back onto the

Beautiful Corruption

bed. I loosened my grip on Odin and Tristan's hands, the pain finally over. "You did great Lilith."

"I love you so much," Tristan said in my ear. "I'm finally a dad." The tears in his eyes falling to mimic my own.

"I love you too."

"Here you go mommy," Ambi said handing me Elijah.

"He is perfect," I said kissing his little head. He had a head full of black hair just like Odin's. He also had his glowing green eyes.

"Want to meet your daughter?" Ambi asked me.

"Of course." I handed Elijah to Tristan, so I could hold Ava. She was just as perfect as Elijah. She had my red hair and my gray eyes. I looked over at Tristan, my heart warming at the sight of him loving our son. "Want to hold your daughter?" He nodded, and I took Elijah back while he took Ava. I spoke to Tristan with my mind and he nodded in response to my question. I looked at Odin, "Would you like to meet your son?"

"Really?" he asked shocked.

"Yes. You were right. They can have two dads." His face lit up as I handed him Elijah. "They will have the best two dads in the world." Our family wouldn't be the normal family but the way I see it, my two babies would have unconditional love from so many people. They are lucky to have so many people in their lives that will love them no matter what. We would make this work and we would all survive as a family. My heart couldn't get any fuller than it is at this moment. The ugly, painful corruption that my heart felt from Odin's deceit, has now turned into the most beautiful corruption that anyone could ever feel.

Jessica Manson

Chapter Nineteen

Odin let Tristan and I stay together. He didn't lock him back up in his cell, but we did have to stay locked up downstairs in my room. I didn't care though; I was just happy that we could finally be together. Odin came to visit the babies several times a day since I've had them. Today when he came, he brought Bristol and Parker with him. He let them come see the babies. He even let them stay locked in the room with us.

We were all starting to unite as a family again. The guys and Ambi would come see the babies as much as they could as well. Everyone was getting along like we did before I left Odin. Despite being locked up, our life was peaceful, but I know it wouldn't last. Tristan and I still had many obstacles in front of us. Our first mission is to get out of this place. We still needed to kill Draven, so I could take his place and I still had the witches to deal with. Not to mention that Slaaneth would be back soon since I had the babies.

I think our best option at the moment is to take Slaaneth out first. As long as I'm locked up in this room his army can't get to my babies. My mom said that the answer is within myself and if I listened to my inner self, I would find the answer on how to kill him. If I could convince Odin to let me out of this room long enough, I could search for the answer, but I can't do anything without my magic. And there is no way I can use my magic in this room without killing myself.

With the day winding down Bristol and Parker lay at the foot of the bed on the floor while Tristan and I lay cuddled in each other's arms. Ava and Elijah lay in their bassinets peacefully sleeping. "I've missed this," I said snuggling deeper into his chest.

"Missed what baby?" he asked.

"Cuddling with you. Hearing your heartbeat. Feeling the warmth of your body against mine."

"I've missed it too baby." He wrapped his arms tighter around me and kissed the top of my head. I lay there letting the rhythm of his beating heart sing me into a much-needed sleep.

Beautiful Corruption

When I woke up Tristan, Bristol and Parker were gone. Odin and Draven stood over the babies. Odin wore a guilty look on his face when he noticed I had woken up. I jumped out of bed and walked over to protect my babies from Draven. "Get away from them," I told him before turning toward Odin, "What is he doing here?"

"I came to see my grandchildren," Draven said answering for Odin. He wore an evil mischievous smile that made my stomach turn.

"You have no claim to them and Odin you had no right to let him near them."

"It's not like I didn't try to stop him Lilith. He wouldn't listen to me," Odin said.

"I'm not here for chit chat. Odin grab the babies and let's go," Draven said.

"Excuse me? You are not taking my babies anywhere," I said stepping between Odin and the babies.

"You didn't think you would get to keep them, did you? Now that you have had them you will need to face your punishment as well as the others. We have put it off long enough don't you think?"

"Do what you want with me, but you are not touching my babies."

"Very well. I don't have time for this today. I will be back with reinforcements," Draven said leaving Odin and me alone in the room.

"How could you bring him down here Odin?"

"I told you I tried to stop him. There was nothing I could do."

"Do you remember that day when you took me to your dad's house, so I could see where you worked?" I asked.

"Of course, I remember. How could I forget? That was the day my mother spoke for the first time in over a year."

"When we were leaving, and she pulled me in for a hug, she warned me Odin. She told me to not let Draven get my baby. She knew he would try to take them. We can't let him have them. He will kill them or raise them to be monsters like him."

"Trust me Lilith. He will not get his hands on our babies."

"What are you going to do?"

"You said you were going to take his spot as a Luminary, how were you planning on doing that?"

"I'm going to kill him."

"Then we need a plan. Only problem is, everyone in this house works for my father. We won't know who we can trust to keep quiet about our plans."

"If I can get out of this room, I will be able help with that. All I have to do is read everyone's minds when we tell them the plan."

"That may work. But what if they know how to block their thoughts?"

"They don't know I can read minds. If they don't know that why would they try to hide their thoughts?"

"Good point."

"Where is Tristan, Parker and Bristol?" I asked remembering they were gone.

"When my father called to tell me, he was on his way I had to lock them back up." He didn't need to be able to read minds to tell what I was thinking. "No worries. I'll let them out now."

"You better. You wouldn't want to push the limits of this friendship already, would you?" I asked jokingly.

"I would never," he said acting offended.

"Come on. Let's go get my man," I said pulling him toward the door.

After Odin released Tristan, Parker and Bristol, Tristan and I grabbed Ava and Elijah and we all headed for the dining room. When we arrived, everyone was already sitting at the table waiting for us. Gunner jumped up from the table and walked over to me. He looked at me smiling, "Give me my niece. She needs time with her uncle." Gunner was starting to warm up to me since I had the babies. Even before I left Odin, he didn't have much to do with me. In fact, I think he even hated me at one point.

"Uncle Gunner," I said teasing. "I like it."

"Me too," Gunner said snuggling Ava.

Odin walked over to me and pulled me to the side and whispered as silently as he could in my ear. "Are you ready to listen?" I nodded. He turned to everyone in the room. "We have asked all of you to meet us here today because my father is trying to take Ava and Elijah away from us. We can't let that happen. There is only one way to stop him." He looked at me to make sure I was listening to the responses from everyone when he said these next words. "Lilith has to kill him."

All at once everyone started talking but no one moved their lips.

"I knew this was coming," Cal said.

"Son of a bitch. A war with a Luminary. Are they crazy?" Dex said.

"No one will hurt Uncle Gunners baby girl." I couldn't help but smile at Gunners words. It wasn't like him to be so sweet.

"Oh, baby you…" This must be Cal's favorite song. It is always playing in his head.

"Hell yeah, finally some action," Brant said.

"I'd love to take that bastard out once and for all," Latham said.

"You got what I need. You say you're just a friend, you say you're just a friend but baby you, you got what I need." I had to stop myself from laughing out loud at him singing.

"I can't take much more of this attention seeking bitch. I need to get rid of her once and for all. Draven will kill her before she even sees what's coming. I just need to find a way to protect Odin." My heart fell for Odin as I heard Ambi's plan. Did she want to hurt me only because she was still jealous? I didn't want Odin. I would never love him the way I used to.

I nodded at Odin when I had the information we needed. I knew who would betray us all. She was willing to sacrifice two innocent babies just to get rid of me. She was a heartless bitch and if I ever got the chance, I would take her out as well.

"Odin, can I see you for a moment?" I pulled him out into the hallway where we couldn't be heard. I whispered as low as I could. "I am going to cast a spell on you, so you can hear their thoughts. You won't believe me if I tell you who the traitor will be. You need to hear it for yourself."

"Can't you just tell me who it is?"

"No. You would never take my word for it. Just let me do this."

"Okay."

I began my chant:

To seek the truth,
And not to find,
Heed these words,
Within my rhyme,
He hears the thoughts,
Within their mind,
He shall hear them,
Within his mind.

"Ready?" I asked. "They will all be speaking at once so be ready. Don't make any facial expressions. And do not laugh when you hear Cal singing."

"Singing?"

"Yes, Cal likes to sing, and he seems to like only one song. Keep a straight face. Show no emotion."

"Alright, let's get this over with." When we walked back into the room everyone was waiting for Odin to finish. "As I was saying, Lilith will have to kill my father. We will need everyone's help for her to be successful. My father is a very powerful man with a lot of reinforcements. He will have the numbers, but we have something better. We have the element of surprise."

"You are wrong Odin. Draven will know her plan. I will get rid of her once and for all and I will use Draven to do it. The fucking whore of a bitch needs to pay for what she has done to you." Ambi's words cut like a knife. How could someone turn out to be so cruel?

Odin didn't let what she said phase him in the slightest. He held himself well in front of everyone. "I need to know who will help Lilith. Who will help save my children?"

"Lilith will die. I will raise your children as my own. I will be the only mother they know. They will never even know she existed."

I couldn't stop myself. I flew across the room and tackled Ambi to the floor. "You will never raise my children. I am their mother, not you," I screamed at her as I punched her in the face over and over. "You will have to kill me to get to my babies you fucking bitch."

She tried to fight me off, but it was no use. "Draven will kill you, you fucking whore. What will happen to your precious babies then?"

"No one is killing me." I punched her in the face again. "Not you." Another punch. "Not Draven." One last punch from me and she blacked out. "That bitch has lost her fucking mind if she thinks she will get her conniving ass hands on my babies," I said to no one as I got myself off of her.

"Brant, Latham, lock Ambi in one of the cells downstairs," Odin said as an order.

"But she is one of us," Brant said.

"No, she is not. Lilith put a spell on me, so I could hear everyone's thoughts. We needed to know who we could trust. And trust me, Ambi is not one of them. She is going to tell my father our plans. I will take out anyone that interferes with the safety of my children. Now, lock her up." With everyone else on our side Brant and Latham locked Ambi up in one of the cells below us.

Jessica Manson

Chapter Twenty

After Ambi was locked up we immediately started going over ideas on how to kill Draven, but no one could come up with any good ones. We knew we had to get him when he was alone. We wouldn't be able to attack him as long as his reinforcements were around. I did have one idea, but I wasn't sure if Odin would go for it.

Everyone was throwing ideas around all at once, so no one heard me when I tried to speak the first or second time. Frustrated I yelled, "I have an idea." Finally, everyone shut up and looked at me.

"What's your plan baby," Tristan said walking up and placing his arm around my waist.

"Odin, I need to speak to your mother," I said.

"What for?" he asked confused.

"Because she will tell us when Draven is home alone. She won't speak to anyone else, but if I talk to her maybe she will do it. The only way for us to have the upper hand is to catch him off guard."

"How do you suppose we get you there without being seen? My father has this place surrounded." I looked at him and smiled. "What?" Without saying a word, I made myself go invisible.

"Holy shit," Brant said.

"Girls got talent," Cal said.

"I know. Isn't she amazing?" Tristan said placing a kiss on my invisible forehead.

I turned off the invisibility and said, "That's how. Now when can we go see her?"

"Want to go now?" Odin asked catching me off guard.

"Can I change first?" I had no intention of going to see his mother in my pajamas.

"Of course."

I left everyone in the dining room while I went down to shower. The bathroom was steaming when I stepped into the hot water relaxing my body instantly.

140

I had just finished washing my hair when I felt two familiar arms grab me from behind. I didn't need to turn around to know Tristan had joined me. Instead I leaned into him resting my head on his shoulder. He kissed the side of my neck gently causing my body to scream for him to make love to me.

He slowly ran his fingers up my stomach until he cupped one of my breasts. A moan escaped me as he pinched my nipple between his fingers. I could feel him growing hard against my back. I lifted my hands to his head and tangled my fingers in his hair slightly pulling it. He growled into my ear.

He turned me to face him. When our eyes locked, my heart skipped a beat. His eyes were filled with love, passion, desire. He wanted me just as bad as I wanted him. He pressed our bodies closer together and kissed me softly at first then he kissed deeper, more passionately.

My body wasn't healed enough for sex yet, but that didn't mean I couldn't please him. I pulled away from him and pushed him against the wall. I dropped to my knees and took his hardness in my hands. I caressed him softly at first, gently kissing his tip. I kissed his thighs making the anticipation grow. When he looked like he couldn't handle much more of my teasing I took him into my mouth. He leaned his head back as he accepted the pleasure.

I sucked just enough to make him moan. I kept my hands busy as well. They massaged him pulling all of him into me. Slowly sucking while gently licking him. My hands were wet and slippery sliding up and down on him. I knew he wasn't going to last much longer. He was moaning and panting uncontrollably. He wrapped his large hand around the back of my head as he was getting ready for his release. I pulled back, my mouth full of him.

As he leaned back against the wall not looking at me, I spit him out of me. "That was amazing," he said caressing the back of my head. I stood up and he pulled me into his arms. I rested my head on his chest. We stood locked in each other's arms until the water ran cold. "I love you Lilith."

"I love you too Tristan. More than you could ever imagine."

When we got back upstairs Odin didn't hear us walk into the room. He was cuddling Ava and Elijah at the same time. With his back to us he started talking to them. "You know you two are the luckiest babies in the world. You have the best mom you could ever ask for, two dads that would do anything for you and a whole lot of uncles that are going to teach you things that will drive your mom crazy. You have a lot of love in your lives already. Your mom and I may not have been able to make our relationship work, but we did get one thing perfectly right, the two of you. Ava Faye, you are daddy's little princess and Elijah Eugene, you are my little slugger. I love you both so much. And I love your mom for blessing me with the two of you. Don't tell anybody I said this, but I love Tristan too for letting me be a part of your lives. He didn't have to accept me being friends with your mom, but that man has a big heart. Sleep my babies. I love you."

When Odin laid the babies down in their cribs, catching him off guard I gave him a hug. "What is this for?" he asked.

"For just being you," I said. He wrapped his arms tighter around me. "Thank you."

"For what?" he asked pulling away from me.

"For everything. For accepting Tristan and me, for agreeing to let Tristan be a part of Ava and Elijah's life, for being a great dad and for standing beside me when it counts the most."

"Come here," he said pulling me in for another hug. "You know I would do anything for you. No matter what happened between us Lilith, I still love you. And I'll be here waiting if shit goes south with Tristan," he whispered in my ear and when he pulled away from me, he was smiling.

I playfully hit him on the arm, "Let's go asshole."

"I'm just saying, offer is always open," he said laughing.

I walked over to Tristan, "Are you going to be okay with the babies while I'm gone?"

Beautiful Corruption

"Of course. They are in perfect hands. Besides, I have Gunner looking over my shoulder in case I need help."

"Damn right. You don't have to worry Lilith. I'll make sure they are well taken care of," Gunner said walking into the room.

I kissed Tristan before turning myself invisible. "Let's get this over with Odin." Odin walked toward me, "Ouch. Watch where you're going."

"Sorry. It's not like I can see you."

I placed my hands on his shoulders and placed him in front of me. "I'll hold onto the back of your shirt. Remember, I'll be sliding in on your side of the car. It will look mighty funny for your passenger door to open and shut by itself."

Odin led the way to the car and when we were about to get in a short brown-haired guy walked up to us. "Are you leaving the property Mr. Odin?"

"Yes. I will be out for a while," Odin said. I went ahead and slid in while the guy was distracted.

"I'll call down to the gate and let Justin know you are heading out."

"Thanks Michael," Odin said as he got in the car. I watched Michael speak into a walkie talkie as we drove off. I assumed he was letting Justin know we were on our way. When we got to the gate Odin rolled down his window and spoke to another guy. I couldn't see his face, but I assumed it was Justin. When they were done speaking the gate opened.

When his window was rolled back up, I said, "Your dad really does have this place on lock down."

"Just a precaution so you can't escape."

"If he only knew that his very own son was driving me right out the front gate."

"Very funny. He would kill us both if he found out."

"Yeah, lucky for you, you have gotten on my good side lately. I guess I won't tell on you," I said teasing him.

"You keep teasing me and I'll start to think you are flirting."

"I am a married woman Odin," I said pretending to be offended.

143

Jessica Manson

"That didn't stop you from hooking up with Tristan." I could tell he regretted the words as soon as they left his mouth, but that didn't make it hurt any less.

"Ouch," I said and turned to look out the window.

"I'm sorry Lilith. I shouldn't have said that."

"You know Odin there comes a time when you have to choose between turning the page and closing the book." We rode the rest of the way in silence. His words hurt me even though I didn't feel bad about being with Tristan. Life doesn't give you the people you want, it gives you the people you need. The people that will help you, love you and make you the person you were meant to be. Tristan is my person.

I didn't feel bad for being with Tristan, but I did feel bad for Odin. I know he truly loved me. I guess he couldn't stand the silence and awkwardness between us because he said again, "I really am sorry."

"Odin, I hope you know I really did care about you. I loved you without reason."

"Are you still mad at me?"

"I was never mad at you."

"Then what were you?"

"Hurt." I watched his shoulders fall from disappointment in himself. "The worst feeling in the world is being hurt by someone you love." The tears started to fall. I think my heart was finally ready to bleed. "Stop the car Odin." He didn't hesitate. He pulled over and let me cry. The pain I locked away was finally surfacing. It felt like I was crying with my whole body. My heart ached so much I couldn't take a breath, I couldn't talk, I couldn't move. My mind was set on my pain.

I had locked my feelings away for so long, not facing them when I should have. It consumed me now. I had lost my parents to the guy I loved more than life itself. I loved him with every single heartbeat in my body. Odin was my world and my world crumbled and fell to pieces. It felt like I had found out the truth all over again.

When I finally collected myself, I looked over at Odin. He was staring out the driver side window. "Odin," I called his name to let him know we could go now. When he looked over at me my heart fell again.

His eyes were red and swollen. He was crying as well. "Odin," I whispered his name heartbroken for the both of us.

"Lilith, I can't tell you how truly sorry I am. I never meant to hurt you. I love you so much and when you left you took my heart with you. Seeing you hurt makes me hurt. You were my everything and I lost you. I lost the only good thing in my life. I miss the time when I actually meant something to you. It's sad how you were such a big part of my life and now you're just gone."

"I'm not gone Odin. Sometimes people fall in love but aren't meant to be together and that's okay. We can be friends and doing so shows how mature we are. We can get over the fact that we weren't meant to be together. And I will never forget you were my first love Odin. You will always have a special place in my heart. I have forgiven you for what you did. And I think it is time we move on and raise our babies as a family, an unconventional one, but all the same we are a family. And I will always love you, it's just a different kind of love now."

"I will always love you too just in the same way I always have. If being friends with you is the only way to have you in my life, then that is what I am willing to do. I will quietly watch you love someone else. I will silently watch you go on with your life while I love you secretly. And I will wait patiently for the only girl I have ever loved to come back to me."

"You honestly believe that I'm coming back to you, don't you?"

"Mark my words Lilith Rose, one day you will be mine again."

I rolled my eyes at his confidence, "Come on, let's get back to the mission at hand." With that Odin pulled back onto the road.

Jessica Manson

Chapter Twenty-One

When we got close to Odin's father's house, I made myself go invisible again. The closer we got the more active my nerves were. My fear was in overdrive. I couldn't imagine what would happen if Draven was home. Odin pulled into the driveway and we both took a deep breath before he got out of the car. He acted like he dropped something on the ground to give me time to crawl out of his side of the car.

I grabbed the back of his shirt again as he led the way into the house. "Stay here. I'll go check the house for my father," he whispered to me. While he was gone, I stood as still as I possibly could. I was almost too afraid to breath. "He's not here," Odin said coming down the hallway.

"Who's not here?" Draven said coming down from the stairs. All of my fears were coming to reality. I was so scared I didn't even blink.

"You. I thought you were gone," Odin said.

"No. I am here in the flesh. What are you doing here?"

"I just came in to catch up on some of the paperwork I'm behind on."

"Well, I'm heading out. You will have to work on it alone."

"I think I can handle it. Where are you off too?"

"I have a couple meetings in New York. I won't be back for a few days. Tell me Odin, do you think you can handle Lilith while I am away?"

"Of course, I can."

"Good. I knew I could count on you. I'll see you when I get back."

"Be safe."

"Always."

When Draven walked out the door, I finally started to relax a little. I watched through the window as he left. I didn't want to take any chances of him returning. "That was close," I said to Odin who was standing right behind me watching too.

"Too close. Let's get this over with. I'm ready to get out of here."

Odin walked over and knocked on the same door that was in the living room. No one answered, but he pushed the door open anyways. "Mom," he called out for her, but she didn't seem to notice he had even entered the room. She was sitting in the same place she was sitting the last time I saw her, in a chair in front of a TV that wasn't on.

I walked around Odin and made myself visible. I sat on the floor in front of her. When she finally noticed me, she smiled. "My precious Lilith. How have you been?"

"I have been just fine. What about you?"

"Why have you waited so long to come see me?"

"I know it has been a while. I'm sorry for that. But I am here now."

"How has my boy been treating you?"

"He's been just fine."

"Adreana, I need a favor. Can you do something for me?"

"Sure dear. What do you need?"

"I am going to kill Draven, but I need your help to do it."

Her eyes lit up. "I'll help you. What do I need to do?"

"I will need to know when he is alone. He can't have any bodyguards around. It needs to be just him. Can you do that for me? Can you call Odin when he is alone?"

"Yes. I can do that."

"Thank you."

"No sweetie. Thank you. I can't wait to get out of this hell I'm in."

"Okay. You understand the plan, right?"

"Yes. I will call when he is alone."

"Okay. Great. Since Draven is out of town would you like for Odin and me to spend some time with you?"

"Oh, that would be lovely."

Odin sat on the floor next to me and we spent the next two hours watching a TV that wasn't on.

When we left, Odin was smiling so big. "What has you smiling like that?"

"You."

"Why me?"

"Because, no one can get to her the way you do. It's amazing to watch the effect you have on her. She doesn't even talk to me when I visit her, but you just got her to let me watch TV with her. It may have been a blank screen, but it was the best two hours of my life. If you weren't married, I would kiss you right now."

"I'm glad you're happy. It's nice to see you smile again."

"It's all because of you."

"Get us home. I'm ready to see my babies."

When we walked into the house everyone was yelling and frantic. We ran to where their voices were coming from. Everyone was downstairs where the cells were. "Oh no. Ambi," I said running down the stairs. When we reached the bottom and noticed what the commotion was, my heart fell. Ambi had Tristan with one arm wrapped around his neck.

"There that bitch is," Ambi said when her eyes landed on me. "You made it just in time to watch me rip his fucking head off."

"Let him go Ambi. You don't want to do this," Odin said.

"No. I think I do."

"Let him go. I'm the one you want," I said trying to convince her to let him go.

"I'll kill him first while you watch. Then I will slowly take my time killing you."

"You're not going to hurt him, Ambi. Let. Him. Go."

"Fuck you," she said as she dug her fingernails into Tristan's chest. I panicked as I watched blood drip to the floor. "A little harder and it's bye-bye to lover boy here Lilith."

"What do I have to do for you to let him go?"

"I'm not letting him go. I'm just having fun watching the fear build up in you."

I couldn't let her hurt Tristan anymore, but I knew I couldn't get to him before she killed him. A chant formed on my lips before I knew what I was doing.

Time stand still- I order you,
No minutes' pass until I'm through doing what I must do,
Time stand still- I order you.

When the chant was finished, everyone in the room was frozen in place. I walked carefully over to Ambi and released Tristan from her grasp. I shut the cell door locking her inside and as the lock clicked into place everyone unfroze.

I could see the anger radiating off Ambi. She was pissed beyond measure. "Bitch, one day I will kill you and everyone you love," she said, and I believed her. She would try to kill me, I knew that. But that doesn't mean she would be successful.

"How did you do that?" Odin asked.

"I'm not exactly sure, but I froze time, so I could free Tristan. It was the only thing I could think to do to save him."

Tristan walked over to me and wrapped me into his arms. He kissed me on the top of my head before saying, "Thank you for saving me yet again."

"What do you mean again?" Odin asked.

"Do you remember the bear shifter you sent to find her?"

"Yes. I sent him to track the two of you, but I never heard from him again."

"Well that's because she ripped his heart out when he tried to kill me."

"That explains why he never returned. It seems like you will do whatever it takes to save the ones you love Lilith."

"I'm willing to kill your father, aren't I?"

"Indeed, you are."

"Where are my babies?" I asked Tristan.

"In the room with Gunner. They are safe."

Jessica Manson

I was walking into the room when Odin stopped me, "Hey Lilith."

"Yeah."

"Would you and Tristan like to move upstairs? You can take Tristan's old room, or you can have ours."

"Tristan's room will be perfect. Thank you." Tristan and I grabbed Ava and Elijah while everyone else started grabbing our things to move us upstairs. "Hey Odin, can I talk to you for a minute?"

"Sure."

"What about Parker and Bristol? They can't stay down here."

"We will move them upstairs too."

"What about Fate? Before we came here Fate was supposed to come back, what happened to him?"

"My father kept him on the mission longer, so he wouldn't know he had Bristol locked up."

"Can you get him out of whatever mission he is on? Can you bring him here?"

"I will see what I can do."

"We will need all the help we can get when it comes time to fight your father. I have a feeling it isn't going to be as easy as we hope it will."

"I'll do everything in my power to get him here."

"Thank you."

"No problem. Now give me my little princess," he said taking Ava from my arms.

"One more thing."

"What's that?" he asked between making cooing noises at Ava.

"Can we bring Tuls here also? She helped us once maybe she is willing to help us again."

"Okay. Get Parker to give her a call but he will have to use my cell phone. It is the only phone in the house that isn't bugged."

"Thank you." He nodded as he walked away. Gunner took Elijah from Tristan leaving us alone. I walked over to him "Come here. What the hell happened?" I asked pulling him into my arms.

150

"Gunner and I came down here to put the babies to bed when Ambi acted like she was hurt. I went in to check on her and that's when she attacked me. Luckily, the lock locked when I went in and she wasn't able to get free. Gunner ran up to get help, but she wouldn't let anyone near the cell without killing me."

"I'm just glad the witch inside me knew what to do and I was able to save you."

"You are my own personal superhero."

"She could have killed you. I don't know what I would do if I lost you."

"You aren't losing me anytime soon baby."

"I better not or I will bring you back to life just, so I can kill you again for leaving me."

Jessica Manson

Chapter Twenty-Two

Within the next few days Odin kept his word on his promise. Fate and Tuls arrive tomorrow. Odin called us into the dining room for a meeting. When I got there Daveh and Razi were seated at the table. "What are they doing here Odin? They work for your father."

He didn't get a chance to answer. "We would like to help," Daveh said.

"Help with what?" I asked confused.

"We want to help you take down Draven."

"Why?"

"You aren't the only prisoners here Lilith," Razi said catching me off guard. He normally didn't speak, to anyone.

"Draven has kept you prisoner?"

"Yes. He will not let us return to our realm. We are fairies, if we do not get back to our realm soon, we will no longer exist as such."

"You mean you won't be fairies any longer?"

"No. We will turn human, but we will not live for very long once we turn."

"How long does it take you to die after turning human?"

"Longest any fairy has lived after turning is a week."

"Why do you have to get back to your realm? I mean why do you turn human if you don't return?"

"Our realm is called Land of Lore. The waters are clearer there. The trees, grass, flowers are brighter. The air is unpolluted. The land untouched by humans. There are fields and fields full of nature. It also grows the Huath tree. We must eat the bark of this tree in order to stay fae. The Huath tree is like your Hawthorn tree that grows in Ireland."

"Can't you just eat from the trees we have here?"

"No. Our tree is full of magic. The bark of the Huath is what gives us our powers, our strength."

"What powers do you have?"

152

Beautiful Corruption

"Same as you mostly. Invisibility, telekinesis, teleportation and strength. We can also fly, and we can tell if a person has a soul or not. We are also immortal as long as we eat of the tree."

"So, do you have weaknesses like in the books?"

"Such as?"

"Iron?"

"Iron will hurt us, but it will not kill us. Silver burns our skin. Cream is a weakness and a delicacy for fairies for the same reason, it gets us drunk. And the worst weakness of all fairies is salt or sugar. If you spill it onto the ground, we have no choice but to count every single grain. We can't resist it."

"That is the craziest thing I have ever heard. You mean to tell me that if I spilled some salt right now the two of you would have to count it? No matter what?"

"Yes."

"That definitely is not in any books I have read."

"We don't like that fact to be known. It is the easiest way for our enemies to kill us. It's the best way to distract us so they can then cut our heads off."

"That's horrible."

"So, will you help us get home? Can we fight with you?"

"Sure. We could use all the help we can get."

"Great," Daveh said jumping up and down.

"So, tell me, what else lives in the Land of Lore."

"Goblins, Gnomes, Elves and Leprechauns to name a few."

"I am reminded every day that this world is not what I knew it was."

"What do you mean?" Razi asked.

"When I was a child, fairies, goblins, elves and leprechauns were the monsters in fairy tales. And fairytales weren't real. Gnomes are things you put in your yard for decoration. Vampires and witches were things in scary movies. Not in real life. And now, every day I live my very own horror show."

"Not all things scary are bad."

Jessica Manson

"Let me ask another question. In every book I've read and every movie I have seen, vampires and fairies can't be around each other. Vampires can't resist your blood. How have you been living here for months and are still alive?"

"It is true that fairy blood is more appealing to vampires, but we have been around for centuries. We have learned to control our cravings for them." Odin answered this time.

"So then why haven't I tried to feed from them? How come I can resist them too?"

"You did try, remember?" Tristan said. "I stopped you. Back then you wanted Daveh because she was fairy. But now we gave you so much blood in a feeding tube while you were in a coma that you shouldn't need it for a while."

"Once all the blood we gave you leaves your system, you will want to feed from Daveh and Razi more than you want to feed from a human," Odin said.

"But it has been weeks since I came out of my coma."

"We gave you a lot of blood."

"Well, not to change the subject, but when does your father return?" I asked Odin.

"In a few days."

"How much time do you think we have before we can take him down?"

"I'm not sure. Hopefully we can do it soon. The longer we wait, the more dangerous it becomes."

"Well hopefully with eleven vampires, two fairies and a vampire-witch hybrid it will be easy to take him out. We just need a solid plan."

"Have any ideas?"

"Not yet."

"Then it looks like we are stuck at square one."

"For now." Tristan, Daveh and Razi left the dining room leaving me and Odin alone. "Can I ask you for a favor?"

"Depends on what it is you want," he said with a smile.

154

"I want you to teach me how to fight. I need to be able to defend myself if I need to. I can't always rely on a spell to just pop up."

"When?"

"Yesterday."

"Sure. Meet me in the back yard in ten minutes."

"Wait. I can't go outside. Someone will see me."

"Oh yeah." He thought for a minute. "I know a place we can go. Meet me at the front door in ten minutes instead. And be invisible."

"Okay."

I stood by the door waiting for Odin. After waiting fifteen minutes instead of ten he finally walked down the stairs. He had replaced his jeans for track pants. "Ready?" he asked.

"Yeah, five minutes ago."

"Go invisible so we can go." I did the same as last time. I went invisible and climbed in the car from his side. We drove in silence until we pulled onto a dirt road and pulled into a clearing. "I'm excited," he said.

"About what?"

"I get to kick your ass."

"You wish." We got out of the car and walked into the middle of the clearing. "Don't go all witchy on me while I'm trying to teach you."

"I'll try not to."

"First I am going to teach you some basic self-defense moves." He grabbed my wrist, "If your attacker grabs you by the wrist don't try to pull away. Instead, rotate your wrist so your thumb lines up with where your attacker's thumb meets his fingers. Jerk sharply by bending your arm at the elbow. Your wrist should slip right of his hand. Now try it," he said gripping my wrist harder. I did as he showed me and broke free from him.

Jessica Manson

"That was good. Now this next one is good to buy you time to run away from your attacker. Thrust the sole of your foot toward your attacker's knee. This will incapacitate them. This area works better than the groin or face because it is nearly impossible to block. Plus, the attacker will need both legs to chase you. Ready to try it?"

"What if I hurt you?"

"Just try it, I trust you." Catching me off guard Odin lunged for me. I wasn't expecting him to run into me and we both fell to the ground him landing on top of me. He stayed there looking at me longer than I liked. I could feel the old heat I used to feel for him try to resurface. Nope, I shut that shit down really quick.

I pushed him off me, "I wasn't ready. Let's try again."

"You won't know when your attacker will strike. You should always be ready."

"Okay then let's try something else." He lunged at me again, but this time I was ready. I kicked at his knee and he fell to the ground.

"That was better, but you weren't supposed to use all of your strength," he said as he got up limping.

"I didn't. Are you okay?"

"I'll be fine." He walked off his pain for a moment before walking back over to me. "Alright now we are going to try a nerve strike."

"That sounds dangerous."

"It could be." He touched the space located slightly below my ear on my neck. "A weak blow to the vagus nerve will cause intense pain and involuntary muscle spasms. A strong blow will cause your attacker to black out or die. Ready to try it?"

"No freaking way. Are you kidding me? I could kill you."

"You won't kill me. Come on and stop being a baby. Try it."

"No."

"Try it," he said stepping closer to me.

"No way."

"Lilith damn it. Stop being such a..." I cut him off when I punched him in the same spot, he just touched on me. He fell to the ground once more, but not in pain or in a spasm. I knocked him out.

156

Beautiful Corruption

"Fuck. Damn its Odin. I told you," I said as if he could hear me. I sat down beside him and tried to wake him up. "Get up," I yelled into his ear. He didn't budge. I sat there and played with some blades of grass while waiting for him to come too. After fifteen minutes, he finally stirred. "Thank goodness. I was starting to worry."

"You weren't supposed to hit that hard."

"I didn't even hit you that hard."

"Yeah, then why was I laid out on the ground?"

"Are we done for the day?"

"No, just give me a minute."

I waited and when I thought he was done being butt hurt I said, "I thought you were going to kick my ass."

"Shut up. Do not hit me on this one. Just act like you are going to hit me."

"Okay."

"This one is the palm strike. You want to position your attacker's nose with your palm." He placed his palm on my nostrils. "This will break your attacker's nose. But if you hit hard enough it could also cause death. Remember, just act like you are going to hit me."

I forced my palm up toward his nose just like he showed me only I didn't stop in time. "Oh, my gosh. I'm so sorry," I said instantly.

"Son of a bitch, whore. Damn it." He pulled his hand away from his nose, blood poured from it. "Mother fucker."

"Odin I..." he cut me off by holding up his hand to me. He walked away from me leaving me to wallow in my guilt. He finally walked back over to me, "Odin I think this is enough for today."

He took his shirt off and pressed it to his nose. My body reacted to the sight of his ripped abs in a way that I didn't want it to. "You giving up already?"

"I keep hurting you," I said forcing myself to look at his face and not at that sexy V thing leading right into his pants. His eyes were starting to turn black from the hit.

"Are you doing it on purpose?"

"No. I swear."

Jessica Manson

"Then let's keep going."

"Are you sure?"

"Yes."

"I really am sorry about your nose and knee. And for knocking you out."

"Don't worry about it. At least I know you can take care of yourself." He touched me in the area right below my breast in the middle of my stomach. "This is your solar plexus. A hit here will knock the wind out of your attacker. It will give you enough time to run or get the upper hand. Try it."

"I don't think that's a good idea."

"Just do it," he said sounding frustrated.

"Fine," I said as I punched toward his solar plexus. I hit him with a force I didn't know I had. He leaned over trying to catch his breath and started coughing. "I'm done. I will not hurt you again. Once you've caught your breath, take me home." He didn't fight me this time. I think he was tired of getting his ass kicked as much as I was tired of doing the ass kicking.

Odin didn't speak to me the rest of the way home. I felt bad for hurting him. I didn't mean to do it. The worse his eyes looked the worse I felt. They were completely black now and starting to swell. "Are you okay to drive like that?" I asked.

"Yeah. We are almost home."

"Why haven't you healed yet?"

"I will. It will just take a couple of hours."

"Want me to use a spell on you?"

"No thanks. I wear my battle scars proudly."

"You know the guys are going to make fun of you."

"I know. I don't care. They will all know what a badass you are."

"I'm not a bad ass. I hurt you."

"This is nothing compared to what I did to you."

"Odin."

"I know. Can I just ask you one thing? If your answer is no, then I will never say anything about it again."

Beautiful Corruption

"What?"

"You felt it, didn't you?"

"Felt what?" I asked knowing exactly what he meant.

"The electricity between us. You felt it?"

"Odin. I…"

"Did you feel it? Yes or no?"

"Don't do this."

"Do what?"

"You know what. I am married to Tristan. I am your friend Odin. We can't be together."

"You were mine first."

"Yes. Then you betrayed me in a way that was worse than what Cody did to me."

"Lilith, I have told you I am sorry about that. I know sorry doesn't begin to make it right, but I need you to know that I would never ever hurt you in any way ever again."

"And I believe you, but I am still married."

"Yeah well I know you felt it," he said confidently.

"Thank you for teaching me a few moves today," I said trying to change the subject.

"Any contact with you is worth getting my ass kicked for."

"Stop that."

"What?"

"Flirting."

"Technically, I'm not wrong for it. You are my wife by the laws I follow."

"You are so frustrating."

"I know. But you love me," he said wiggling his eyebrows.

"I can't believe I'm saying this, but yes I do love you. But *do not* read too much into it. I'm still a married woman Odin."

"Yes mam' Mrs. Rose." He said sarcastically as I went invisible and we pulled into the driveway.

Jessica Manson

Chapter Twenty-Three

As soon as we walked into the house Cal started laughing, "Damn dude. Lilith beat your ass."

"Shut up she did not."

"Tell that to your two black eyes," Brant said.

"So how did the training go?" Tristan asked.

"It was good for me. Not so much for him. I ended up taking out his knee, busted his nose which led to the black eyes, I knocked him out for fifteen minutes and knocked the air out of him when I hit him in the solar plexus." Everyone immediately started laughing. I looked over at Odin, he looked embarrassed. "I'm sorry Odin, I didn't realize they were listening."

"It's alright."

"I told you my girl is a badass," Tristan said.

My eyes were still locked on Odin and he was still looking at me. I still felt really bad for hurting him then I go and embarrass him in front of everyone. "That she is," he said never breaking the eye contact. "She is definitely badass." I had to break the eye contact. His glowing green eyes were starting to get to me. His eyes were the first thing about him that I fell in love with. And they were starting to have the same effect on me as they used to.

Oh, my God, what is wrong with me? I can't be having these feelings about him again. He betrayed me, he hurt me. I am married. But those eyes. Those beautiful glowing green eyes. That body, that hair that is dying for me to run my fingers through it. Jesus, Lilith, snap out of it.

I had to walk away. My body was not listening to my mind. It was heating up in ways it should only heat for Tristan. I was getting feelings in places that only Tristan had access to. I went upstairs and took myself a cold shower needing to remove the heat that was building up inside my body.

When the feelings washed away, I got out, wrapped myself in a towel and checked on Ava and Elijah. They were still sound asleep in their cribs, so I decided to lay down and watch a movie. I didn't make it past the credits before falling asleep.

I was taken back to that bridge in Maine. Slaaneth was standing there waiting for me. "Welcome Lilith. It is nice to see you again."

"Can't say the same."

"How are my babies?"

"*My* babies are just fine. What do you want?"

"Do you always have to ask me that? You know what I want."

"Yeah, you want me dead and to steal my babies. Why am I here?"

"That's a better question," he said through laughter. "I called you here to warn you."

"Warn me about what?"

"The witches are coming. They have planned an attack."

"When?"

"Now." Just as the word left his mouth, I was woken up by glass shattering. I jumped out of bed, grabbed the babies and ran out of the room. "Gunner," I yelled. "Gunner," I yelled for him again and he ran out of his room.

"What's wrong?"

"Take the babies down to the cells. Keep them safe. When it is safe, we will come get you. Do not leave them Gunner. I'm trusting you with my baby's life."

"I will take care of them. I promise."

"Good. Now go. Hurry." I ran down the hall. "Odin, Tristan." I ran down the stairs as they were running up them. "The witches are here. They've planned an attack." Everyone came running downstairs when they heard the commotion.

Suddenly the front door flew open and three witches stood in the doorway. Odin and Tristan stood in front of me protectively, but I pushed them out of my way. I walked closer to the witches, "What do you want?"

"We wanted you to join us, but since you drained me of my powers now, we just want you dead," The leader said with so much hate in her voice.

Jessica Manson

"I see. And how exactly did you think this would play out when you come to my home that is full of vampires that are willing to risk their lives for me? How successful do you think you will be?"

"Oh, Lilith, you underestimate us. Rosita, freeze," she said to the girl on her left. Rosita lifted her hands and everyone in the room except me, froze. They could still hear and see everything going on. They were just frozen in place. "Nissa, strike." The leader said to the girl on her right. Nissa lifted her hands ready to strike me. I flicked my wrist and she went flying across the room. Rosita tried to strike me next, but again I was too fast. When I threw her across the room her concentration was broken, and everyone unfroze. It didn't take her long to recover. Everyone only got to take a couple of steps before freezing again.

I lunged for the leader. She jumped out of the way just in time for me to miss her. While I was distracted, Nissa attacked. I was hit with a bolt of electricity that she shot from her hand. I fell to the floor in pain. Nissa struck me again and again. Her hits were causing anger now instead of pain. The leader knelt down in front of my face. She was smiling. "You should never underestimate the power of a witch."

"You're not a witch. I stole your power remember?"

She back handed me then leaned in closer, "How could I forget?"

"Wrong move bitch." She looked at me confused right before I sunk my teeth into her neck. I used her body to block Nissa's attacks draining her of her blood at the same time. Once every ounce of her blood was drained, I felt a power flow through my body and out through my fingertips. The power was so strong; I couldn't hold it in.

I pointed at Nissa and Rosita, suddenly they were screaming in pain. I walked closer to them. Nissa tried to attack me again, but her hits didn't faze me. "Look at her eyes. What's wrong with them?" Rosita asked Nissa.

"I don't know but help me. My strikes aren't hurting her."

"Fear," I said to Nissa. She fell to the floor screaming. I had projected her worst fear onto her. She thought she was burning in a fire. I looked at Rosita, she was next.

Beautiful Corruption

"Please no," she begged.

"You come into my house and attack me then expect me to have mercy on you."

"Please. I am sorry we attacked you."

"Unfreeze my family now." She did as she was told. Everyone started to run toward me, but they didn't get far. I had put up an invisible barrier between us and them. They wouldn't get to us until I was done. I pointed my two fingers at Rosita and brought her to stand in front of me. "Tell me something Rosita."

"Anything."

"Why did your leader really want me to join your coven so badly?"

"Don't Rosita. She will kill us," Nissa said through tears and screams of pain.

"Don't make me ask again. My patience is wearing thin Rosita."

"She was going to steal your powers and divide them between the three of us."

"I see. And what exactly was she planning to accomplish here today?"

"We were going to steal your powers for her and give them to her. She wanted to be a witch again."

"How old are you?"

"Twenty."

"If I let you leave here today with your life, what will you do with it?"

"I don't know. I've been a part of the coven for so long. I guess I will have to find another one to join."

"No, you won't be able to do that."

"Why not?"

"Because if you leave her today with your life, you leave with no powers. I will trade your powers for your life. Your choice Rosita."

"Don't do it. We can take her," Nissa said.

"No, we can't. I will give you my powers if you promise to let me live."

"Of course, I will. Nissa the same offer stands for you as well."

163

Jessica Manson

"You will have to kill me before I give you my powers."

"Fine," I said as I shot fire from my hand and watched as she burned.

She screamed bloody murder as the flames engulfed her. "Okay, I'll give them to you. Just please make it stop," I snapped my fingers and the fire went out.

I brought Nissa to stand beside Rosita and began to chant. I used the same chant on them that I used on their leader.

Powers of the witches rise,
Course unseen across the skies,
Come to thee, I call you here,
Leave your witch, leave her bare.

Tears fell from their eyes as I continued the chant.

Powers of the witches rise,
Course unseen across the skies,
Come to thee, I call you here,
Leave your witch, leave her bare.

I let the barrier drop when the girl's powers were gone. I grabbed them both and pulled them in for a hug. "You girls are young and very bright. And today you have been given a second chance. Take this chance and do something with it. Go to college. Make something of yourselves."

"I have always wanted to be a nurse," Nissa said.

"That's great. Do that. Become a nurse and save lives instead of taking them."

"I will," She said.

"If you really want to do this, if you are willing to make the sacrifices to go to school, I will help you. When you choose a school, I want you to contact me. I will pay for it. You won't have to worry about a thing. Same goes for you Rosita."

Beautiful Corruption

"You would do that for us."

"Yes."

"Why?"

"Because I see a lot of me in the two of you. And unlike you I didn't have a choice in what I became. But you do, you have a choice today. And no one should be limited to what they were. You can be better than that."

"Thank you," they said in unison as they pulled me in for a hug this time.

"Your welcome," I said hugging them back.

As the girls left, Tristan and Odin walked up beside me. "That was very kind of you Lilith," Odin said.

"I felt sorry for them. They are so young and headed down the wrong path."

"You could have killed them, but you chose not to. That was amazing to watch," Tristan said.

"It didn't feel amazing. It felt wrong to take their powers, but they wouldn't change their ways if they kept them."

"You're right. They wouldn't have changed. You did the right thing Lilith. You should be proud of yourself for changing two lives for the better today."

Latham cleared his throat causing us three to turn around. "Lilith your towel." I looked down at myself horrified. I was standing in front of everyone naked. "You dropped it when you lunged for the leader."

"I hadn't realized I dropped it," I said as I wrapped myself up. I was so embarrassed. Everyone had seen me naked. "I'm going to go get some clothes on. Tristan, will you go get Gunner and the babies?"

"Sure," he said placing a kiss on the top of my head. He walked away to get my babies.

Odin leaned in and whispered in my ear, "You were so sexy fighting those witches naked. I may have been frozen, but there was a certain body part that didn't care."

"I hate you." He pulled away from me laughing. "It's not funny. You have to stop doing this to me."

165

Jessica Manson

"Doing what exactly?"

"Driving me crazy."

"Am I starting to make you feel things again my Lamia Mea?"

"Don't call me that?"

"Why not Lamia Mea?" My body felt like jelly at his words. His voice seductive in my ears. Tingles were in places they shouldn't be. Feelings formed in my middle and it called for him to touch me there. I could feel myself wanting to open up to him. When he kissed me on my bare shoulder, I felt like my body would melt right into him.

"Odin don't do this. Please," I said needing him to stop but wanting him to kiss me again.

"You should get some clothes on before I take you to our room Lamia Mea. I can't take much more of seeing you wrapped in that towel." I made the mistake of looking into his eyes. They were filled with just as much desire as my body was. He leaned in and kissed me gently on the lips. "Lilith," he whispered my name, but it spoke volumes.

"Odin. I can't do this." I turned away from him and ran upstairs. I grabbed my clothes and locked myself in the bathroom. Once the door was shut, I slid to the floor as tears streamed down my cheeks. How was it possible that I loved two men at the same time? How could I want two men to touch me? They both have something I want. Something I long for. Something I couldn't get from just one man. Odin had the passion my body needed while Tristan had the trust my heart longed for. I wouldn't be able to have one and not the other. I needed them both. Selfishly. Undeniably.

Chapter Twenty-Four

I didn't get up until someone knocked on the bathroom door. "Give me just a minute." I looked at myself in the mirror. My eyes were red, puffy and swollen. There is no way I could hide the fact that I have been crying. I threw cold water on my face to try and help, but it didn't.

Someone knocked again, "Babe, dinner is ready. You coming?"

"Yeah, go ahead. I'll be down in a few minutes." I put my clothes on and brushed my hair out. I put on light eye shadow and some mascara to try and cover the redness. It helped a little bit, but if you looked hard enough you could still see the evidence of tears.

When I got to the dining room my heart sank. The only spot left for me to sit was in between Odin and Tristan. I could tell Odin was not going to make this easy for me. When I sat down Tristan gave me a kiss on the cheek. And Odin stared at me like he could tell I was crying. Tristan didn't notice, thankfully.

Ava started crying when I started to get up to get her, Tristan stopped me. "I'll get her. You eat."

When he walked away Odin leaned into me. "What's wrong?" he whispered into my ear.

"You," I said as a single tear slipped out of my eye. He wiped it away.

"I'm sorry I upset you. I didn't mean to make you cry."

"Why are you doing this to me?"

"Doing what?" I started to answer, but Tristan walked back over to us. I kept my head down as we ate dinner. If any of the others noticed Odin and I, they didn't say anything. It was hard to hold myself together in front of everyone when all I wanted to do was cry. A few tears slid down my cheek throughout dinner, but thankfully Tristan was too distracted playing with Ava. Odin noticed though. He looked heartbroken for me. He wanted to console me. He wanted to wrap his arms around me, to hold me, to kiss me. I know because I wanted to do the same thing to him.

Jessica Manson

Odin reached over under the table and grabbed my hand. His touch made it worse. The tears were about to come in streams instead of drops. I jumped up from the table and excused myself. I ran upstairs, but not to the comfort of Tristan's room. Instead I ran into Odin's. I looked around, everything was the same as I left it. I ran my hand over the dresser and stopped when I saw a picture of us. It was from our honeymoon in Croatia. We took it in front of one of the waterfalls right before I attacked that woman.

That was all it took. The tears poured out of my eyes. I didn't understand how my heart could be so conflicted. I had hated Odin for what he did. I should still hate him, but I can't. I love him. I have always loved him. And right now, at this moment, I wanted his arms around me. I needed the comfort of them.

As if someone granted my wish, two arms wrapped around me from behind. I turned around and leaned into Odin's chest. He picked me up and carried me over to the bed. He let me cry on him for as long as I needed. I knew he would, he always did. He always knew when I just needed to cry.

He rubbed the back of my head and kissed my forehead. "I can't do this to him Odin. I can't break his heart."

"I know baby. I know."

"Just the thoughts I have of you are enough to make me feel so guilty I can't stand it."

"I was only flirting with my wife, but if it is causing you this much pain I will stop. I hate to see you hurting. It kills me Lilith."

"Do you know what kills me?"

"No what?"

"The fact that I want you more than I want him."

"Our time will come baby. Maybe not today, tomorrow or next year. It may be a century from now, but we will have our time to be together. And I will wait for you forever."

"I can't ask you to do that."

Beautiful Corruption

"You didn't. Waiting for you is my choice. You are the only girl for me. It has always been you. Do you remember my vows to you when we got married?"

"Yes."

"I meant every word I said that day. My heart belongs to you forever Lamia mea. You are truly my counterpart and without you I am nothing. So, Lilith, today I make a new vow to you. I will wait forever until the other half of my heart returns to me. I will wait until you return to me."

"Do you remember my vows to you?" I asked him.

"Of course, I do. They are forever etched into my mind."

"I meant what I said too. I may have forgotten for a while, but I meant it. I want you. I want your flaws. Your imperfections. Your mistakes. I want you Odin."

He kissed me tenderly at first. When he realized I wasn't going to pull away, he kissed me deeper. I know I should have pulled away from him, but I needed to feel his lips on mine. He tasted like the same familiar mint that always left me craving more of him. He tangled his hand in my hair and I leaned my body into him. His other hand started to slip under my shirt. When his fingers made contact with my skin electricity shot through me causing a moan to escape me.

He threw me onto the bed and climbed on top of me. He kissed me again with so much hunger. He lifted my shirt and his mouth found my nipple. He sucked and licked it vigorously. "Stop," I said. He didn't. I didn't want him to, I needed him to. "Odin, we can't do this." Finally, he paused. He lay his forehead on my stomach, catching his breath.

"I'm sorry I got carried away."

"It was both of us. But I can't do this. I'm married to Tristan and I don't plan on breaking my vows to him."

"You are married to me too so technically you aren't breaking any vows Lilith," he said frustrated. He got up from the bed and started pacing. "How do you think it makes me feel to see you kiss him? How do you think I feel seeing his arms around you? To know that you lay

Jessica Manson

right next door in his bed every fucking night. It's fucking killing me Lilith. Every day you rip another piece of my heart out when I see the two of you touch. You are my wife. You should be with me, not him."

"I'm sorry," I whispered as I pulled my knees into my chest. I have been so caught up in my own pain that I haven't noticed his. How could I be this person? How could I do this to both of them?

"I know you're sorry, but it doesn't stop the pain," he said through tears. His heartbreak was killing me. This isn't the first time I have hurt him. First it was him and Parker and now it's him and Tristan. How could he still love me after all the pain I have caused him?

"How can you still love me after everything I have done to you?" I asked him.

"How can you still love me after what I have done to you?"

"Because my heart doesn't know how to beat without you."

"Exactly."

"What do we do about it?"

"Nothing. I love you Lilith, but I won't make you choose. You will come to me when you are ready."

I made myself invisible before leaving Odin's room. I didn't want anyone seeing me. I went downstairs to get Ava and Elijah. They would be a good distraction from my broken heart. Gunner was playing with Ava while Tristan was feeding Elijah. "Mind if I take them for a bit?" I asked them both. I loved how Gunner acted like he was a father too. It was sweet.

"Sure. Is everything okay?" Tristan asked.

"Yeah. I just needed time to deal with everything that happened today. Thank you for giving me the space I needed."

"No problem, baby. But you know I'm here if you want to talk, right?"

"Yeah I know. Thank you. We will be in the library if you need me."

The babies and I went into the library. All of the medical things had been removed. I lay the babies on one of the bean bags in the middle of the room and walked over and grabbed a book from the shelf. It was a book from my favorite poet, Edgar Allan Poe. I turned to the page that

Beautiful Corruption

held my favorite poem, Annabel Lee. I read the words to Ava and Elijah aloud one verse standing out more than the rest.

But our love it was stronger by far than the love
Of those who were older than we-
Of many far wiser than we-
And neither the angels in Heaven above
Nor the demons down under the sea
Can ever dissever my soul from the soul
Of the beautiful Annabel Lee;

I read that passage over and over realizing that my soul was connected to Odin and nothing could dissever it. Not the Gods in heaven or the demons in hell. Not Draven nor my love for Tristan. Yes, I love Tristan and I would stay with him, but my soul belonged to Odin. There is no changing it.

Tears fell at my new revelation. Not because I was sad, but because I finally understood my love for two men. I have always heard that if you love two people at the same time that you should choose the second. Because if you really loved the first one, you wouldn't have fallen for the second one. But that's not true. You can love two people at once, just never at the same level. And sometimes two people need to fall apart to realize how much they need to fall back together. Odin was right, one day, we will find each other again. Maybe when we are slightly older, our minds less hectic. That's when we will be right for each other. But right now, he is chaos to my thoughts and I am poison to his heart.

My heart belongs to Tristan while my soul belongs to Odin.

Finally feeling like a weight had been lifted from my shoulder, I curled up next to the babies. I love the way babies smell. So sweet and innocent. I envied them. They didn't know the pain of a broken heart yet. And it would be a long time before they did. I missed my innocence. I missed my solitude. I missed the time before my heart knew pain. But I regret nothing. I wouldn't be who I am today without

171

Jessica Manson

my sufferings. And my babies make my life complete. I wouldn't have them without knowing the love that broke my heart.

As my babies slept so innocently on the bean bags I walked over to the desk. I pulled open the bottom drawer and did something I haven't done in a long time. I did what I promised Odin I would never do again. I slid the blade of my hidden razor across my arm; I watched as my blood fell to the floor. It felt like every pain that I have felt in the last twenty-four hours seeped out with my blood. It was a release I needed. A release that only I could give myself. My own personal escape. My therapy.

Beautiful Corruption

Chapter Twenty-Five

It was well after midnight and I was still sitting beside my babies reading over Edgar Allan Poe's poem when I heard a knock at the door. "Come in."

"Hey baby," Tristan said peeking his head in. Odin walked in behind him.

"Hi."

"Are you okay? You have been in here a while."

"Yeah I've just been reading and spending time with the babies."

"What are you reading?" Odin asked.

"Edgar Allen Poe."

"I didn't know you liked poetry," Tristan said.

"Yep. I actually used to write it when I was younger, but I haven't written in a very long time."

"Tell us one."

"No way."

"Why not?"

"Because it is stuff, I wrote as a kid."

"So."

"It's embarrassing."

"Come on baby. For me please," he said batting his eyes. "Please," he begged.

"Come on Lilith, share a poem with us." Odin joined in on the begging.

"Okay fine. But you better not laugh."

"Scouts honor," Tristan said as they both held up two fingers.

I thought back to the last poem I wrote:

I long to feel his lips on mine,
No longer causing my heart to pine.
The feel of his arms around my waist,
A kiss from him, I long to taste.
Suddenly, my dreams come true,

Jessica Manson

My heart would no longer cry blue.
He was everything I dreamt of and more,
He made me happy, made my heart soar.
One day I became his secret,
Only I never knew it.
His betrayal came in the form of violence,
Embarrassed, I kept my silence.
He is out roaming free,
While the demon is locked inside of me.
I treat myself to therapy with a knife,
It's the only release I get from my strife.
He damaged my spirit, he has broken me,
I'll never be free of the demon inside of me.

Tristan sat in silence as tears ran down my face. Odin looked heartbroken. He knew the story of my rape. He understood the pain in that poem.

No one spoke for a few minutes, but when they did it was Tristan that broke the silence. "Lilith, what happened to you?"

I looked at Odin. I didn't want Tristan to feel sorry for me. "Nothing. It was about a friend," I lied.

"Then why are you crying?"

"She was a really close friend."

"I think we should call it a night," Odin said. I was thankful for the change in conversation. "If you don't mind Lilith, I would like to help you get Ava and Elijah ready for bed."

"It's past midnight, I'm not going to bathe them tonight."

"That's okay. I'd still like to help."

"Okay." I grabbed Ava while Odin grabbed Elijah. We headed up to Tristan's room. We changed their diapers and clothes then fed them both. Once they were asleep, we laid them in their cribs.

Before Odin left, he pulled me in for a hug and whispered in my ear, "The only demon you need to save yourself from is you." He pulled away from me and rubbed the fresh cut on my arm. He looked at me with disappointment in his eyes before he turned and left the room.

We got up early so we could welcome Tuls and Fate. I was exhausted after staying up so late last night. Cinzia made breakfast and had it ready for us lined along the wall in the dining room in warmers. She made eggs in four different ways, scrambled, over easy, over medium and poached. There was bacon, sausage and ham. Pancakes also came in four different ways, blueberry, raspberry, chocolate chip and regular. There were biscuits and toast. There were also cinnamon buns.

When I smelled the cinnamon buns, memories came flooding back. It brought me back to that morning in Maine when Odin brought over cinnamon buns for breakfast. It was the day he told me he wanted to be with me. I couldn't help but smile at the memory as I placed one on my plate. "What's got you smiling this morning?" Tristan asked.

"Nothing. Cinnamon buns just bring back memories." I glanced at Odin. He had his head down filling his plate, but he was smiling. I knew the same memory came back to him as well.

"Want to share your memory?"

"Na. Just a breakfast I had with my aunt." I needed to change the subject, "Odin what time does Tuls and Fate arrive?"

"Sometime after ten." I looked at my watch. It was eight forty-five.

"Hey Lilith after breakfast how about a game of Mortal Combat? I practiced while you were in a coma. I think I can actually whoop that ass now," Cal said.

"You're on. But you know you will never beat me."

"I don't know about that baby girl. I've improved my skills."

"We'll see."

"I got winner," Brant said.

"Unfortunately for you Brant, that's going to be me."

Jessica Manson

"One of these days someone is going to beat you at that game," Odin said.

I looked at him with one eyebrow raised, "Is that a challenge?"

He leaned in closer to me, "Bring it."

"You're going down." I haven't played against Odin before. I was secretly hoping I wouldn't be eating my words later.

After everyone ate, we all gathered in the living room. Odin and I took our spots in the floor in front of the TV. I was ready to kick his ass. Tristan, Bristol and Parker were rooting for me while everyone else rooted for Odin. We started the game with full focus and intent on beating each other.

When Odin won the first four rounds, I became nervous. "Damn, looks like you have met your match Lilith. Odin's kicking that ass," Cal said playfully.

"Games not over yet," Tristan said in my defense.

We were on our last match and the game was tied. Everyone sat in silence waiting with anticipation to see who the winner would be. Odin didn't hold back either. He used as many special moves as he could. Last five seconds of the round I made Kitana do her signature move, off the top. Odin's character fell to the ground with his throat sliced. "In your face," I said as I jumped up and did a little dance. "Undefeated. Ain't nobody got game like me," I sang as I danced around Odin rubbing his losing in his face. Everyone laughed.

"She got game and some sexy moves," Cal said.

"Yeah. She does, doesn't she?" Odin said.

"Who's next?" I asked. Cal took the controller from Odin. The guys spent the next hour trying to beat me at the game but none of them could. We didn't stop playing until a knock sounded at the front door.

Odin got up to answer it and came back in the room with Tuls and a man I had never seen before. I assumed it was Fate. When Bristol noticed him her eyes immediately filled with tears. She ran to him and their embrace was filled with so much love it made tears burn at the rims of my eyes. You could feel how much they belonged in each

Beautiful Corruption

other's arms. Their embrace and kissing made you feel like you shouldn't be watching, but it was impossible to look away.

With my focus on Bristol I hadn't noticed that Parker and Tuls had connected as well. They stood off to the side hugging each other. Their embrace didn't feel as intimate as Bristol and Fate's, but you could still tell they missed each other.

"Come on, I want you to meet Lilith," Bristol said to Fate as she walked him over to me. As they made their way to me all of the guys stopped Fate welcoming him home with handshakes and hugs. When they reached me, Bristol introduced us, "Lilith, Fate. Fate, Lilith."

"It's nice to meet you," I said holding out my hand.

He took my hand as he said, "Nice to meet you."

When our hands locked, his words faded into the background. Suddenly, I could see Fate talking to someone that had their back turned away from him.

"Tell me, how important is your wife to you?" the man asked Fate causing me to recognize his voice. Draven.

"What do you want me to do?"

"I'm sending you on a new mission. My son will call for you to come home while I am away. I want you to accept his offer."

"How do you know he will call for me."

"I have someone working for me on the inside. They are watching their every move. I knew I couldn't trust my son to keep his wife locked up. He loves her too much. He is a fool."

"That's all I have to do is accept his offer?"

"No. I want you to make nice with them, especially Lilith. She needs to trust you which shouldn't be too hard. She is even a bigger fool than my son. She trusts too easy and believes every word out of anyone's mouth. Once you have her trust, I want you to kill her."

"I can't kill her."

"You can, and you will. You want to save your precious wife, don't you? Your wife has betrayed the coven and has yet to face her punishment. I will pardon her if you kill Lilith. Otherwise your wife dies. Your choice."

Jessica Manson

Fate hung his head, "Fine. I'll do it."

Finally, my hand slipped from Fate's. Tears filled my eyes as I backed away from him. I tripped and fell. Odin and Tristan both rushed to my side, "Baby what happened? Are you alright?" Tristan said.

"Your eyes were completely black. We couldn't get Fate's hand free from you. What happened Lilith?" Odin said almost cutting Tristan off.

"I need some air."

"Go invisible. I'll take you outside," Odin said.

Once we were outside Odin walked me over to a patio area where we both took a seat on the swing. "Do you want to tell me what happened?" he asked.

I was afraid someone would see him talking to himself or hear my voice, so I spoke to him with my mind. *"Use your mind to talk to me."*

"Okay. What happened Lilith? Your eyes went completely black. You just stood there staring blankly for at least ten minutes"

"I had a vision when I touched Fate's hand."

"Do you want to tell me about it?"

"Yes and no."

"Why not?"

"Because if I tell you what I saw you will overreact."

"Was it bad?"

"Yes."

"Then why aren't you overreacting?"

"Because I understand why he is doing it. Love makes us all do stupid things."

"Tell me about the vision."

"Only if you promise to keep your cool. We have to be smart about this. There is a traitor in the house besides Ambi. Someone is telling your father our every move."

"So, he knows."

"He knows everything," I said cutting him off.

"Okay. So, what happened?"

"Fate was sent here by your father to kill me."

"That son of a bitch."

Beautiful Corruption

"Calm down and let me finish. Your father told him you would call for him and that he needed to accept. He told him if he didn't kill me, he would kill Bristol. He didn't want to, he argued with your father, but it was no use. Fate would do anything to save Bristol and Draven would do anything and use anyone to see me dead."

"Do you know who the traitors are?"

"I think so."

"Who?"

"Daveh and Razi. They work for your father. They fed us their story about needing to go back to Land of Lore, so we would feel sorry for them. They needed our trust, so we would tell them our plans. It has to be them. I've read everyone else's minds. They are all on our side."

"How do we address Fate trying to kill you?"

"We need to talk to him. He needs to act like he is still going to kill me. At least until we can figure out what to do about Daveh and Razi."

"Okay."

"Can I ask you something?" Seeing Parker and Tuls together made a few questions run through my mind.

"Of course."

"When I was having to choose between you and Parker, I had feelings for you and felt a strong attraction to Parker. How come I don't feel that way about him anymore if he was truly supposed to be my mate?"

"Because attraction was what it was. You were attracted to him based on your human feelings. Mates most of the times can't even stand each other let alone be attracted to one another. Take Bristol and Fate for instance. She didn't love him at first. She had to learn to love him."

"I loved you the moment I saw you."

"One look at you lamia mea and I was head over heels. Our attraction came from our souls. We weren't chosen for each other, but I knew instantly we were destined to be together. Even though my father lied to put us together it was still meant to be."

"So why have the Sacrament if no one wants to do it?"

"I've told you this before. It's because there are so few women born in the coven."

"Yeah, yeah I know. Ten to one."

179

Jessica Manson

"You have a good memory," He said through laughter. The look on his face changed instantly. It went from happy to downright sad.

"Odin what's wrong?"

"Just thinking back to the way things used to be between us. Before we moved here, and things got complicated with us."

"Things have always been complicated with us."

"Yeah, I know, but I was thinking about how much we used to love each other. The times we spent together."

"Odin..."

"I really want to kiss you Lilith."

"Fight it Odin. What happened last night can never happen again. I am with Tristan and I will not betray him like that."

"Even though you really want to be with me instead of him?"

"Yes Odin. Even then."

180

Chapter Twenty-Six

Once we were back in the house, I locked myself in the library. I sat on the floor behind my desk pulled out the razor and cut across my skin. I hated myself for what I was doing to Tristan and Odin. How could I allow myself to become this person? How could I hurt them both like this?

I watched the blood trickle down my arm while I waited patiently for my relief to come. But it never did. I cut myself again and again. Each new cut came with a new rage that was building inside of me. A rage directed at myself. A rage that wouldn't pour out with the blood no matter how many times I cut myself.

As I peered down at my bloody mangled arm tears streamed down my face. Between the pain in my heart and the anger in my body I felt like my mind was going crazy. It hurts when you have someone in your soul but can't have them in your arms. It kills me to realize that I can't be friends with someone I am madly in love with.

Odin and I need distance. But there is no way I can distance myself until Draven is dead. Being around him, I'm afraid of what will happen between now and then. I'm afraid I will hurt Tristan. I'm afraid that I will end up giving into my feelings for Odin. But what scares me the most, is a life without Odin.

Tristan walked into the library and I tried to cover my bloody arm. "What the hell happened? Lilith you're bleeding," he yelled as he ran over to me. It wasn't long and everyone in the house was standing in front of me.

"What happened?" Latham asked.

"Is she okay?" Gunner asked next.

I felt exposed and embarrassed with everyone standing there staring at me. The tears started to fall harder. "Everyone out. Now," Odin said coming to my rescue. "Tristan go get a wet towel." When everyone was out of the room, he turned on me. "What the fuck Lilith? Why do you keep doing this to yourself?"

Jessica Manson

"Odin, I can't handle what's going on inside of me. I hate myself for what I'm doing to you. To Tristan. I can't do this anymore."

"So, then what's the plan? Kill yourself instead of facing what you really want?" His anger was laced with fear causing my heart to break even more.

"No."

"Then killing yourself is better than breaking one fucking heart?"

"No. Odin…"

He cut me off. "Then what is it Lilith? Why do you keep doing this? What do you think a world with you not in it would be like? It's not a world I want to be in. I can't lose you again. I won't. Do you hear me? Do you fucking hear me lamia mea?"

"Yes."

"Then don't do this again. Promise me."

"Odin I…"

"Don't give me fucking excuses Lilith. Promise me."

"I promise"

He pulled me into him and wrapped his arms around me. He whispered in my ear, "Please don't ever do that again. I can't live in a world you're not in. I can't lose you."

"I promise I won't do it again."

"You promise you won't do what again?" Tristan asked watching us from the doorway.

"Tristan, I have something I need to tell you." He brought over the towel, Odin took it and started cleaning up my arm.

"What do you have to tell me?"

I didn't hesitate. I came right out and said it. "I'm a cutter."

"What do you mean you're a cutter."

"I self-harm in the form of cutting. I cut myself when I'm stressed, angry, frustrated. When I feel emotions, I don't know how to deal with, I cut myself."

"Why?"

"It's a form of therapy for me."

"How long have you been doing this?"

"A long time."

"So, that's where all of your scares came from?"

"Yes."

"And you knew about this?" he asked Odin.

"Yes."

"For how long?"

"I knew before we started dating."

"Why haven't you stopped her?"

"I tried."

"Obviously not hard enough."

"Lilith is a grown woman. It doesn't matter how many times I beg her to stop if she wants to cut, she is going to."

"Tristan I…" Tristan cut me off and started yelling at me.

"No Lilith. What you are doing is stupid. It's selfish. Do you not realize you have two little people depending on you? Do you not care that you have people that love you?"

"Of course, I…" He cut me off again and continued yelling louder this time.

"What would happen if you cut yourself in the wrong place? What would have happened if I hadn't walked in on you today? Tell me Lilith, what would happen if I walked in here and found you dead?"

Tears streamed down my face and the guilt was killing me. I already felt like a horrible person he didn't need to make me feel worse. That's why I came in here to cut in the first place. "Tristan I'm sorry but…"

"I don't want to hear it," he said as he turned and walked out of the room.

"Maybe I should go talk to him for you," Odin offered.

"No. Give him some time to cool down. I'll talk to him in a little bit."

"Can I say something?"

"No."

"Well I'm going to anyways. You know he wasn't wrong. I mean he was wrong for yelling at you like that, but not for what he said."

Jessica Manson

"You think I don't know that? It's not like I can just stop. You don't understand. None of you do."

"Don't understand what?"

"Why I do it. Why I cut."

"Tell me."

"Just leave me alone."

"I don't think that is a good idea."

"Odin please."

"No." He pulled me into his arms again and let me cry on his chest. "How does your arm feel?"

"It's fine."

"Tell me what made you cut today Lamia mea."

"You."

"Why me?"

"Because Odin, I miss you, not the 'I haven't seen you in a while kind of miss you but the 'I miss us' kind of miss you. Before I met you, I never knew what it was like to look at someone and smile for no reason. You taught me how to feel the butterflies over and over. And I still get butterflies even though I've seen you a hundred times. I love that feeling I get just from seeing you smile. You are my favorite place to go when I need peace. I want to touch you more than I want to breathe. I am much more me when I am with you. You found parts of me that I didn't know existed.

There is always going to be that one person that you can't walk away from and you are that person to me. I want you today, tomorrow, next week and for the rest of my life. It's you Odin. It has always been you. And because I have these feelings about you, guilt has poisoned my veins. It has me trapped in a place I don't want to be. It has my heart paralyzed."

"Lilith, you can't destroy yourself for the sake of someone else. You can't let the guilt consume you. It's your life, don't let anyone make you feel guilty for wanting to be happy. You deserve happiness."

"I can't hurt him Odin. I won't."

Beautiful Corruption

"So, you are just going to keep living in hell for the rest of your life all because you don't want to hurt his feelings?"

"No. I plan to live in hell only until we kill Draven."

"What's happening after that?"

"I think it would be best if Tristan and I moved out after we kill him. I can't keep living like this and I refuse to give into any feelings that I have for you."

"Why? Why can't we be together?" he was starting to sound frustrated.

"You are not making this easy for me."

"And you think this is easy for me? You run into my arms every chance you get. You pour your heart out to me and tell me you have feelings for me and expect me to just sit back and watch you be with Tristan when we both know you want to be with me instead. You are the one making this hard on both of us."

"You're right. It is my fault and I'm sorry. I'll do my best to keep my distance while we are here, but when all of this is over, we will be leaving." I walked out of the library not letting him respond. He was right, all of this was my fault. I did run into his arms every chance I got. I was the one having feelings for him that I shouldn't be having. I am the one sending him mixed signals, every minute of every day. My guilt was caused by myself and only I could put a stop to it.

185

Jessica Manson

Chapter Twenty-Seven

Tristan didn't speak to me for the rest of the night, so he ended up going to bed mad at me. It was hard to fall asleep. I felt bad for upsetting him earlier. He was also right about the things he said to me today. I was being selfish when I cut myself and I vowed to myself that I wouldn't do it again. I can't chance my life when I have two beautiful babies that depend on me. At around two a.m. I finally dozed off.

I was standing on the bridge in front of Slaaneth. "You know meeting you here is getting really old."

"Shall we meet somewhere else?"

"What do you want this time?" I asked my patience wearing thin.

"You know the security at your castle isn't as good as young Odin would like to think it is."

"What do you mean?"

"Time will tell my dear."

"What are you planning?"

"Again, time will tell."

"I can't stand riddles or half sentences. What do you want?"

"It won't be long and little Ava and Elijah will set me free from this hell."

"What type of person can be willing to kill two innocent babies?"

"I'm not a person. I'm a demon. And those innocent babies are the key to my freedom."

"You will not get your hands on my babies."

"So young, so naive. Such a fool," he said with a wave of his hand.

"Fuck you Slaaneth. I will kill you if it is the last thing I do." Laughter filled my ears as he vanished. I jolted awake and ran over to check on Ava and Elijah. I couldn't get Slaaneth's words out of my head. *Security isn't as good as Odin thinks it is.* Does that mean his people are already near? Will they strike soon? Will they try to get in to take my babies? Panic filled me as these thoughts raced through my mind.

Anger filled me at the thought of anyone laying a hand on my babies. I knew it was time to meditate so I could find the answer on

Beautiful Corruption

how to kill him. I headed for the door, so I could go into the library where I knew there would be peace and quiet, but Tristan stopped me. "Where are you sneaking off too?" He still had anger in his voice.

"I'm going to the library."

"Why? So, you can go cut yourself some more?" He practically spit the words at me. I have never seen him this angry before and I didn't like to see him like this.

"Can we talk?"

"What's there to talk about? You are selfish and aren't going to listen to what I have to say."

I walked over and sat beside him on the bed. "Listen, you were right. I was being selfish. I shouldn't have done it. I don't know if you will believe me, but I promise you here and now that I will never ever cut myself again."

"Do you really mean that?"

"Yes. I promise I will never do it again."

"Okay. I forgive you." I couldn't help but laugh. "What's so funny?"

"You're easy to win over."

"That's because I love you so much, it's hard to stay mad at you."

"I love you too Tristan. I really do."

"So, what were you going to the library for?" I told him about Slaaneth coming to me again and about what he said about the security. He had the same concerns I did. He instantly went on high alert.

"I need to find out how to kill him. It's the only way to protect our babies."

"You can't do it here if I promise to be really quiet?"

"I guess I can, but I will need complete quiet."

"I promise. But first come here." He pulled me into his arms and kissed me gently on the lips. He started to pull away from me, but I grabbed the back of his head holding him in place. I wasn't ready to let him go just yet.

I opened my mouth up to him letting our tongues touch slightly. He groaned at the touch. He kissed me deeper with more passion

187

sending tingles down my spine. He rolled me onto the bed placing him on top of me. He pulled my shirt off and started trailing kisses down my neck until his mouth found my breast. He sucked gently on my nipples, giving them both equal attention.

He kissed my stomach all the way down to my belly button. He paused long enough to remove my pants. He looked up at me with concern. "What is it?" I asked.

"Do you think you're healed enough?"

"Yes."

"Good. I don't think I have it in me to stop."

"Then don't."

He climbed back on top of me and kissed me again. I slid his boxers down and dug my nails slightly into his butt cheeks causing him to growl at me. I could feel the hardness of him against my leg, so I opened myself up to him. He inserted himself slowly causing me to winch in pain. "Are you okay?" he asked concerned.

"Yeah. It's just been a while."

"Trust me, I know." He was moving slowly in and out of me, but it was causing me more pain than I cared for.

"Tristan."

"Yeah."

"I'm not a china doll, fuck me." He didn't hesitate to speed up. He moved faster and faster inside of me causing the pain to be replaced with pleasure. Even though Tristan was moving faster I could tell he was still holding back. He needed to release the animal within him. His primal beast needed to be brought to the surface. "Tristan, look at me." When we made eye contact, I said with as much conviction as I could, "Let go and fuck me."

"Are you sure?"

I reached up and grabbed his face between my hands, "I am your wife. You can let go with me." A smile formed across his face. Then he did something I wasn't expecting. He flipped me over and forcefully inserted himself inside of me. He made a fist in my hair and pulled my head back while he pounded into me roughly.

Beautiful Corruption

He smacked my ass catching me off guard. He reached up and wrapped his hand around my neck and squeezed slightly while the other hand was still wrapped up in my hair. I liked it. I was moaning uncontrollably and on the verge of my release. He wasn't ready to stop; he had eight months of pent up sexual frustration to get out.

With a few more times of him moving in and out of me at the pace he was moving my toes curled and I threw my head back as he sent my body over the edge. He continued to move at his fast and hard pace causing me to climax two more times. When I was on the verge of my fourth one, he came with me this time.

He let me go and we both fell onto the bed. We were both covered in sweat, but we were both fully satisfied.

"Wow," was all I could say.

"I know."

"That was…"

"Amazing," he said cutting me off. "I didn't hurt you, did I?"

"No. You were perfect. Why haven't you ever done it like that before?"

"I don't know. You just didn't seem like the type."

"What type would that be?"

"The type that likes it rough."

"Well, I guess we both learned something new about each other tonight."

"I guess we did."

With Tristan exhausted he fell asleep fast. I was tired but I still needed to find out how to kill Slaaneth so I headed to the library. Everyone was asleep leaving the castle quiet giving it a creepy feel. Once inside the library I lit a few candles and sat in the center of the room on the floor. I closed my eyes and began to concentrate on what I wanted to know.

I searched within myself for ten minutes and came up with no answer. I was getting discouraged. I let out a loud breath and tried again. I closed my eyes once more, sat up straight and touched my

189

Jessica Manson

thumbs to my pointer and middle fingers. I positioned my head in a downward angle and took breaths through my nose.

I concentrated on my breathing. After another five minutes, I started to see flashes of what I was looking for. The flashes sped up until they became one constant flash. I was finally seeing the answer in front of me. I finally knew how to kill Slaaneth.

Excitement filled me, and I could hardly contain it. I stood up and jumped up and down in circles proud of myself for figuring it out. I wanted to shout but was too afraid I would wake the whole house. I needed to tell someone, so I decided I would try to wake Tristan and tell him. He wanted me to find the answer as bad as I did so I assumed he wouldn't get mad.

I left the library in a hurry and ran upstairs taking two at a time. Halfway up Odin stopped me, "Where's the fire?" he asked teasingly.

"Oh, my God Odin I figured it out."

"You figured what out?"

"How to kill Slaaneth."

"Are you serious?"

"Yes." I told him about my dream and everything that Slaaneth said.

"I will handle security. So, tell me, how are we supposed to kill him?"

"Can we get everyone together for breakfast and I will tell everyone then because I will need everyone's help to do it?"

"Sure."

"Where were you headed?" I asked curious.

"To the kitchen. Care to join me?"

"I'm not sure that is a good idea."

"Come on. I can hear your stomach growling from here. I promise to behave."

"Okay." We headed for the kitchen to grab something to eat. Once we had our bowls of fruity pebbles we sat at the island. The next hour was followed by friendly banter between the two of us. Odin kept his word and behaved himself. He didn't flirt with me and I didn't spill my heart out to him. We sat there until my eyelids grew heavy. When I couldn't hold them open any longer, we both headed up to bed.

Jessica Manson

Chapter Twenty-Eight

When I woke up, I was eager to meet with everyone and tell them about me finally finding out how to kill Slaaneth. I quickly got myself dressed before getting Ava and Elijah ready. I then headed down to the kitchen with both babies in tow to make them their bottles. I walked past the dining room where everyone was already waiting for me. When I didn't go in, Gunner came running out. "Need some help?"

"Sure, want to take one of them so I can get their bottles ready?"

"Of course." He took Ava from my arms and started talking to her. "How's Uncle Gunner's little princess?" He started making cooing noises at her and my heart melted.

"You are so different."

"What do you mean?"

"You used to hate me. You were quiet. Now you are so caring and loving with my babies. You are even nice to me."

"Lilith, I never hated you."

"Gunner you thought I was a monster."

"No, I didn't."

"Let me let you in on a little secret, I can read minds."

"Listen, you were just changing so fast. You were becoming someone I didn't know. No one, not even you, understood your powers. And yes, it was a little frightening."

"I understand. So, how do you feel about me now?"

"I thought you could read minds?"

"I can. But I also like staying out of people's heads. Everyone is entitled to their privacy. And I don't think I have the right to just go listening in whenever I want to."

"I appreciate that. And I like you... enough," he said with a smile.

"Would you like to feed her?"

"I'd love to help."

"Well, come on helper, let's join the others in the dining room. I have some very exciting news to share."

We both made our way to the dining room. When we entered, Odin walked over and took Elijah from me and Tristan came over and wrapped me in his arms. "Good morning, beautiful."

"Good morning."

He leaned down and whispered in my ear, "I can't stop thinking about last night. It was amazing." I couldn't help but giggle as my cheeks burned red.

I wrapped my arms around his neck and whispered back in his ear, "Maybe we can have a replay later."

"Mmm…Mrs. Rose, you drive me wild."

"Okay, okay enough with the lovey dovey mess. What's this big news you have?" Cal asked.

"You did it, didn't you? You figured out how to kill Slaaneth?" Tristan asked.

"Yes. I did. I know how to kill him. But it will take all of us."

"What do we have to do?"

"In order to kill him, I will need to summon him here. Odin, I will need you to get me some supplies."

"Done. What do you need?"

"Five black candles, some salt, a lot of it, and some holy water. I will also need five of you to actually participate in the summoning. The rest of you will be there just as a precaution in case anything goes wrong. Who will help me?"

"How will we have to help you summon Slaaneth?" Latham asked.

"All I will need you to do is stand on one of the five corners of a pentagram and chant with me."

"I'll help," he said.

"Me too," Gunner said.

"Actually, Gunner I was hoping you would stay with the babies. Slaaneth's main goal is getting Ava and Elijah. I will need for you to keep them in the highest part of the house away from him."

"Sure, I can do that."

193

"Thank you. Bristol and Fate, I would also like for the two of you to stay with Gunner and the babies. If anything happens and Slaaneth gets loose, I will need someone that can help keep them safe."

"Of course," Bristol said.

"You already know I'm going to help you," Tristan said.

"Me too," Odin said. "That bastard is going to get what's coming to him."

"I need two more people." No one said anything. "Come on guys, this is to save Ava and Elijah."

"Count me in," Parker said.

"I'm always down for a good ass whooping," Brant said.

"Good. Okay, Dex, Cal, Tuls, Daveh and Razi I will need for you to stand sporadically around the room and make sure Slaaneth doesn't break free."

"What will you do?" Tuls asked.

"I will have to be standing right in the middle of the pentagram leading the chant. When Slaaneth appears, I will have to kill him."

"How are you going to kill him?" she asked.

"That's the tricky part. I have to find something called a demon's knife."

"Well this mission just became impossible," Daveh said matter-of-factly.

"Why?" I asked confused.

"Do you know what a demon's knife is or how you have to get it?"

"No, but I take it you do?"

"Yes, I do. And it is impossible."

"What is a demon's knife?" Everyone sat quietly waiting for Daveh to explain what it was.

"It is a blade made out of dragon scales and demon eyes."

"Tell me how to get it."

"Well first you have to find a dragon."

"Like a real dragon? Like with giant wings and breathing fire kind of dragon?"

"Yes, a real dragon."

"Where can I find a dragon?"

"Land of Lore has one."

"That's perfect."

"How is that perfect?"

"Because you and Razi can take me there and lead me to the dragon."

"Are you kidding me? You can't face a dragon. It will kill you before you even get the chance to get close enough."

"I have to at least try."

"You're crazy."

"Let's say I get past the dragon, what do I have to do to get the demon's knife?"

"Usually the person seeking the demon's knife has to take a witch with them, so they can cast the spell. But since you are a witch, you will be able to do it yourself. If you last long enough, you will chant to make the blade. I don't know what the chant is though."

"I do."

"You do? How?"

"I heard it last night when I had my vision. So, that's it? We just go to the Land of Lore, find the dragon, say a chant and find the demon's knife?"

"Basically."

"Sounds easy enough."

"You are serious about doing this?"

"Yes. It's the only way."

"Okay, Razi and I will take you to the Land of Lore."

"Yay," I said giving her a hug. "Thank you."

"Don't thank me until this mission is over."

"Hey, how are we supposed to get demon eyes?"

"When we get to the Land of Lore, we will have to go see a leprechaun. You can get the demon eyes from him, but he will need something in return."

"What will I have to give him?"

Jessica Manson

"Either gold or something shiny. Leprechauns can't resist either. As long as you have one of those things to give you, he won't ask for your soul."

"Why would he want my soul?"

"Leprechauns are soul collectors. They collect souls from people that need items, like demon eyes, that are impossible to get. They feed off of the souls to keep them young."

"Well then. Guess not everything can be easy."

"So, Lilith will have to face a leprechaun then face off with a dragon?" Tristan asked with concern.

"Yes. I think that was all explained already," Daveh said sounding like she was starting to get frustrated.

"I don't think you should do this. It's too dangerous."

"Tristan, I have to. It is the only way to save Ava and Elijah."

"Then I am going with you."

Razi spoke this time. His voice was firm. "No, you will not go. Vampires are not permitted into the Land of Lore. We are risking a lot by taking Lilith."

"She can't go alone."

"I won't be alone. Razi and Daveh will be with me."

"Lilith, can I see you for a minute? Privately?" Odin asked. We headed to the library where no one would be able to hear us.

"What's up?" I asked.

"I am with Tristan, I don't think you should go alone with Razi and Daveh."

"Why not?"

"Have you forgotten that they are traitors? They will probably kill you for my father the first chance they get. You can't go alone."

"You're right. I was so excited I forgot."

"We have to convince them to let one of us go with you."

"Do you think a convincing spell would work on them since they are fairies?"

"Yes. Fairies may have similar powers as you, but magic can still be used on them."

196

Beautiful Corruption

"Okay I think I might have a spell I can use. If you give me time to say the spell, I'll let you know when to ask if one of you can come with us."

"Okay. But I think I should go, and Tristan should stay with the babies."

"That will be between the two of you. I will call him in here," I called for Tristan to join us with my mind. I wasn't going to choose which one would be going with me.

Tristan joined us in the library and we filled him in on what we knew about Daveh and Razi. "If they are traitors and working for Draven then why are you even considering going?"

"We were thinking I could use a convincing spell on them and get them to let one of you go with me."

"Okay. Then I'm going with you."

"I think I should go, and you should stay here with Ava and Elijah," Odin said.

"Why shouldn't I go? She is my wife."

"She is also mine." At that statement from Odin I walked out of the room and let them discuss who would be going. I didn't want to hear them fight over me. It made me uncomfortable. It didn't matter who went with me as long as one of them did.

I was waiting outside of the door when they walked out of the room laughing. "So, who will the lucky guy be?" I asked.

"I'll be going with you," Odin said.

"And you're okay with this?" I asked Tristan

"Yes baby. Odin should be the one to go with you. He is the only person that can get you off the property."

"Okay. Since it is settled let's get this over with." We headed back to the dining room. Everyone was still gathered around the table but now the food was finally served. The smell of bacon and eggs filled my nostrils making my stomach growl.

"Yo, when do you plan on going on this mission?" Cal asked.

197

Jessica Manson

"We will need to go today. Once I go to sleep Slaaneth will know what we are planning. So, when we get back y'all will need to be ready to summon him. This will all happen fast."

"Considering if you make it back alive," Daveh said.

"I'm not scared of a dragon or a leprechaun. I've faced much bigger demons." Truthfully, I was a little scared, but I wouldn't let them know that.

Once I took a few bites of my food and everyone was silently eating, I focused on Daveh and Razi and whispered my chant to them:

Son of day, moon of night,
Give Daveh and Razi the gift of sight,
Let them hear and understand,
They shall follow my command,
A friend can join us unlike before,
He shall accompany us to Land of Lore.

"Now Odin," I said with my mind.

"So, are the two of you sure I can't come with Lilith on this mission?" Odin asked Daveh and Razi.

"Of course, you may come," Daveh said.

"She would be much safer if you were to join us," Razi said.

"After breakfast we should get ready to go. The sooner we get there the sooner we can get back," I said eager to get this over with.

We finished our breakfast in silence. When it was over, Odin, Daveh, Razi and I all went to our rooms to get ready. I was starting to get nervous. This was my first mission and I'm not sure what to expect.

We all met downstairs and said our goodbyes to the rest of the team. Daveh, Razi and I went invisible while Odin led the way to the car. He pretended to put something in the back seat, so they could get in without raising suspicion. When Odin opened his door, I did as before and climbed over the driver seat. We took off toward our destination.

Chapter Twenty-Nine

We pulled down the same dirt road Odin took me to when he taught me some self-defense moves and we walked to the same clearing. "This is where the portal is to Land of Lore?" I asked.

"Yep," Odin responded.

"Where is it?"

"Over there inside that tree."

"We have to go inside a tree?" I asked with a raised eyebrow.

"Looks that way. Come on let's go."

We walked up to the tree and it turned out to not be a tree at all. It was a doorway. "How the…"

"Someone that didn't know it was here would only see a tree, not a doorway. The only way to know it is here is if, well if you know it's here," Daveh said.

Razi walked in front of us and started speaking in what sounded like Latin.

Hic mihi: Dimitte me ut transeam

"What did he say?" I asked Odin.

"Passage before me; let me pass."

The doorway opened to reveal the most magical land I have ever seen. I wasn't the only one impressed either. Odin wore the same silly expression on his face as I did. We were both completely in awe of this place.

There were trees lining the entry way, each one a different color of the rainbow. The grass we walked on wasn't green but blue. And I don't mean the kind of green that looks blue; this grass was a bright vibrant blue. It looked so fluffy like clouds and it took everything I had not to take my shoes off and scrunch my toes in it. There were multitudes of flowers in every color anyone could ever think of. Anemones, Roses, Lilies, Blood Roots, Bleeding Hearts, and

Jessica Manson

Ranunculus' in every shade of pinks, purples, blues, yellows, oranges, and reds.

Butterflies floated around carelessly, and they too were different shades of color. Everything was so beautiful and bright. It filled me with so much joy. I felt like a kid on Christmas morning after Santa left the only gift I ever wanted.

We walked deeper down the path until we came upon a clearing. It was miles of beautiful landscape. Fields filled with flowers, rolling hills and I think I even spotted a stream in the distance. Now that we were out of the trees, I noticed the sun even seemed to shine brighter here.

As I was looking around taking everything in, I noticed a small area off to my right that was dark and foreboding. There was no sun shining in that area. The air looked foggy and the trees looked dead.

"What is that place over there?" I asked.

"That is where we go to get your demon eyes. The dead forest," Razi said.

"Great because that place looks so welcoming."

"It's not," Daveh said.

"I was being sarcastic."

"Oh, well come on. We don't want to waste too much time lingering." We walked toward the dead forest. The closer we got the more on edge I became.

Once inside the forest I started to feel claustrophobic. The trees were very close together and towered over us forming a tunnel. The branches were bare and looked like arms ready to reach out and grab us. The air felt chilly against my skin. The only sounds were my racing heartbeat and out of control breathing.

"This place is creepy," I whispered to Odin too afraid to talk too loudly.

"What gives you the right to call my home creepy dear?" We spun around to find a man standing in front of us. He was only about two feet tall. He had red hair and a red beard that covered most of his face. The only feature I could make out on him was his eyes. They were shiny and gold.

Beautiful Corruption

"I'm sorry. I didn't mean to offend you."

"Very well. Daveh, Razi, why have you brought vampires into my home?"

"She seeks demon eyes," Daveh said sounding afraid.

"Did you bring something for me?" I started to panic. How could I forget to bring something shiny or gold?

"Yes," Odin said pulling a block of gold from the bag he was carrying.

"Follow me," the leprechaun said with a smile on his face.

We followed him into a small area of the trees that opened up wide enough for the man to have a small bed, a fireplace that was made out of large rocks, a table that looked only big enough to sit one person and a large shelf along one of the trees walls. The shelf was filled with small boxes and vials of things I couldn't make out. Some even held different colors of liquids.

The small man climbed a ladder to the top of his shelf. He started moving things around until he found what it was, he was looking for. "Here it is. How many eyes do you need dear?"

"Two, I guess," I said uncertain.

"Let me see the gold again." Odin pulled the gold block from his bag again and held it up for the man to see. He dropped the eyes and the brick of gold floated up to the man. Odin caught the eyes just before they hit the ground.

Odin walked over to Daveh and Razi so they could make sure the leprechaun gave us the correct eyes. Daveh said leprechauns could be tricky and I didn't want to take any chances. The man stepped down from the ladder and walked over to me. "What is your name dear?"

"Lilith. What is yours?"

"You can call me Gold deary." I couldn't help but laugh at his name. He held his hand out for a shake; I took it.

"No!" Daveh screamed to stop me, but she was too late. Gold had already taken my hand in his. My head felt like it was being pushed in from both sides. There was so much pressure I fell to my knees. Gold never lost his grip on me. I winced in pain as his eyes started to roll in

201

Jessica Manson

the back of his head. He started taking in deep breaths as if he was trying really hard to smell something.

Odin tackled Gold causing my hand to slip away from him. The pressure in my head released as soon as my hand was free. "What did he do to me?"

"He isn't just a soul collector. He also collects memories."

"He stole some of my memories?" I asked as Odin helped me up to my feet.

"Not just any memories. He stole memories that were filled with love. Leprechauns aren't capable of showing love, so they steal the memories from others. It's their only way of feeling what love could be if they were able to feel it."

"Such sweet memories," Gold said licking his fingers as if he had just finished a bucket of fried chicken.

"I'll still remember the memories he took, right?"

"No. Once he has taken them you won't be able to remember them at all."

"What memories did you take?" I asked Gold.

"Just the ones of your love."

"But I remember Odin. He is my husband. If he took my memories how come I can remember Odin?"

"Because he didn't take memories of Odin. He took your memories of Tristan."

"Why Tristan? I don't love him like that. He is just my friend."

"No sweetie, he is your husband."

"Don't be silly. Odin is my husband."

"I think for now we should proceed with the mission. We will figure Lilith's memories out later," Odin suggested.

"Good thing you tackled him when you did, or her memory of Tristan would be lost forever," Razi said to Odin.

"Come on, let's go," I said walking over to Odin and grabbing his hand. I intertwined our fingers together. The familiar spark of electricity surged through me. Suddenly, a feeling of sadness came over me. It felt like I had missed this feeling but wasn't sure why. It was like I hadn't felt it in a very long time even though I'm sure I had.

Daveh looked at Odin accusingly and I couldn't help but wonder why.

We finally made it out of the dark forest and headed toward another pathway. "Are you ready to face the dragon Lilith?" Razi asked me.

"Yes."

"Good, cause this path leads straight to him."

When we entered the path, I was awestruck. The trees looked like ballerinas frozen in a dance pose. It was breathtaking to see. As we walked farther down the path the trees looked like the trees had become knotted together. It was as if the trees were forming some type of chain along the path. They just got more enchanted after that. The trunks of trees had holes in oval shapes all the way through it in a very intricate design. Some trees looked like it had faces grown into them and some were even in the shape of seats.

"That's the entrance to the cave. The dragon will be waiting for you, so you have to move fast," Daveh said pointing to a cave.

"Wait...you're not coming with me."

"No, we can't. We will be waiting for you here." She handed me the demon eyes and said, "When you get close enough to the dragon you will have to throw the eyes down its throat then stab it in the heart. It will not kill the dragon, but it will piss it off. Once you have stabbed it, say the chant and the demon's knife will form and fall out. You must retrieve it quickly before you get burned alive." She hugged me and wished me luck. Razi nodded at me as if to say goodbye. I walked over to Odin and pulled him in for a hug.

"I'll be waiting for you right here," he whispered in my ear.

"I love you."

'I love you too lamia mea." I kissed him gently on the lips before walking away from my safety net.

The entrance to the cave was more beautiful than any other part of the Land of Lore. There were weeping willows of shades of pink and

Jessica Manson

purple that formed a protective circle around the entrance. Weeping willows are my absolute favorite tree and to see them in these colors was magical.

Inside of the cave was dark. Had I not had the vision of a vampire I wouldn't have been able to see anything. I walked for a few minutes until my foot bumped into something. When I looked down, I had to keep myself from screaming. Under my foot lay a skeleton of someone that had gotten charred to death.

I focused my vision down the pathway and realized there were hundreds more skeletons in front of me. My heart sank as I realized I had to walk through them to get to the dragon. I tried my best to tiptoe around them without stepping on them. I didn't want to step on them and disturb them. It was disrespectful.

After what felt like an hour of slow navigation through the skeleton's graveyard, I finally made it through. I stepped into an opening that lead to two more pathways. I wasn't sure which path to take so I played eenie meenie miney mo. When I was done, I was left to choose the path on the right. So, I headed off toward that path until I was stopped dead in my tracks.

Just as I was about to enter the path a loud ear-piercing roar sounded from the path to the left. Guess eenie meenie miney mo was wrong. I headed down the path with my knees shaking. My hands began to sweat, and my breathing quickened. I was nervous before, but now, I am downright scared.

Just when I was about to chicken out my thoughts flashed back to Ava and Elijah. My body started to fill with a courage I didn't know I carried. I would do anything to save my babies even if that included facing a dragon and killing a demon. I marched forward with a purpose.

Chapter Thirty

I walked for what felt like miles; the path was very long. I was starting to think I had taken the wrong path after all. I had lost the sense of time and it felt like I had been in this cave for hours now. I was tired from the long walk and needed a break. My throat was dry, and I needed water. Why hadn't I thought to bring some? I tripped on a rock and landed on my face. I could taste blood as it poured from my lip. I rubbed my eyebrow and it too was bleeding.

I tore a piece of my shirt to stop the bleeding above my eye. I took a seat on a large rock and sat there until my body temperature cooled off. When my body felt rested enough, I got up and started on my journey again.

It wasn't but a few minutes later that I reached a large opening. The sun was shining inside from an opening in the ceiling of the cave. It illuminated it. Inside the walls of the cave were different types of crystals. Rubies, emeralds, ambers, amethyst, aqua aura; there were so many different types and when the sun hit them, they formed a rainbow inside of the cave. It was the most beautiful thing I had ever seen.

I was so fixated on the way the sun hit the crystals I hadn't realized the dragon was behind me. It roared causing me to cover my ears. I looked at it just in time to realize it was about to breathe fire at me. As a safety reflex, I laid flat on the ground. The fire missed me, but the heat was enough to make my skin burn. I jumped up and went in for an attack, but the dragon hit me with its tail sending me flying across the cave. My body slammed into the rocks with so much force I was sure I had broken something.

The dragon didn't waste any time. It was getting ready to blow more fire toward me. I jumped out of the way just in time to keep me from going up in flames, but not fast enough to keep the ends of my hair from catching on fire. I patted the flames out as quickly as I could.

Jessica Manson

The witch inside of me was begging to be released and I let her. I looked the dragon in the eye, moved my finger in the shape of a figure eight over and over and then started chanting:

Dragon, dragon
I mean no harm
In peace and goodwill
I cast this charm.

I knew the spell would only last a few minutes, so I had to move fast. Once the calming spell took effect, I walked over and threw the demon's eyes into the dragon's mouth. I walked very carefully underneath it and stabbed it in the place I was sure its heart was located. The calming spell had worn off and the dragon was madder than ever.

It didn't work. The knife didn't turn into the demon's knife. I quickly realized what I had done wrong. *The spell.* I forgot to say the spell. Hoping that the knife wouldn't fall out, I tried to say the spell:

Dragon scales and demon eyes
Combine to create the…

I didn't see the dragon's tail coming toward me. Suddenly, I was thrown against the wall of the cave again and the breath was knocked out of me. I tried to sit up while coughing and gasping for air. The dragon flicked its tail at me again. This time the tip of it hit me across the face leaving a long cut down my cheek. Blood poured from it, but I didn't let that stop me.

I stood up with the help of the wall and started the spell again.

Dragon scales and demon eyes
Combine to create the demon blade inside.

Dragon scales and demon eyes

Combine to create the demon blade inside.

The knife started to glow inside of the dragon. It must have been painful to the dragon because it started whimpering. I couldn't help but feel sorry for the poor animal.

With each second the knife glowed brighter. When it got to where it was almost unbearable to look at the light, the dragon let out a loud ear shattering roar. Then suddenly the knife fell from the dragon's chest. While it was distracted in its own pain, I ran over and grabbed the knife.

As I was running away its tail caught me one last time. This time it twirled me into its tail before sending me soaring into the air. It was as if twirling me up like that gave the tail more throwing power. I hit the ceiling and one of the crystals that was sticking out stabbed me in the shoulder. But that was nothing compared to what I was about to feel.

The fall from the ceiling had to be at least fifteen to twenty feet. When I hit the ground, I heard a snap. Pain shot through my body and the wind was knocked out of me. Something was definitely broken. Blood poured from my shoulder and face and my ankle seemed to be twisted. I tried to stand, but it was no use. The dragon was getting ready to breath fire straight at my face. I wouldn't be able to run this time.

Get me out of here. I said to my inner witch. Suddenly, as if the witch inside of me had taken over my body, I pointed to the pathway that I entered from and started chanting:

I am here, I am there
Teleport me over there.

Instantly, I landed in the pathway. I forced myself up using the wall. The pain was unbearable, but I didn't let it get to me. I couldn't. Not if I wanted to survive.

I wasn't going to die in this cave away from Ava and Elijah. With tears streaming down my face and what felt like two hours later, I finally reached the exit of the cave. I could see the sun and the weeping willows from where I stood.

Once I made it outside and into the sun I collapsed. I had lost a lot of blood and my body was becoming very weak. I could feel the darkness of my unconsciousness coming on; I spoke to Odin with my mind. *"Odin help me please. Come to the weeping willows."* That's all I could get out before the blackness of the abyss took over.

When I woke up, I was back at the castle. Tristan and Odin were sitting on either side of the bed. "Hey," I said with a raspy voice.

"Hey," they both said in unison as they got up and leaned over me.

"How are you feeling?" Odin asked

"What happened after I left the cave?" I asked a little confused as to how I got back home.

"You blacked out once you got out of the cave. When we got to you, you were nearly dead. Lilith, you broke three of your ribs and your ankle. You got stabbed in the shoulder and it caused you to lose a lot of blood. I haven't even mentioned the burns on your back yet. And…" Odin trailed off.

"And what?"

"Well don't get mad but we had to… well we…"

"Just spit it out already," I said annoyed.

"We also had to cut your hair. It got burned pretty bad."

I reached my hand up to feel just how much hair I had lost. I was upset that my hair was now to my shoulders, but there really isn't much I can do about it.

I didn't recall getting burned until I remembered when the dragon blew fire at me the first time. "How long have I been asleep?"

"Six days," Tristan said sounding pained.

I reached for Odin's hand and interlocked our fingers. "Where's Ava and Elijah?"

Beautiful Corruption

"Gunner has them. He has been taking really good care of them since you have been out."

"Will you take me to see them?"

"How about I bring them to you? You probably shouldn't be walking yet. I will also get you some water."

"Thank you." When Odin left the room, Tristan sat on the bed next to me. He rubbed the top of my head and kissed my forehead. "Baby I was so worried you wouldn't wake up. I love you so much."

"Tristan what the hell are you talking about?" He kissed my lips causing me to panic. "What the fuck Tristan? Odin will kill you for kissing me like that," I yelled at him as I pushed him away.

"What?" he asked confused.

"Odin is my husband. Why in the hell did you kiss me like that?"

"Lilith, I am your husband, not Odin."

"What are you talking about? Of course, Odin is my husband. You have no right to kiss me that way," I was shouting by now.

"Hey what's going on in here?" Odin said barging back into the room.

"What the hell happened to her Odin? She doesn't think I am her husband," Tristan shouted at him.

"Oh, that."

"What do you mean "Oh that"? What the hell happened?"

"I had forgotten all about the leprechaun with the way her health was. Her memory loss was the last thing on my mind when I found her."

"What do you mean?"

"When we went to see the leprechaun to get the demon eyes, he stole some of Lilith's memories. He stole her love memories." I think the guys forgot I was in the room and could hear them.

"What do you mean he stole her love memories?"

"He stole the memories of her love for you. She thinks you are just friends."

"If he stole her love memories, why didn't he still the ones of you too?"

209

Jessica Manson

"What do you mean?"

"Please Odin, you know exactly what I mean. Do you think I am actually that blind? I see the way the two of you look at each other. I see how she runs into your arms when something is bothering her. I know why she cut herself Odin, and it wasn't because she was stressed. It was because she is in love with you and can't bring herself to tell me. I'm not stupid. I saw how much it was killing her."

"Then don't you think that now is the time to let her go?"

"Let her go? Are you kidding me?"

"She doesn't remember your love for each other. And she never will Tristan."

"Then I will spend every day helping her to remember."

"I know this is hard for you, but she only remembers being married to me."

"I love her. I can't, no, I won't let her go."

"Excuse me," I said bringing both of their attention to me. "So, I'm married to both of you?" I asked confused.

"Technically yes. You married Odin first under the coven's laws. Then when you left Odin, you married me under human laws," Tristan said.

"I loved you? But I thought we were just friends."

"We were at first. But our friendship grew into something more. You are now Lilith Rose."

"Rose?"

"Yes. Do you remember why you named Ava and Elijah their names?"

"Because I liked them?"

"No. You named Ava after my mother and Elijah after my father. Their last names are also Rose."

"But Odin is their father?"

"Yes. Odin is their biological father, but you named them after my family."

"This doesn't make sense. Why can't I remember any of this?"

"Because the leprechaun..."

Beautiful Corruption

"I know about the leprechaun," I said cutting him off. "I just don't understand why I can't remember this love that we supposedly shared." I was so confused. Tears slowly started to stream down my face.

"Are you okay?"

"No. I need a minute alone with Odin please."

"Okay. I'll go get that water for you."

"Thanks."

"Odin, I'm so confused," I said once Tristan was out the door.

"I know Lamia mea."

"I remember running away from you with Tristan's help. I remember everything. Except I don't remember ever being with him. I don't remember marrying him. Is what he said true?"

"Yes."

"Then we aren't together? You and me?"

"No."

Tears streamed down my face rapidly as my heart broke into a million pieces. How could I live my life without Odin? How could I survive without him? He was my world. I thought we had gotten past his betrayal. "How do I live a life that you are not a part of?"

"I'm still in your life. I'm just your friend now."

"So, I'm just supposed to be with a guy I don't remember being with? I'm just supposed to cuddle up next to him at night? Let him touch my body? Have sex with him?"

"You can have my room until you are ready to make whatever choice you choose too. I will sleep in the library. You don't have to do anything you are not ready for."

"But I want you here with me. In my bed is where you belong."

"I know baby. But right now, Tristan isn't ready to give you up."

"I'm not his to give up," I said getting frustrated. "I need you Odin."

"How about I sleep up here, but on the couch?"

"How about you sleep up here in my bed?"

"Lilith, I can't do that."

211

"Can't or won't."

"You know I want to."

"Then what is the problem?"

Letting out a sigh he said, "Fine. I'll sleep next to you, but only on top of the covers."

"I guess that is better than nothing. Now bring me my babies please."

Chapter Thirty-One

I spent the next few days getting used to walking around with crutches. It wasn't a very easy task especially with my shoulder having a hole in it. But luckily for me, I had the love of my life to help me. Odin was by my side every step of the way. He cared for me even when I didn't ask him too. Tristan tried to help as well even though I kept reassuring him Odin was more than enough help.

My recovery time was taking longer than I had time for and it was becoming frustrating. I had Odin help me down to the library, so I could meditate. For some reason, I couldn't remember how to heal myself. Odin propped me up carefully on one of the bean bags in the middle of the floor. He was so close to me I could feel his breath on my skin.

"Is this comfortable?" he asked. Not taking my eyes off of him I nodded. "Why are you looking at me like that?"

"Like what?"

"Like you want to devour my body."

"Maybe because I do."

"Lilith. We…" I cut him off by pressing my lips to his. I kissed him feverishly. I wanted him. I needed him. I pulled him on top of me letting him know what I wanted. "Lilith, what about Tristan?" I didn't say anything. One flick of my wrist and the door locked. I flicked my wrist again and the chair from my desk flew across the room and barricaded the door. I didn't need to speak to tell him my intentions.

I ripped his shirt open and ran my hands over his chest. I dug my nails in just deep enough to make him growl with pleasure. I unbuttoned his jeans while he pulled my dress over my head. Our lips found each other again. He kissed me with so much passion, longing, hunger, and want. He kissed me like it would be the last time our lips would ever meet.

He ran his hands through my hair then pushed it to the side exposing my neck to him. He slowed us down when he slowly kissed me from behind my ear down to my collar bone. He kissed me going

Jessica Manson

back up the front of my neck until our lips met. Kissing me gently he said, "I've missed you Lilith."

"I've missed you too baby." He laid me back onto the bean bag and climbed on top of me. He kissed me starting from my forehead, then my nose, my lips, my chin. Then he slowly made his way down my neck, to my chest, stopping to linger on my breast. He caressed one gently while kissing the other. Once he was done there, he continued kissing my body. He kissed me down my stomach, made a circle around my belly button with his tongue and then continued to kiss me until he reached my panty line.

He removed my panties kissing my leg as he pulled them down. On his way back up, he kissed my other leg showing each one equal attention. He crawled his way back up to my lips. While he kissed me, I slid his pants off. I ran my hands over his body feeling each muscle in his back and then on his stomach and chest.

Odin is a beautiful man and just looking at him made my mouth water. I opened my legs up to him letting him know I was ready for him. He looked me in the eyes and asked, "Are you sure about this?" I nodded.

"I love you Odin."

"I love you too Lamia mea." He kissed me one more time before he slowly entered me causing a moan to escape me. He moved slowly in and out letting me feel every inch of him. He pulled himself out of me and kissed my neck. He was teasing me, and it was killing me. After a few minutes, he entered me again and moved slowly once more.

He teased me a few more times until I was begging, "Odin please." He smiled at me like that was what he had been waiting for. He inserted himself inside of me again. He moved slowly at first then he quickened his pace. His body felt so good against mine. It felt like our bodies were meant to touch in this way. We were just two puzzle pieces that fit perfectly together.

We made love for the next hour. We were sweaty and tired and were finally ready for a release. With our bodies in sync with each other, we came at the same time. Odin laid down beside me to catch his breath and I rolled over to rest my head on his chest.

My body felt completely satisfied. But the feeling I loved the most, was the feeling I had in my soul. My soul felt like it was dehydrated, and it just got a big cold glass of water. It felt like my soul had awaken from a long dark sleep and it was finally seeing the sun for the first time. Odin is my light in the dark, my sun in the rain and my rainbow after a storm.

Still naked I sat up, "What are you doing?" Odin asked.

"I'm fixing to meditate. That is what I came down here for remember? Now, shhh. I need complete quiet."

"Yes mam'."

I closed my eyes and concentrated on what I wanted. It was hard to do since every time I closed my eyes all I saw was Odin's naked body. A smile formed across my lips. *Damn it Lilith, concentrate.* I scolded myself. I tried again. When the images of Odin popped in my head, I pushed them to the side. I focused on what I wanted to do and after a few minutes the spell I had used once before to heal myself after my aunt and Jacan had kidnapped and tortured me came rushing back flooding my memory.

I opened my eyes and began to chant:

By the light of the moon
And the path of the north
Let the pain of my wounds be purged
And let healing flow forth.

Let not this simple spell coerce
Or make my situation worse
Hear now my humble plea
As I will it, so mote it be.

My body started healing as soon as I was done with the chant. "Help me remove my cast and these bandages please," I said to Odin.

Jessica Manson

"Are you sure? Don't you want to make sure you are healed before taking everything off?"

"Trust me; I'm healed." He sat up and pulled the bandage off my shoulder first. As the wound was healing it pushed the stitches out of my skin. Next, he removed my cast, the purple and green bruises began to fade. He reached up and touched my cheek where it had been cut open. That wound had healed as well.

"You are truly an amazing creature," Odin said still rubbing my cheek.

"So, I'm a creature now."

"Aren't we all?"

"Some more than others," he laughed at me. I got up and walked around the room. "Oh, how I have missed being able to walk." The spell worked wonders because my body felt better than it ever has. I felt full of energy. I felt awake for the first time in a long time.

I slipped my dress on and searched for my panties. "Did you have to get dressed?" Odin asked with a smile on his face.

"Yes, we still have work to do."

"I got some work for you," he said wiggling his eyebrows.

"I bet you do." I wrapped my arms around his neck and kissed his perfect lips. He laid down on the bean bag and pulled me on top of him. With me in control this time we lost ourselves in each other one more time before leaving the library.

By the time we joined the others, it was dinner time. We all met in the dining room. "Dude, how did you heal so fast?" Cal asked.

"A spell."

"Why didn't you do that days ago?"

"Because I didn't think about it."

"You're a witch with the ability to heal yourself and you didn't think about it."

"Nope," I said taking a bite of my spaghetti. "Plus, I didn't remember how to."

"So, when is this going down with Slaaneth?"

"Hopefully today if everyone is ready."

Beautiful Corruption

"We're ready."

Suddenly there was a big bang at the front door as if someone was trying to break in. We all jumped up on guard. "Gunner, Bristol, take Ava and Elijah and hide. Don't let them get my babies. Fate go with them. If anyone comes near them that isn't one of us, kill them," I ordered.

"Who is at the door Lilith?" Odin asked.

"Slaaneth's army." With a snap of my fingers my outfit changed from a dress to a black leather outfit. The top fit perfectly to my breast with two straps that formed an x around my stomach and tied in the back leaving most of my skin exposed. The leather pants hugged every one of my curves. My shoes changed from flip flops to knee high black combat boots. The guys stood there looking at me with their mouths open. "What? I need to be able to fight and I can't do that in a dress."

"I'm not sure I'll be able to fight with you looking so sexy in that outfit," Cal said.

"He's right. You are smoking hot," Brant said.

"Shut up and get ready to fight. There is at least fifty people out there."

"How can you tell?" Latham asked.

"X-ray vision."

"Smoking ass hot and more powers than we can count on one hand. My dream girl," Cal said.

"We should gather at the door. Be ready when they enter," I instructed. My witch and my vampire was ready for me to call upon them. I was ready for their attack.

"Hey Lilith, I think you need to decide which one of you will fight," Odin said looking at me sideways.

"Why?"

"Because your eyes look like they are having a fight of their own. They are red one minute then yellow and swirling the next. They just keep going back and forth." Even though my eyes changing like this is pretty cool, it is also frustrating because I can never tell when they change. It doesn't feel like anything and it doesn't affect my vision.

Jessica Manson

"That's because I'm going to use them both," I said with a smile. I turned my focus back to the door and used my x-ray vision to see what they are doing. "They are almost through the door. Everyone get ready." Everyone bared their fangs and growled in unison. They were ready. These humans wouldn't know what hit them. "Daveh, Razi, you two go invisible and take them out. If they don't know you're there, they can't fight you off." I scanned the area once more, this time going out a little further just to be safe. "Oh no."

"What? What's wrong?" Odin asked.

"Tainted ones are waiting in the trees."

"How many?"

"At least a hundred."

"Fuck."

"Man, with that many Tainted Ones we should have some type of weapons," Cal said.

I snapped my fingers, and everyone had a sword in their hands. "How's that?"

"Hell yeah. You are a badass for real."

"What about you? What weapon will you use?" Tristan asked me concerned.

I smiled at him, "I am my own weapon."

Chapter Thirty-Two

The humans finally broke through the front door. As soon as they got through, I raised my hands and pushed them backwards with force using an energy wave causing them all to fall to the ground. "Do you even need our help?" Cal asked sarcastically.

"Of course, I do. I just thought I'd get us a head start." Everyone charged toward the fallen group and took them out one by one. I went past them and headed straight for the Tainted Ones.

A few ran toward me, but they didn't stand a chance. I hit the first in the nose the way Odin had shown me knocking him backwards. I ran a clothes line on the second one throwing him into a flip before he landed on his ass. The third one swung at my head causing me to duck. When I dropped to the ground, I spun in a kick making him lose his balance and he too fell to the ground.

Ten more came out of the trees. I was taking them out one by one, but they were starting to gain on me. Once they formed a circle around me the witch had a trick up her sleeve. I dropped to the ground then pushed off of it and flew into the sky. As I came back down, I was spinning at the speed of a tornado. I slammed into the ground in the middle of the circle I just escaped from making the earth shake. It caused them all to fall.

While they were down, I shot fireballs from my hands blasting as many of them as I could. They began to scream in pain. Three big red eyed vampires towered over me. "Hi, boys," I said with a smile. I spun in a circle jabbing my hands three times. When the spin was over, I held three hearts in my hands. "Bye boys," I said as their lifeless bodies fell to the ground.

I had taken out sixteen of the Tainted Ones while the others were still fighting the humans. A group of five came out of the trees this time. While they had me distracted, I didn't see the other group of four that came out as well. One of them grabbed me and threw me against a tree.

Jessica Manson

That shit hurt, but I jumped up and was ready to fight again. I sent a fire blast from my hands burning three of them.

Two more charged at me, I kicked one straight in the chest sending him flying through the air at top speed. He didn't stop until his head hit a tree a few feet away. His head split and blood gushed from the wound. He didn't move. The second tried to grab me but missed when I ducked. I kicked him in his knee causing it to snap backwards. He screamed in pain.

I ran past him and charged at the four that were left. The first one I got to, I ripped his heart out. Without pausing I kept going. The next one I kicked in the face making his head spin. I also ripped the heart out of the third one. When I reached the fourth one, I jumped on his shoulders and twisted his head with my hands breaking his neck.

As his lifeless body fell, I jumped to my feet. When I stood, everyone in the group was staring at me with looks of awe. "What?" I asked wondering why they were looking at me like that.

"I know I have said this before, but I am for real this time. I'm in love," Cal said.

"Girl you got some serious skills," Tuls said.

"I had a good teacher," I said looking over at Odin.

"I didn't teach you those moves. That was all you."

"I've taken out twenty-four tainted ones."

"Only seventy-six more to go," Brant said stating the obvious.

"Well get ready because they are all coming out at once. Spread out but stay behind me. I'm going to send another energy wave."

As the rest of the tainted ones came out from the trees, I lifted my hands and sent an energy wave toward them. The first line of them fell to the ground. I started shooting fire balls at as many as I could. I took out five of them before one attacked me from behind. He wrapped his arm around my neck trying to choke me. I donkey kicked him in the knee. When he loosened his grip, I jumped up and flipped over his head onto his shoulders. I snapped his neck then ripped his head off.

Beautiful Corruption

Another one came at me with speed like I had never seen before. Odin intervened and chopped his head off before the Tainted One even knew what happened. "Thanks, sexy."

"Any time," he said with a wink. I watched Odin for a second as he took out three more vampires. He was swift and skillful. He worked his sword like it was an extension of his arm. He had become one with the sword. I was getting hot watching him fight. He was so sexy in the way he moved so effortlessly.

My eyes stayed on him until another vampire came at me. I let him think I wasn't paying attention and when he got close to me ready to attack, I jabbed my hand straight into his chest and pulled out his heart. A few more ran toward me and I easily took them out as well.

With all of us fighting it didn't take long to take the rest of the tainted vampires out. A hundred lifeless vampires lay dead on our front lawn along with fifty dead humans. The yard was a bloody mess. With the flick of my wrist I started moving the bodies into a pile. Once they were all piled up Latham jokingly asked, "Bon fire anyone?"

"Why not?" I said as I snapped my fingers and the pile of dead bodies went up in flames.

"You're really getting a hang of those powers of yours," Parker said.

"Someone once told me that I had to control my powers not the other way around," I said smiling at him.

"He was a smart man," he said teasing.

"I'm just going to say what everyone else here is thinking," Cal said. "Lilith, you are a sexy badass. And you may or may not have given us all wood with your sexy ass moves. And yes, that even includes Tuls."

"I'm not afraid to admit that I got some ladywood watching her. She was flawless in the way she moved. It was beyond sexy. Hell, it was downright beautiful," Tuls admitted.

I couldn't help but smile even though their compliments were making me uncomfortable. "Well, I don't know about y'all, but I would like to wash the vampire off me and go finish my dinner. Odin, will

Jessica Manson

you get Ava and Elijah and let Gunner know it is safe to come out?" I said walking away from the group.

I went into my bathroom, peeled off the leather outfit and stepped into the shower to rinse off before soaking in the tub. Once I was sure there was no more blood on me, I stepped out of the shower and ran me some water for a bath. When the tub was full, I stepped inside. The water was hot against my skin relaxing my every muscle.

Odin came into the bathroom. He undressed revealing his gorgeous body to me. I couldn't get enough of this man. Just looking at him made my whole-body tingle. He got into the shower and I watched him as he washed the battle off of him. Watching the soap run down his body made me crave him. I needed his touch again.

When he had his back turned rinsing the soap out of his hair, I joined him in the shower. When he turned around, I pushed him against the wall dropped to my knees and took him in my mouth. I moved my head back and forth in a quick hungry motion. A moan escaped him causing me to move faster. He tangled his hand in my hair and pulled slightly. When he was almost ready, I stopped pleasing him.

When I stood up, he threw me against the wall, lifted my legs and inserted himself inside of me. Finally, the craving I had for him was getting fulfilled. He kissed my breast feverishly while thrusting into me so hard I was sure we would crack the wall. I began to moan uncontrollably as I was reaching my release. I could feel his grip tightening on me letting me know he was ready too. With our bodies in sync with each other, I ran my hands through his hair grabbing it in my fist and came harder than I ever had before. Odin held me in place for a few minutes before letting me go.

"Lamia mea," he whispered in my ear. I loved it when he called me that. Especially when he whispered it in that sexy deep voice of his. It always sent a tingle down my spine. "You are so beautiful."

"You're not so bad yourself," I said with a smile.

"I'm serious. And when I saw you in that outfit fighting," He closed his eyes and leaned his head back remembering that moment. "I wanted to take you right then and there."

Beautiful Corruption

"Same here baby. When I was watching you, it made me want you so bad it hurt."

"I can't get enough of you. You are like a hunger that can't be filled, and I crave you constantly."

"Then have me." He picked me up and carried me to the bed and he did just what I told him to do. We made love to each other for the next two hours. We made love like we were making up for lost times even though no time had been lost. And we would have kept going, but Ava and Elijah woke up needing to be fed.

When we went downstairs to make their bottles, everyone was in the living room watching a movie. Odin joined them taking Elijah with him while Ava and I went into the kitchen. Wasn't long and Gunner was standing next to me taking Ava from me. I turned toward the sink to make their bottles when Gunner spoke to me, "Can I ask you a question?"

"Sure," I said cautiously.

"What are you doing with Odin?"

"What do you mean?"

"Are you back with him?"

"Of course, I am with him. He is my husband. Why do you ask?"

"Because when you left, it broke him. But when he found out you left him to be with Tristan, it nearly killed him. I had to watch my best friend go through heartbreak. I know some people would say it's just heartbreak; he will get over it. But not Odin. He loves you so much. Like I said, it nearly killed him, and I can't watch him go through that again. Don't break his heart again Lilith."

"I understand your concern. And I'm sorry you had to go through that with him. But Gunner, Odin is my world. He is my life. My air. My heartbeat. I would never do anything to hurt him."

"I hope not." That was the last thing he said as he and Ava left to join the others in the living room. I finished making the bottles and joined everyone else. We watched movies for the rest of the night, just enjoying each other's company.

Jessica Manson

Chapter Thirty-Three

When I woke up, I decided that today would be the day that we summon Slaaneth. We couldn't keep putting it off. He would send another army. And when he does, he would probably send a lot of more Tainted ones than the last time. Not to mention, it is a gloomy and rainy day, perfect for summoning a demon.

As soon as Odin woke up, I sent him out to get the supplies we needed to summon Slaaneth. A knock sounded on my bedroom door, it was Tristan. "Mind if we talk for a minute?" he asked as he entered my room.

"Sure. What's up?" He walked over and sat on the bed across from me and ran his hands through his hair. He looked frustrated, but also sad. There seemed to be a deep sadness inside of him. When he didn't speak, I asked, "What is it? What's wrong?"

"Have you had sex with Odin?"

His question caught me off guard. I didn't understand what business of his it was. "Why are you asking me this?"

"Have you?"

"It's none of your business if I have or haven't."

"I'll take that as a yes then."

"As a matter of fact, yes I have. But it's none of your business. Odin is my husband and that's what married people do Tristan; they have sex together."

"You are my wife. Mine damn it. He had no right to fucking touch you. I understand you can't help it because you don't remember, but he shouldn't have taken advantage of you like that."

"Hold up. I am Odin's wife; he has every right to touch me. And for your information I'm the one that asked for it."

"Maybe so. But he should have said no. Lilith, it is killing me to see the two of you together."

"You don't see us together. We don't kiss, we don't hug, we don't even hold hands in front of you. As a matter of fact, we don't do anything in front of you or anyone else in this house."

Beautiful Corruption

"No, but you are in his bed, laying on his chest, making love to him when it should be me. I should be the one holding you. I should be the one you make love to. It should be my lips pressed to yours."

"Tristan I'm sorry." Catching me off guard, he pressed his lips to mine and kissed me softly. I could remember getting kissed like this before, but I couldn't remember by who. All I knew is that it wasn't Odin who had kissed me like this. I tried to not kiss him back, but the longer his lips were pressed to mine the more I felt like it was right. Like I was supposed to kiss him.

He pulled away from me looking at me with such sadness in his eyes. "Lilith..."

"Why did it feel like we have done that before?" I asked cutting him off. I ran my fingers over my lips trying to remember what my mind wouldn't let me.

"Because we have."

"Impossible."

"No Lilith, it's not impossible. You are my wife."

"But I'm married to Odin."

"Yes. And to me."

"How can that be? I can't be married to two people at once."

"Yes, you can, and you are. You married Odin under the laws of the coven. Then when you left him you married me under the laws of humans."

"Why can't I remember?" I asked more to myself.

"Because when you went to Land of Lore..."

"Tristan, I remember what the leprechaun did. It was a rhetorical question." I got up and paced around the room frustrated. "Tristan, I don't know what you want me to do. I don't know what you expect of me. All I know is, I am married to Odin. All I can remember is loving Odin. I don't remember us ever being together."

He got up and walked over to me. "All I'm asking is that you give me time. Give me a chance to help you remember."

"And what do I do in the meantime?"

"Don't sleep with Odin again."

Jessica Manson

"What if I never remember you?"

"I'll never stop trying. I love you Lilith and I won't give up on us."

"I can't promise you I won't be with Odin."

"Fine, I'll take what I can get as long as you let me help you remember."

"Alright, you can try."

"Yes," he said as he pulled me into his arms squeezing me against his chest. "Thank you."

"Wait and thank me if I remember."

"I promise, you *will* remember."

As I waited for Odin to get home, I took a shower. When I was done, I dried off and wrapped myself in a towel. I nearly jumped out of my skin when I walked into the bedroom and saw someone sitting on my bed. "What are you doing here Draven?"

"I came to check on things. See how my son was doing with keeping you locked up. I see he has failed."

"Did you actually think Odin would keep me locked away? He loves me."

"Yes, and that love has made him foolish." He got off the bed and walked over to me. "I know what you have planned dear and let me just tell you now, it won't work. You can't kill me."

"I can, and I will."

"Here I am. Kill me," he said before bursting into laughter. "I'll let the two of you continue to play house for now. But you still have to face your punishment."

"I'll kill you before you ever lay a hand on me." Suddenly, Draven backhanded me, and I went flying into the dresser causing me to smack the back of my head on the corner of it. Losing my towel was the least of my worries because blood was now pouring from my head.

He started walking toward the door when he stopped and turned to face me, "And don't be expecting Adreana to be calling. She has been let's just say...rendered speechless."

"What did you do to her?" He didn't answer me. He just laughed as he walked out of the room. I grabbed my fallen towel and pressed it to my head. I started seeing black spots and I knew it wouldn't be long before I would black out. I knew I needed to get help. If I blacked out with a head wound, I probably wouldn't wake back up.

I tried to stand but failed miserably. I crawled over to the door as fast as I could. I got the door open and only one arm out before I collapsed and blacked out.

When I came to, I was lying on the bed, Odin was next to me. "Hey," he whispered to me.

"Hey."

"What happened?"

"Your father was here."

"What did he do to you?" I told him about everything his father said and told him about him back handing me. By the time I was done, he was furious.

"Odin, I think he has hurt your mom."

"Why would you think that?"

"Because he told me not to worry about her calling. He said she has been 'rendered speechless'." He jumped up from the bed and started toward the door. "Where are you going?"

"I have to go check on her. What if he has killed her?"

"I don't think that is a good idea."

"Why not?"

"Because I think that is his plan. I think he wants you to rush over there so I am here alone. He wants to separate us."

"I have to make sure she is okay."

"I will check on her for you."

"How? You can't go over there."

"I'm not going to. I will reach out to her with my mind."

"You can do that?"

Jessica Manson

"Yes. It is how I got Bristol and Parker to come get us. We knew we couldn't use the phone to call them because you probably had the phones tapped. I had to reach them another way."

"Okay. Can you do it now?"

"Maybe after I take something for this headache." He grabbed two pills and some water that were sitting on the table ready for me.

"Now can you do it?"

"Okay. I will need complete concentration and silence." He nodded and sat on the bed beside me. Him being this close to me was a big distraction. "Odin, I don't want to sound rude, but can you sit somewhere else please?" He got up and moved to a chair that was beside the bed. "Thank you."

I closed my eyes and started to think about his mom. I reached for her with my mind, begging to make contact. I called out to her, but here was no answer. Just blackness. But in the blackness, I could feel fear. She was here. She was just hiding.

"Adreana, you don't have to be afraid. It's Lilith." There was only silence. As I stood in the blackness, I closed my eyes and focused on her location. I needed to find her. I began to chant:

A location I seek
From the one that is weak
Show me her light
To guide me through this night.

When I opened my eyes, a light glowed in the distance. I walked toward it. Adreana was balled up in the fetal position with tears streaming down her face. She looked like a lost child that couldn't find their missing parent. "Adreana," I called her name, but she didn't even look at me.

I sat down beside her and grabbed her hand with mine. "You don't have to be scared anymore. Odin sent me to find you."

"My Odin sent you."

"Yes. Are you okay?"

Beautiful Corruption

"No. I'm hurt."

"What hurts?"

"My tongue and my legs."

"Where are you?"

"Locked in a dark place. I can't see anything. It's so dark. I'm scared. Will you help me?"

"Yes. We will help you. What have they done to you?"

"Can't you see it?"

"See what?"

"Look at me dear." When I looked at her fear, pain, and regret filled my body. I was horrified at the sight in front of me. It scared me so bad it pulled me out of the vision.

When I was back in the room I was hyperventilating, and tears rushed from my eyes. Odin ran over to me. "What happened?" I couldn't answer him. I was crying to bad. It was my fault she had been tortured. It was my fault she would never be the same again. "Lilith what happened?" he asked me with pain in his voice. "She's dead, isn't she?" I shook my head. "Then what happened?" I held my finger up asking for a minute to get control of myself.

Once my breathing was under control, I began to tell him what I saw. My tears never stopped flowing. "She is hurt, but she is alive. Your father should have just killed her. That would have been the nice thing to do."

"What did he do to her? Just tell me."

"Odin, you don't need to know what he has done to her."

"Damn it, Lilith. Tell me."

"He cut her tongue out. And her eyeballs. He also cut her legs off. He has her trapped somewhere dark. But she doesn't know where."

"That fucking bastard," Odin yelled as he threw the table that was beside the bed across the room barely missing the baby's cribs."

"Odin, you have to calm down. I know this is hard, but hurting our babies isn't going to fix anything." He fell to the floor beside the bed. I got off the bed and sat next to him. I wrapped my arms around him. "We will find her Odin."

Jessica Manson

"How?"

"We will figure it out."

"She will die from her wounds if we don't get to her."

"I know baby. I will keep a check on her as much as I can. I will also try to figure out a way to get a location on her."

A rapid knock sounded at the door. Brant didn't wait for us to let him in. He opened the door and said, "Ambi is gone."

"Draven has her," I said never taking my eyes off Odin.

Chapter Thirty-Four

Needless to say, we would not be summoning Slaaneth today. We had to figure out a way to save Odin's mom first. I know there has to be some sort of spell that will tell me her location. I have tried all day to meditate to find it, but I can't concentrate long enough to get anywhere. I even locked myself in the library, but that didn't help either. I needed a break.

I found Odin and asked if I could take a walk outside. "I'll walk with you if that's okay?"

"I'd like that." I knew he needed a break just as much as I did. It's driving him crazy not knowing where his mom is. Not only is the guilt killing me because all of this is my fault, but to watch him in pain makes it worse. I know he blames me even though he hasn't said it. He hasn't been able to look at me since I told him what happened to his mother. I think the only reason he even wanted to walk with me is for my own protection.

"You're quiet," Odin said breaking the silence. We had been walking around the property for about ten minutes and neither one of us had spoken to each other.

"I could say the same about you." He took a deep breath as if it would help him somehow. "Odin I'm sorry."

"What do you have to be sorry about?"

"This is all my fault."

"How?"

"Because it was my idea to get your mom to help. If I wouldn't have asked her to help us, Draven would have never hurt her. She would be safe right now."

"We both asked for her help Lilith."

"It was my idea."

"Come here," he said as he pulled me into his arms. "I know you think I blame you, but I don't. You didn't make my father do that to her."

"No, but..."

231

Jessica Manson

"Lilith, stop. Don't blame yourself. I don't."

"Odin, I know there is a spell to find her, but I can't focus enough to figure it out."

"You will."

"How are you so sure when I'm not?"

"Because it's you baby. You will figure it out." He leaned down and kissed me on the top of my head. I sensed that he needed to be held so without saying another word I wrapped my arms around him and held him close.

I laid my head on his chest and closed my eyes. I listened to his breathing and focused on his heartbeat. He was what I needed all along to focus. As we stood there holding each other in silence I was able to concentrate. I focused on what I needed to know and as if a light bulb went off inside of me, I had the answer.

I pulled away from him. "I know what to do. I know how to find your mom," I said smiling at him.

"See, I knew you would find the answer." He kissed me and hugged me tight. "Now let's go save my mom."

We went back into the house and into the library. I grabbed the globe from the table. "I need an orange, some apple juice and a knife. Oh, and a bowl."

"Your spells get weirder and weirder. Last time you needed cinnamon."

"Cal, can you be serious for two minutes please?" Odin snapped.

"Alright, I know you're stressed. I'll be quiet."

When Dex brought back the items I asked for, I peeled the orange and then pulled the orange in half. I then I pulled one of the halves into fourths. I put the orange slices and the apple juice into the bowl and mixed them together. I then spread the mix over the globe moving my hand clockwise then I began to chant:

Strength of night, power of day
Let this help me find a way
The pulp and juice of two fruit

Will help me make pursuit.

A location floated into my vision. I had the address to his mother's location. Suddenly, my head was jerked back, and my eyes rolled into the back of my head. I began to levitate off the ground. I no longer saw the address, I saw the building and what was inside. It was dark, but my eyes saw through it. The building had two guards that stood outside and there were two more guarding the front of the building on the inside. There was a room in the back of the building where one guard stood in front of the door. I could see inside the room.

Odin's mother lay in the dark on a table. She is almost lifeless. Her wrist was chained, and blood pooled around her. Someone else was in the room. Ambi and Draven stood in the corner watching Adreana bleed. They began to speak.

"Can't we just kill her? She should have died by now."

"Patience Ambi. Suffering a long and painful death is her punishment for helping my traitorous son and that whore of a wife of his." Ambi ran her hand down Draven's arm in a sexual way. He looked at her and smiled. "You are eager my dear."

"Yes, I am. I know what I want."

"And what would that be?"

"You." Draven grabbed Ambi and pulled her in for a kiss. It was sloppy and wet causing my stomach to turn. They groped each other feverishly. It was disgusting to watch. I was thankful when they finally pulled away from each other.

"Let's go home, shall we?" Draven said with suggestion in his voice.

"Finally," Ambi said biting her bottom lip.

As they walked out of the room I was once again in the library. I stopped levitating and fell to the ground fast. Odin reached out and caught me just in time. "Are you okay?" he asked.

"Yes. I know where they have your mom. And if we are going to save her, now would be the time since your father is a bit preoccupied," I shuddered at the thought of Draven and Ambi together.

Jessica Manson

"What do you mean preoccupied?"

"Let's just say Ambi is keeping your father busy."

"That's just nasty," Cal said.

"Just be glad you didn't have to watch it."

"I think I'm going to be sick. Thanks, Lilith, for the visual."

"We need to go now. There are five guards, two on the outside, two on the inside and one guarding your mom's door. Odin, I think it would be best if you stay behind with Ava and Elijah."

"No way. I'm going with you."

"I don't think that is a good idea."

"I don't care. That's my mom, I'm going."

"Please don't make me put a spell on you. I don't want you seeing your mom like that."

"Lilith this is nonnegotiable. I am going and that's final."

"Fine," I snapped my fingers and changed my clothes. I was once again in my leather fighting outfit. "Let's go."

I gave Odin the address as we piled into the car. Latham, Dex, Cal, and Tristan came with Odin and me. Everyone else stayed back to protect Ava and Elijah.

It didn't take long for us to reach the location with Odin driving as fast as he was. He parked a few blocks away from the building, so we could sneak up to it without being seen. Odin was doing some weird hand motions to the guys. When he was done, they nodded that they understood what they were to do. I, on the other hand, had no clue what orders he just gave them.

The guys took off. Latham and Cal went to the right while Tristan and Dex went to the left. Odin grabbed my hand and dragged me behind him. We walked up to the building casually as if we were just passing by. The guards stopped us. "Can we help you?" One of them asked.

"No thanks," Odin said as he punched the man in the face. The second guard lunged for Odin but was stopped by my foot making contact with his throat. As he was gasping for air the shades, he had been wearing fell off revealing that he was a Tainted One. While he was

234

Beautiful Corruption

distracted trying to catch his breath I ran over and ripped his heart out of his chest.

The first guy had gotten the upper hand on Odin. He had him pinned to the ground. He reared his hand back and was aiming for his chest. He was going to rip Odin's heart out. I ran over and grabbed his arm in mid strike. "I don't think so mother fucker," I said full of rage. I twisted his arm back until I heard a snap. The man cried out in pain then I kicked him in the face sending him flying off of Odin. "Are you okay?" I asked as I helped him up.

"Better now," he said smiling at me. The man came charging back at us. "I got this one," Odin said as he ran toward the man. When they met, Odin flipped over the man ripping his head off in mid flip.

"Yes, you do," I said out loud but to myself. Odin was so sexy in the way he moved.

Odin walked back over to me and said, "You're doing it again."

"Doing what?"

"Looking at me like you want to devour my body."

"Maybe I do want to devour your body."

He smacked me on the butt, "Same here Lamia mea."

Just then the guys came around the building. "It's clear," Latham said.

"Good. Then let's go get my mother."

As we entered the building the two guards, I saw in my vision rushed toward us. I stood back and let the guys take them on. I watched Odin as he took the first guy out. He was skillful and graceful in his movements. Heat flushed through my body.

Without me doing it my x-ray vision kicked in. I could see the man guarding the door to Odin's mothers' room. He was pulling a phone out of his pocket. He knew we were there and was about to call reinforcements. I was standing in front of him within a matter of seconds. He hadn't even had time to dial the number. I casually reached up and placed my hand on his chest. His skin turned gray as I watched the life drain from his body.

Jessica Manson

I don't know where the power came from or what I even did but I liked it. I stepped over his lifeless body and ran into Adriana's room. I felt her neck for a pulse. It was there although, weak. I broke the chains that held her down to the cold metal table.

Adriana's voice entered my mind. *"Lilith kill me please. I can't live like this anymore. Please."*

"I can't," I said as tears filled my eyes.

Odin came into the room. "Is she alive."

"Yes, but barely. She wants me to kill her."

"Mom, if you hang on, we will get you some help."

"Lilith please. You know I won't survive like this anyway. Kill me."

"Odin, she doesn't want to live like this. She's begging me to kill her."

"Mom are you sure this is what you want?" She nodded her head. "Okay."

I looked up at Odin, he nodded for me to go ahead. I lay my hand on her chest and drained what little life she had left from her body. Tears fell rapidly as she took her last breath.

Odin clung to his mother. I watched as tears fell from his face. My heart broke at the sight of his pain. I wanted to wrap him up in my arms, but I could tell he didn't want to be touched. He was hurting and there was no magic spell that could take his pain away.

Odin's face turned from sadness to pure hate. He looked at me with blame in his eyes. My heart sank at the look. If he didn't blame me before he blamed me now. He headed for the door, "Let's go." No one said anything, we just did as we were told.

The ride back to the house was awkward and silent. I was thankful when we got home and out of the car. Odin rushed inside ahead of us. He went straight upstairs shutting himself in our bedroom. I decided to give him a few minutes before checking on him.

Cal started filling everyone else in on what happened. "If you killed the guards then where is Adreana?" Bristol asked.

"Lilith killed her." The room fell silent. Everyone looked at me accusingly. I couldn't take them staring at me like I was a monster, so I went upstairs to check on Odin.

When I entered the room, I heard the water running in the bathroom. Odin was in the shower sitting in the floor. He had his knees pulled up to his chest. I got undressed and joined him. I sat on the floor beside him. "Baby."

"Don't Lilith."

"Okay." I sat silently beside him. I wanted to comfort him, but I didn't know what to do. I couldn't imagine how he was feeling. His wife just killed his mother in front of him. He was probably pissed at me. He probably hated me now. He probably didn't even want me near him at the moment. He just didn't have the heart to tell me to go to hell. I wish he would though. At least then he would tell me how he feels.

I placed my hand on his arm to try and comfort him as much as I could, but he jerked away from me. "Don't fucking touch me." I was shocked at his tone, but I still couldn't blame him. I got up, wrapped myself in a towel and left the bathroom. He needed space and I was willing to give it to him. Didn't mean it didn't hurt though.

I laid on the bed as tears slowly fell down my face. I not only cried because Odin hurt my feelings, but because he was hurting. I cried because I just killed my husband's mother. I cried because all of this was my fault. I wouldn't have had to kill her if it weren't for me. She would have never been tortured if it weren't for me. All of this was my fault. No wonder Odin didn't want me to touch him.

I didn't notice when Odin walked out of the bathroom. I didn't know he was in the room until he crawled in the bed behind me. He wrapped his arm around me and pulled me into him. "I'm sorry I snapped at you," he whispered in my ear.

"Don't be. I don't blame you for hating me."

"I don't hate you baby." He went silent for a moment. "It just hurts so fucking much."

I turned to face him. I ran my fingers through his hair. "I know baby. Trust me, I know." He snuggled his head into my chest and cried.

Jessica Manson

I let him. I let him cry on me the same way he let me all those times. He cried until there were no more tears to cry. He cried until he fell asleep in my arms.

Chapter Thirty-Five

Odin didn't wake up until the next day. He woke up refreshed and acting like nothing ever happened. He wasn't visually sad anymore. I knew he was still hurting, but that cry he had helped a lot. I know the pain of losing a parent would never go away. He would just have to learn to live it. And it seems like he has learned rather quickly.

"Good morning beautiful," he said to me.

"How are you feeling?"

"I'm okay."

"Are you sure?"

"Yes."

"Baby, you don't have to hide your feelings in front of me."

"I'm not. Yes, I'm hurting, but I can't let that stop me from moving on. We still have so much to do. We have to save our babies and kill my fucking piece of shit father."

"Okay. If you're really ready to face the world, then I'm beside you."

"By the way, thank you."

"For what?"

"Letting me cry on you last night."

"You don't have to thank me. Look at how many times I've cried on you."

He leaned into me and kissed me. When he pulled away from me, he was smiling. "Tell anyone and I'll have to kick your ass."

"Like I would and as if you could," I said laughing.

"I'll just have to prove to you who's stronger," He said as he pinned me down to the bed. I pretended to struggle letting him prove he was the stronger one. He kissed me roughly on the lips still holding my arms down.

Neither one of us got dressed from the shower last night so our bodies lay naked against each other. I could feel him growing against my thigh. He moved his kisses down my neck then to my breast. He sucked and nibbled roughly. He treated my body like he was hungry, and I was his next meal.

He forcefully pushed my legs open and thrust into me causing a moan to escape me. He didn't slow his pace making my body move to his rhythm. Our eyes locked causing him to slow down. He leaned down and kissed me softly. "I love you lamia mea."

I wrapped my arms around him and used my strength to roll us over, so I was now on top. "I love you too Odin." I moved my body slowly back and forth causing him to groan with pleasure. He rubbed his hands up my thighs leaving traces of tingles in their place. I continued to move slowly until we were both ready for our release.

I laid beside him on the bed resting my head on his chest. I could have laid in his arms all day, but he sat up and said, "Come on. We have a demon to summon."

When we went downstairs, we gathered everyone in the dining room. When everyone had joined us, Odin began speaking. "Today we are summoning Slaaneth. Is everyone still willing to help?" They all said yes in unison. "Good. Does everyone remember what they are supposed to do?" They answered yes in unison again. "Good. Bristol, Fate and Gunner, take Ava and Elijah and head to the highest peak of the house."

Before they left with the babies, Odin, Tristan and I kissed them goodbye just in case we didn't come back from this. Odin and I grabbed the supplies we needed and the rest of us headed downstairs where the cells were.

"Daveh. Razi. We are about to pour salt. Are y'all going to be able to focus?"

"We will do our best," Daveh answered looking uncomfortable.

"Then Odin, will you help me?"

Beautiful Corruption

Odin and I took the salt and started pouring it along the walls in the room. Then I drew a pentagram in the center of the room with the salt. I placed the bowl of holy water in the center of the pentagram. I placed the black candles in each one of its points. I had Latham, Odin, Tristan, Brant and Parker stand at each one of the points as well. Then I had Cal and Dex stand next to the stairway and I placed Tuls, Daveh and Razi on the other three sides of the room. Davah and Razi looked like they were in physical pain.

"Please watch where you step. Do not break the salt lines. It is the only thing that will keep Slaaneth contained in this room." After I had everyone in their places, I grabbed the demon's knife and stood in the center of the circle. "Is everyone ready?" I could tell everyone was nervous. Even I was scared. Everyone agreed they were ready. "Good. Let's kill a demon." I handed the guys the chant I had written down for each of them to say with me. "We will need to say the chant six times. And remember, no matter what happens, do not leave the points of the pentagram." We began our chant:

Slaaneth, I summon you from hell up to this earth
I call upon you
I summon you to stand before me
Slaaneth
Slaaneth
Slaaneth I summon you.

We repeated the chant six times. After the sixth time, I shouted his name and sliced my palm with the knife letting my blood drip into the bowl of holy water. Smoke started to swirl around our feet. The room grew hot and we all began to sweat. A loud sound filled our ears. It sounded like the ground had split open, but it was still intact.

Suddenly the demon stood before me. He didn't look like the man that met me on the bridge. Instead he was frightening. His skin was shiny and scaly, and it also looked charred. His eyes were crimson red and piercing. There were two horns coming out of his forehead. There

Jessica Manson

were also horns that formed around his eyes, four horns were where his eyebrows should have been, and five horns ran along the bottom of his eyes on both sides of his face. There was also three along each of his cheek bones starting at his ear. His fingernails were sharp like razors. He had fangs at least three inches long. They alone were scary enough to make me regret my decision to summon him.

He towered over me and radiated hate. He wore a sly conniving smile on his face and when he spoke, his voice sounded like fire. His words sounded like the flames of hell flickering from inside of him. "This is so much better than meeting on the bridge."

"Now I can kill you." His laugh was loud and echoed off the walls. It was devious and sadistic.

"Haven't I told you before that you can't kill me."

"So, you say." I lunged at him with the knife. He swatted at me like a fly and sent me flying across the room. When he hit me, Brant flinched and broke the line of salt. Slaaneth laughed harder as he lunged for me. He reached out to grab me. I backed away from him and in the process his long claws scratched my chest. Blood poured from me.

He sniffed the air. "Your blood will taste so sweet on my tongue."

"Fuck you." I lunged at him again. He hit me again sending me flying across the room once more. He came over and towered above me. He kicked me in the stomach knocking the air from me. He kicked me again and this time I heard a snap. He had broken one of my ribs. Anger filled me. I pulled myself up with the help of the wall. I shot fireballs from my hands hitting him in the face causing him to back away from me.

"Do you think fire hurts me? I live in the pits of hell." He came toward me again and I slashed his midsection with the knife. He wailed in pain. "You, stupid bitch," he yelled at me. He charged at me with a purpose this time. He wanted to cause me pain. I went to run away, but I wasn't quick enough. He grabbed me and pulled me into him. He sank his fangs into my neck. I screamed in pain.

His fangs went deep into my skin. The pain was unbearable agonizing. My vision started to grow blurry. He was draining me. I tried to get free, but he sank his fangs in deeper. I closed my eyes and concentrated the best I could through the pain. I chanted:

I am here, I am there
Teleport me over there.

I used the same chant to get away from him that I used to escape the dragon. I landed at Tristan's feet. Tristan went to help me, but I stopped him. "Don't break the circle. Don't worry about me." I stood up and backed away from him. Slaaneth walked toward me but stopped when he got next to Tristan. He looked at me and smiled the most villainous evil smile I had ever seen.

Panic filled me causing Slaaneth to laugh out loud. I knew what Tristan didn't. Suddenly, Slaaneth stabbed his hand through Tristan's back and pulled his heart out. "Noooooo!" I screamed. As Tristan's body fell lifeless to the ground every memory, I ever had of him came rushing back to me. He was right, we were married. I did love him, and I betrayed him.

Uncontrollable anger filled me. I screamed so loud the walls shook and everyone in the room had to cover their ears. While my scream distracted him, I lunged at Slaaneth with the knife piercing him in the heart. He clawed at me one last time slicing my stomach. I smiled at him as he burst into flames and died at my feet. Once he was nothing but ashes, I collapsed next to Tristan's body. I pulled his lifeless body into my lap and began to cry uncontrollably.

Jessica Manson

Chapter Thirty-Six

I sat for hours cradling Tristan's body. I couldn't let him go. The tears had stopped flowing long ago, but my heart didn't stop crying. I sat silently holding his body as if he would come back to me somehow. I begged for him not to leave me even though he was already gone. Everyone left me alone with his body a long time ago. Odin came in every now and then to check on me, but I never responded to him. I couldn't.

The pain in my chest was enough to kill me. My heart was torn from my chest when Tristan's heart got ripped out. My heart died when he died. I will never have him back. He will never know how much I loved him. He died knowing I never remembered him. He never even had the chance to help me remember.

Odin, Brant and Latham came in the room. "Lilith, we have to take his body."

"No."

"Baby we have too."

"No." Brant and Latham reached for him. "Don't fucking touch him," I yelled at them.

Odin squatted down in front of me, "Lilith I know this is hard, but you have to let him go."

"I can't," I said with tears filling my eyes again.

"Baby let me take you upstairs. Please." I didn't answer, but I didn't refuse anymore. Brant and Latham took Tristan's body while Odin picked me up and carried me upstairs. He sat me on the bed while he ran a bath for me. When the tub was full, he undressed me and sat me in the water.

The water was hot, but it didn't relax me. My heart was broken, there isn't enough hot water in the world to heal my pain. My heart hurt so much I had forgotten about the slashes on my stomach. "Lilith, you need to heal yourself." I shook my head. I didn't care about the cuts on my body or about my broken rib. "Please baby for me. For Ava and Elijah." Without giving him an answer, I started my chant.

244

By the light of the moon
And the path of the north
Let the pain of my wounds be purged
And let healing flow forth.

Let not this simple spell coerce
Or make my situation worse
Hear now my humble plea
As I will it, so mote it be.

My body healed, but my heart remained the same, broken beyond repair.

"Thank you, baby," Odin said as he lathered the loofah with soap. "Do you want to talk about it?" I shook my head. "Okay. I'm here when you're ready." He began to wash my back.

"I remembered," I said in barely a whisper.

"What?"

"I remembered," I said a little louder this time.

Odin didn't say anything in response. I didn't want him too. He finished washing me, got me out of the bath, dried me off, and wrapped me in a towel. He then carried me to the bed and tucked me in.

I didn't get out of bed for three days. I didn't eat any of the food Odin brought to me. I couldn't even sleep. Every time I closed my eyes all I saw was Slaaneth ripping Tristan's heart out. The pain has consumed me. I feel cold inside. I feel dead. I am weakened and worn down. I feel like the universe is about to crush me and my heart is about to explode.

Odin came into the room and sat beside me on the bed. "Lilith, I think it is time you got out of this bed."

"No."

"Yes, damn it. You have laid in this bed for three days. Ava and Elijah need you."

"Odin, I can't."

"You have to. Will you at least try?"

Jessica Manson

"It hurts so much."

He pulled me into his arms. "I know baby, but you have to keep living. You can't give up. Tristan wouldn't want you to be this way." The mention of his name sent tears flowing down my face.

"I hurt him so bad. I betrayed him."

"No, you didn't. He knew you loved him."

"Odin, he died thinking I didn't remember him. He died knowing you and I made love. He died never hearing me say I love you. He never even got the chance to help me remember our love."

"Come on let's take a walk." He helped me get dressed then took me for a walk around the property. Once we were away from the house, he spoke to me. "Lilith when you left me you took my heart with you. I felt like the air had been sucked out of my lungs. You were my breath, my heart beat. I felt like I was going to die when you left. But then you came back. Even though you were with Tristan, you came back. I accepted the two of you together even though it killed me to watch you with him. But that didn't matter because you were here.

Then you almost died, and I again felt like I would die too. I have watched you almost die then survive so many times and each time it never gets any easier. Every time I died with you. Then I got you back. You came back to me. You loved me again. And for the first time in a long time I remembered how to breathe. My heart didn't ache anymore.

Now I watch you in so much pain and there is nothing I can do to help you. Watching you dying from losing Tristan is killing me all over again. The air has been sucked out of me once again. I fear what will happen to you every day. You don't eat. You don't sleep and when you do you have nightmares. You are wasting away Lilith. And I fear that you will hurt yourself every second of every day. I need you back. Ava and Elijah need you back. You were there for me when my mother died and I am trying to be there for you now, but it is hard to do when you aren't trying to help yourself."

"Okay." Even though my heart was broken I knew I had people that counted on me. Odin was right, I had to learn how to deal with my heartache or it would kill me. Ava and Elijah needed me. Their father died to save them. He was a hero. I should start remembering his life instead of constantly thinking about his death.

"Are you sure?"

"Yes."

"Good. What do we do now?"

"We kill your father."

Extras

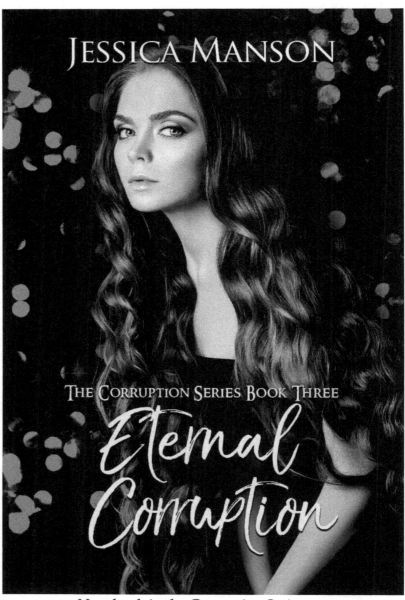

Next book in the Corruption Series
Eternal Corruption
Coming Soon!

Printed in the USA
CPSIA information can be obtained
at www.ICGtesting.com
LVHW051748281023
762324LV00014B/491